A Bag
Full of Stones

A Bag
Full of Stones

A. Molotkov

Apprentice
House Press
Loyola University Maryland

Library of Congress Control Number: 2025932539

First Edition

Casebound ISBN: 978-1-62720-587-0
Paperback ISBN: 978-1-62720-588-7
Ebook ISBN: 978-1-62720-589-4

Internal Design by Maxx Lao
Cover by A. Molotkov and Apprentice House Press
Edited by Matthew McCarney
Editorial Development by Sarah Gilmour
Promotional Development by Emily Metheny

Published by Apprentice House Press

Apprentice
House Press
Loyola University Maryland

Loyola University Maryland
4501 N. Charles Street, Baltimore, MD 21210
410.617.5265
www.ApprenticeHouse.com
info@ApprenticeHouse.com

For all immigrants

FRIDAY, NOVEMBER 8, 2019

1. Maharani Kapoor

Maharani could feel her bones, myriad coarse white particles. After her body was cremated, the white powder had been scattered over the Willamette. By now, most of her bones had been carried out to the Pacific, picked up by the California Current system, and eventually pushed west toward Indonesia. Several particles had made it to the Atlantic Ocean and traveled on. A grain landed on a coral reef, observing the endless dance of the colorful fish, a lava lamp of nature.

The water molecules released by Maharani's body continued their endless perambulations around the globe, following quite different trajectories than the particles of her bones. The water traveled up to the sky and rained back down. Maharani could feel every place her body had touched.

Even distributed in this way, she could sense her house near Portland and the place in Oaks Bottom Wildlife Refuge where the killer had left her body a year ago. She observed the killer in his pink house with peeling paint and a boarded-up window on the second floor. She could also see an elderly man lying on the ground, her killer's second victim.

She saw all of it without knowing how this seeing was possible. It seemed that the world wouldn't let her go as long as her killer was able to hurt others.

2. Brenda Smith

The dry spot on the pavement vaguely resembled a human shape.

"Where's the body?" Detective Brenda Smith asked.

The residential street was lit with soft yellow lights floating over a long hedge. The moon sat on top of a building on their left. The air smelled of water: rain, rot, autumn. It was 6:17 a.m., and Brenda was cold, her skin tight from the sense of dread and responsibility.

"What?" The homeless man stared uncomprehendingly.

"The body," Brenda's partner, Dmitry Volkov, said. He seemed frustrated, too, a frown on his face.

"The body?" The man shrugged. "It's gone."

"Gone?" Dmitry's eyebrows rose. "What do you mean, gone?"

Dmitry's mane of graying hair was more disheveled than usual. He was tall and athletic: broad shoulders, strong arms, his neck twice the size of Brenda's. In the last few years, he'd put on a few pounds around his midriff, but the weight looked okay on him. With his broad frame, he could get away with more, especially with his long black overcoat on.

"What's your name, sir?" Dmitry's Russian accent hadn't lessened since Brenda met him six years ago.

"Stan Michalski."

"You have any ID?"

"ID?" Michalski waved dismissively. "Stolen. It was in this shirt pocket right here." He patted an area around his heart. "One morning, gone, just like that. I had twelve bucks in there. Could've at least left the ID. It's twenty-five dollars to get it replaced." He seemed to run out of steam and stood there, mouth half-open.

"Tell us one step at a time what happened to the body," Brenda said.

"They picked it up." The man's voice was flat.

He wore a long black sweater, loose sweatpants, and immense black boots without bootlaces. White, early sixties. Medium height, round face. By his feet, a beat-up black nylon backpack stuffed to the brim. His body odor overpowered Brenda. She stepped back, trying not to make her move so abrupt it might be offensive.

"Who picked it up?" Brenda asked.

"There was a car parked over there." The man pointed. "I'm just standing here, right? Just looking at the dead guy. Then boom, the car lights come on. And then they go off again. Shit." His face looked surprised even now. "Then the door opened. I knew I was dead if he got to me. So, I ran over there to the 7-Eleven, you see." He pointed with his thumb. "Just waited it out. Finally, he drove away."

"He?" Dmitry asked.

"Just saying." The man made a broad gesture with both arms as if the entire world could be responsible. "Hell if I know for sure."

"So they just pulled up and collected the body?" Dmitry still sounded skeptical.

The man shrugged. "Couldn't see from the 7-Eleven."

Dmitry stared at him for a few seconds as if considering something. "And the car? What make and model?"

The man shrugged again. "I bet you it was dark blue or gray or something."

"Sounds like a bunch of bullshit to me." Dmitry turned to Brenda. "Let's get out of here."

"I took a picture." The homeless man insisted. "Here. I have this phone, see?" He held up a beat-up, old-fashioned flip phone. "You can take pictures with it, too." A huge grin lit up his face. "You didn't know that, did you?"

He seemed so proud of his device. He laughed, his face collapsing into each short, smothered sound. Dmitry watched him with a surprised expression.

"Can I see?" Dmitry extended his hand for the phone.

The detectives stared at the picture for a while. A body, true enough, on its right side on the pavement in a semi-fetal position. Dark jacket, the hood on. The picture looked grainy on the tiny screen; Brenda couldn't distinguish the face or gender.

"Text it to me." Digit by digit, Dmitry gave Michalski his number and waited as the homeless man fiddled with the buttons.

"Was the body male or female?" Brenda was still unsure what to make of this story.

"It was a dude, no doubt. I saw his face. I was going to take another picture, but that's when I had to run."

Brenda was counting the minutes until her morning dose of caffeine. She'd been deep in dreams when the call came. Her stomach gurgled. Embarrassing. She needed a proper breakfast. It was awkward to feel hungry and human next to this homeless person, this empty, dry spot on the pavement. Still, not having a dead body on their hands was a gift. As if there'd been no murder.

"They give these out for free to low-income folks," Michalski said.

"What?" Brenda tried her best to focus.

"The phones."

"Oh, yeah. Right. They distribute free phones." Brenda handed him a card. "Give me a call if you think of something else."

Michalski examined the small paper rectangle as if debating what it was.

"Good luck then." He offered something resembling a military salute, his limp palm up in the air next to his right temple.

"Thank you." Dmitry winked at Brenda. Why the hell did he wink?

Michalski picked up his backpack and began walking away, casually swaying from side to side and clearly in no hurry. Brenda's brain was as blank as this bodyless murder scene. They lingered in the middle of the small street. There was no traffic at this hour.

"Do you believe him, Detective?" Brenda used a British accent she and Dmitry employed for their role-playing game, to help pass the hours of driving around or waiting for some warrant.

"It smells a little fishy to me, Detective." Dmitry did his best, but his accent sounded more Russian than British. "Such a bloody shame."

The last bit cracked her up, and Dmitry laughed too. A deeper layer of his face remained serious. Brenda was used to that.

"A bit of an odd bird, I'm afraid," she continued in the accent, then dropped it. "He seemed a little out of it. Could it be someone just lying on the pavement?"

"Yeah..." Dmitry sounded unconvinced. "We gotta take a look on a bigger screen."

Brenda scanned the scene. A quiet street, with only a few windows lit. A full moon above the buildings—too large, like a backdrop in a high school theater production. In one of the windows, she briefly saw a shadow obscured by the curtain, and then there was nothing again, just a faded light.

"Should we call forensics?" she asked.

"Forensics?" Dmitry's broad face expressed humor, confusion, and who knows what else.

"According to Mr. Michalski, we have a murder scene."

"Come on, Bren. We'll be a laughing stock forever if we call forensics to a murder scene with no body."

"So you think he's made the whole thing up?"

"I'm not sure. The picture is vague, is all I know."

"Come on, dude. Jim's guys would love to start their morning examining this nice little street."

"Tough one." Dmitry pulled out a latex glove, knelt, and picked up a small object. A black BIC lighter, the cheap kind sold everywhere, including the 7-Eleven down the block. "OK, call them."

"They always find something." Brenda was happy that Dmitry didn't argue, even if she could already hear the other cops' stupid jokes in her head. *Hey, Detective, where's your body?* Whatever. She called forensics as Dmitry packed the lighter in a small evidence bag and stuffed it into his jacket pocket.

"I could swear someone was watching us from that window over there." Brenda pointed at the salmon-colored house across the street.

"Let's talk to them as soon as forensics get here." Dmitry seemed in a good mood for no reason Brenda could understand.

"Let's get some breakfast first. I'm about to pass out from hunger."

3. Dmitry Volkov

Dmitry was hungry, too. He and Brenda ordered their burgers and sat at a diner around the corner from the crime scene, sipping coffee. If there was a crime. Dmitry didn't get the whole American thing about eating certain types of food at certain meals. It made no sense to him. His preferences had rubbed off on Brenda.

It was 6:51 a.m. The diner was sturdy and old-fashioned like he'd seen in old American movies, with laminated counters and cracked red faux leather seats a guy could drown in. The smell of coffee and grease was invigorating, just what Dmitry needed at this hour.

He bit into his burger, and the taste spread through his mouth, the perfect mix he'd loved since he made it to America in his early twenties: the vegetables, the cheese, the mayo, and the beef all fused into one. They sat a while at the diner, discussing the crime scene. Neither had any good theories for the disappearing body.

Brenda Smith was skinny, about five eight. Athletic. Her short hair curled around her expressive face, making it look even more animated. Despite a few wrinkles, she looked young for her age. Forty-four. Or was it forty-seven? Unlike his wife, Rita, who was cheerful and full of a positive vibe, Brenda brimmed with nervous energy, a spring compressed too tightly. She wore her puffy blue jacket and a pair of jeans.

It was 7:35 when they rang at the door of the salmon-colored house. They didn't wait long. A middle-aged woman no taller than 5'2" opened the door. She wore a long black dress and a pair of matching sandals that looked unconventional. The woman's necklace shone with all sorts of colors. She was dressed too exuberantly for someone at home early in the morning. Was she getting ready for work? Curly black hair hung loosely around her ears, much like Brenda's.

"Morning." Dmitry produced his badge. She looked resigned as if she'd expected as much. "I'm Detective Volkov. This is my partner, Detective Smith. Mind if we ask you some questions?"

"Questions? About what?" The woman spoke with a slight accent. Middle Eastern? Asian?

"Were you watching us earlier when we examined the scene?" He pointed.

"The scene?"

Something off about her demeanor—a kind of nervousness. It meant nothing. Most people reacted that way to the police.

Dmitry thought of Ivan, his pal from the Leningrad years. Ivan had worked for *militsia*, the Soviet police. They'd get together occasionally for a few drinks or to watch a hockey game. Often, Ivan would share a gruesome or funny story. A drunk who fell asleep in the pipe trench and was buried alive. A guy with a false passport arrested for the crimes of the original passport holder. Nonsense Soviet stuff but often brutal as hell.

"You were looking out the window, weren't you?" Brenda used her friendly voice.

The woman hesitated a little too long. "I just saw you out there, that's all."

"What's your name, Ma'am?" Dmitry asked.

"Yasmin Haddad. H. A. D. D. A. D."

Dmitry was no stranger to spelling out his last name, also six letters. Through the open front door, the hall looked small and tidy: beaded curtains led to a short corridor of wall rugs. One featured a red dragon spiraling out from the center like a crazy volcano erupting with a pattern of double triangles around the perimeter. Dmitry made an effort to refocus on the conversation. A faint smell of incense reached his nostrils.

"Are you the owner," he asked. "Or just renting?"

"Just renting."

Dmitry couldn't shake the feeling that she was hiding something.

"So, you didn't see anything unusual this morning?" Brenda asked.

"No. I was sleeping."

"What time did you wake up?"

"Around 5:30."

"That's pretty early." Brenda smiled.

"I'm an early riser. Have always been."

The morning light had arrived. The forensic team in white suits were busy working the scene, their lights on, their voices cheerful and annoyingly optimistic in the crispy air. It had rained again while he and Brenda were having breakfast. No trace remained of the dry spot that had suggested a missing body.

4. The Corrector

The Corrector reached under his mother's body and lifted her middle. With his other hand, he pulled out the plastic bedpan, careful not to splash Mom's piss. He tried not to look too closely. The stink and the smell of Mom's body were like polish remover. He held his breath against it. Her old body was shutting down. A nurse came three times a week to check on her; other days, it was The Corrector's job.

Mom's condition had worsened. It'd been a couple of weeks of this sorry state. Couldn't get up or anything. Oh well. At least she wasn't afraid of dying, the old bat. The Corrector would cry for her when she was gone, that was for sure. She was what, sixty-two, sixty-four? But she was always going to die young. Everyone knew that. Drinking ran in the family; none of them lived long.

The living room was shady. That's how Mom liked it. The blinds were drawn, but enough light seeped in to see all she needed to see. The white walls, the beige carpet. Just a standard room.

A mess, though, that was for sure. All sorts of medical shit: wrappers, pillows, bed covers. He really should clean up, but who cared? The technicians had pushed the couch and the chair, and the coffee table aside to make room for the damn high-tech bed. There was no room left to stand. Outside, it was raining the fuck out of a dreary day.

At least she'd outlived Dad. Dad would've made her last years hell, like he'd done with the rest of her life. Dad had been great, but together, his parents were like a broken old TV. No picture, just a lot of weight.

"Thank you, dear," Mom said in her crinkled old voice as he walked around the high-tech bed and headed for the bathroom. Her hair was gray on the pillow, grayer than last week.

"Sure, Mom." He didn't turn to look at her. He had to watch his step. The other day he'd stumbled and splashed the whole damn load on the rug. It still smelled like piss in that area.

Yep, Dad had kicked the bucket first. He should be grateful to his son for taking care of things. Now The Corrector was the one left to see his mother off into the shit that happens next, the afterlife or whatever. She had a few weeks tops. The docs were wishy-washy about the whole thing; you never knew if you could trust them.

In the bathroom, he dumped the contents of the pan into the toilet.

The Corrector's lungs weren't in top-notch shape anymore. He couldn't hold his breath long, and the stink hit his nostrils, sharp and clear. He flushed, feeling a grimace of disgust on his face. His arms shook a little, strained from getting the bedpan from under Mom. He rinsed the bedpan and set it on the floor beside the sink. As he washed his hands, he looked down at them. The stupid white bubbles of soap.

He took a piss himself and flushed again. Time to get lunch for Mom. The Corrector stood there, staring at himself in the mirror. His face was okay: firm and weather-worn. A neat, short haircut and a cool beard. A deep crease sat in the middle of his forehead from all the fucking worries in his life. Huge bags under his eyes. What else was new?

The Corrector stood tall as he examined himself. He still had vigor and energy in his muscles. He was ready for his mission.

When he came out, Mom was all present, her mind clear.

"You shouldn't have to do this, taking care of me like this." She looked embarrassed, her voice still cracking from pain and sleep.

Sleeping was something she did a lot of these days, with all the drugs she was on.

"Someone has to do it, Mom. That's what they say, ain't it?"

"At least I'll be dead soon." She constantly repeated that as if this was supposed to make The Corrector feel better.

"No rush," he said with a big smile.

"You're still young. You should marry, have children. Now, your hands will be free to do whatever you want."

"Mom!" He hated that business of her trying to fix his life.

"Okay, okay." She settled into her broad white pillows.

The bed unit's back was tilted. Mom half-sat like a queen, her thin arms over the covers like a kid's. The bed smelled of oil, like machine equipment. The panel was full of buttons to move each section around and tilt it this way or that. The technicians who'd installed it kept blabbering about Bluetooth and shit like that, but The Corrector barely followed half of it.

TUESDAY, NOVEMBER 12

5. *Brenda Smith*

"The pavement pattern is a match." Jim Lundstrom puffed on his pink e-cigarette as he talked, his thin, intelligent face engaged and animated. Smoking would kill him one day. Jim was a lovely loner, a kind and quiet person.

The rain hadn't stopped all day.

"I took some pictures and compared these prominent lines here and here." Jim pointed.

On the screen, two photos sat side by side, one of the alleged body, the other of the pavement where the body was supposed to have been. White arrows pointed at the lines that matched. Jim's thick eyebrows converged at the nose as if he were puzzled by the positive results.

"I'll check the missing person reports," Brenda said.

"Let me know if I can help with anything." Jim nodded before walking out.

Missing person cases depressed Brenda. Most were either murdered, dead from natural causes, or stuck under the bridge somewhere in a drug addiction relapse. Either way, no one deserved that fate. Brenda couldn't help feeling that things could have been better if others—especially people with all the money—cared a little more.

She opened the database and searched the state of Oregon. 432 people. It was hopeless. Faces, descriptions—how was she supposed to find the right person, especially without either? It might be too early, anyway. Only two days had passed. Brenda scrolled through pages and pages of reports; no one had mentioned a nondescript jacket. It was difficult to get the case out of her head.

"What's your feeling?" she asked. "Is it real? Is it a prank?"

Dmitry's fingers played with his prominent chin obscured by the beard. He shook his head from side to side as if to an internal rhythm, as he often did when he was thinking.

"I say it's real."

"Why? Is it that lighter? Why do you like that lighter so much?"

"I don't know. Something about it. But it's not just that."

"Yeah." Brenda hesitated. "And that woman, Yasmin Haddad. She knows more than she told us."

6. Dmitry Volkov

Through the fourth-floor windows, the day poured its even light on his office desk, the computer, and the chairs. All that light. That's what God must be to his brother Boris unless Boris was bullshitting him about the whole still believing in God thing. It made no sense to argue with Boris.

In Dmitry's line of work, belief didn't come easy. He didn't need God to watch over his shoulder like an insecure father. If God cared at all, he wouldn't let people do the crap they do.

Spacious for two detectives, the office was the size of their family apartment back in Leningrad. Their two identical desks faced a pair of windows that could use some cleaning. Dmitry's desk was clutter-free, while Brenda's was covered in paperwork, books, and old coffee cups. They both hated the carpet's indefinite beige. A row of fluorescent lights hummed overhead. Dmitry got out of his chair and turned them off.

His phone buzzed. Another text from Misha.

Where's my money? :)

An actual smiley face at the end. Motherfucker. What was Dmitry supposed to say? He didn't have the money yet, but he'd pay it back, he would.

It was better to think about the case. Something about the case didn't add up.

"Bren, you have a minute?"

"Sure thing." She swiveled in her office chair to face him, turning her attention away from her pile of uncleared cases.

"Let's think backwards." That's what his wife, Rita, would recommend. *Let's retrace our steps. Let's go back.* He pictured her whispering this mantra to herself as she looked for her car keys, left in the freezer or beside the toilet. He imagined Rita's muscular body, cheerful face, and long strands of blond hair in permanent motion, surrounding her face in a halo. What would Rita say if she found out about Misha's threats?

Dmitry forced his thoughts back to the conversation. "Let's say it was a prank. Why play dead for a picture? To attract attention? But to what? There's no clear goal, no target."

"Fair enough," Brenda pursed her lips, thinking. "Let's say the body was real. Does it mean the crime happened right there?"

"Maybe the body fell out of a moving vehicle?" Dmitry was already laughing. "I've heard of this happening in Stalin's times back in Russia."

"Stalin's times?" Brenda laughed, too. "Give me a break. Unless the killer was transporting it in a wheelbarrow."

She pulled a tissue from the box on her desk, blew her nose, and tossed the tissue into the paper basket filled to the brim. The tissue balanced precariously on the pile, ready to slide to the floor.

"We might have to wait." Dmitry shrugged. "Unless the body turns up, we don't have a case."

7. The Corrector

Rush Limbaugh's voice on the radio warmed up the small break room as The Corrector chewed his ham and cheese sandwich and sipped his Coke. The Corrector loved the man and had been listening to him for years.

> *If any race of people should not have guilt about slavery, it's Caucasians. The white race has probably had fewer slaves and for a briefer period of time than any other in the history of the world... And yet white guilt is still one of the dominating factors in American politics. It's exploited, it's played upon, it is promoted, used, and it's unnecessary.*

"Damn right," Daniel smiled at The Corrector. Daniel was a nice, conservative dude in his sixties from Eastern Oregon. Another part-timer at Straight Nail Hardware on Sandy Boulevard. Daniel had moved to Portland to be close to his daughter, but the city's liberal vibe didn't work too well for him. The Corrector, too, was disgusted by what the city had become.

The small table with three chairs was tucked in by the wall, opposite a pile of new deliveries to be unpacked, which weren't supposed to be stored in this area. A bunch of stupid cardboard to empty, break down, and dispose of—their job for the rest of the shift. This wasn't the worst part. The worst was manning the fucking counter, trying to explain simple stuff to whiny new Portlanders who couldn't tell an axe from a shovel. These assholes should have stayed in fucking California or wherever it was they came from.

"I've heard this one before. Must be a rerun." The Corrector frowned, trying to remember when he'd first heard Rush's comment.

Just then, the manager, Juan, burst in. "You two. I've asked you to keep this stuff down." Juan looked back toward the sales floor, concern on his face.

Daniel didn't protest, just turned the volume down a notch or two. It was good that the thing was next to Daniel. Had it been up to The Corrector, he wasn't sure what he would've done. Too bad they had to obey that clown. That wasn't fair at all. Fortunately, all The Corrector had to do was get through four hours of this three times a week.

"Wanna grab a beer after work?"

He already knew Daniel's answer.

"Nah. Wife's going to be waiting on me for dinner. Thanks, though."

The rejection didn't bother The Corrector because Daniel presented it as a matter of fact without apologies. Might as well get back home anyway, check on Mom. Sure, not much could happen to her that wouldn't happen in a week or two, but shit, he wasn't ready yet.

He continued chewing his sandwich, listening to Rush's voice.

Soft, but not subdued.

8. Naseem Nazari

Naseem stared at the gray sky as it rushed overhead. As it rained, he watched the water drops on their way down. Their long fall.

He lay on the roof where he had been dumped a few days ago.

He had plenty of time.

He couldn't help feeling irritated. On Saturday, he'd planned to trick his friend Igor Pechorin with a Queen's Gambit, which he'd researched and practiced all week, playing both sides and keeping notes. Pechorin was the most outrageous guy Naseem had ever met, and this was putting it mildly. Yet, the Russian's exuberance was appealing. Naseem could never imagine himself going on and on about things like Igor did: stuff he knew and didn't know, all mixed up in a verbal hurricane. Performing for the audience of whoever happened to be around. They call it verbal diarrhea in English.

Yet, Igor was a caring person, willing to listen and keep track of others' problems. So many evenings they'd shared, drinking Naseem's strong coffee, playing chess, and discussing their pasts. Naseem was an engineer born in the wrong place, and Igor, a dissident in the USSR and on the KGB watch list if one were to believe him.

He wouldn't be surprised if Igor knew him better than anyone alive.

The frustrating thing about chess was that Naseem didn't excel at it. It would have been nice to visualize the board several moves ahead or keep it in his mind. But he'd never had the intelligence or the patience. He'd stare at the pale and brown squares as diverging possibilities ran off in unpredictable directions and eluded his control. Before too long, he found himself thinking about the matters that occupied him most: his life, memories, and books he read. He was good with words and with his hands. Chess wasn't his talent.

Extraordinarily unfair, considering how much Naseem loved it, with its incredible effort of tracking sixteen pieces and its myriad outcomes even a genius couldn't predict. As hard as Naseem tried, Igor won 90% of the time without ever studying the game. Even when he went off on one of his monologues and lost a piece, invariably, he managed to save his sorry Russian ass, bringing the game at least to a draw.

His sorry Russian ass. Naseem giggled to himself. He loved the expressions they used in this language. He was getting surprisingly good at English after six years. But poor Moby Dick, so far in the past. The thick volume put Naseem to sleep with its unnecessary whale and its pointless sacrifice. By contrast, he cherished his Ernest Hemingway and Toni Morrison novels. There was so much more to read.

The thing was, it didn't look like Naseem would get to show off his Queen's Gambit or read another book. He couldn't move any part of his body. Not even his chest, to do the work of breathing. Nor had the unclenched fist of his heart retained any beating aspirations.

He was dead. This conclusion was undeniable.

9. Brenda Smith

Brenda pulled the half-full bottle of Smirnoff from the freezer and poured two or three fingers' worth into a glass, adding a fair amount of orange juice. Dmitry had gotten her into vodka years ago. It goes well with anything.

She sat on a small round stool by her kitchen table, resting her eyes on its glossy blue surface. The kitchen smelled clean. Outside, a few large clouds dominated the sky. Brenda remembered sitting in the kitchen with her ex, Jessica, who'd dumped her two years earlier, an outcome Brenda was still processing. She needed fresh air. She rose and cracked the window open, letting in a cold drift. It smelled of autumn.

Jessica had blamed the danger of Brenda's job—but so few detectives were hurt. It'd been something else—the emotional toll of her work, the burnout of dead-end cases. To make things worse, all over the country, the police did awful things she kept reading about every day, making her doubt her line of work. Still, someone had to solve murders. It was a bag full of stones, and someone had to carry it to the river.

With a missing body to account for and no clues, this week may have been the worst yet. Brenda closed her eyes. Jessica's face remained clear in her mind. Brenda was tempted to scroll back in her phone to look at the pictures from those years. She resisted, aware that this memory trip would only bring more pain. Vodka was more dependable against mental distress. She finished her first drink and poured another.

The drink had warmed her, but she still felt restless. Spending the night at home in a state like this would be pure torture. She had to get out. Being able to do anything anytime a whim struck her was one advantage of living alone. She pulled on her cool red capri pants and her black leather jacket. Her shoes were red and black. In this outfit, no one would take her for a cop.

Brenda was already drinking and didn't plan to stop; she opened the Lyft app. Only seven minutes for the nearest driver. She pressed the button. As she waited, she rinsed her glass and filled it with water. She downed it quickly and placed it on the rack next to the sink as she watched the driver's avatar on her smartphone approach her location.

The driver was friendly but not effusive—exactly what Brenda wanted. She stretched out in the backseat, letting Portland's streets wash over her. As they drove across the Morrison Bridge, she said hello to the river in her mind. Her thoughts were scattered.

Gertrude's buzzed, like most nights. Named after the famous writer, the club had a stellar reputation the modern era had not tarnished. Brenda looked around: a few familiar faces, but no one she knew by name. Just as well. The music and the lights made everything easy, overpowering every kind of silence. As she walked over to the bar, Brenda found her body moving in time with the music.

Her eyes fell on a striking woman at the bar: prominent lips, large hazel eyes, hair down to her shoulders dyed pink. She wore a blue tunic, a small thing that helped one imagine her body underneath. The seat next to her was empty. Brenda nodded as she sat down, and the girl nodded back and looked Brenda up and down. Excellent. Brenda wasn't into formalities either.

WEDNESDAY, NOVEMBER 13

10. Dmitry Volkov

Natasha made loud gurgling noises, a habit she had recently perfected. A precocious six-year-old, she cracked up each time, her curls shaking as she laughed. Dmitry and Rita had made the mistake of laughing along a few times, and now the girl performed the action incessantly, hoping for a reaction. They did their best to ignore it.

"Mommy, mommy, can I watch TV until we have to go to school?"

"Ask your dad." Rita had finished her breakfast and floated about the room, getting ready for work. "It's his turn to take you."

"Okay, okay," Dmitry huffed.

Natasha's show pierced the morning quiet with a pack of high-pitched, overexcited voices. Rita looked great in her dark blue office suit, sexy but formal. Seeing her, Dmitry felt terrible about his debt. He was tempted to tell her as he sat at the sturdy kitchen table, his breakfast of bacon and eggs with toast before him. The smell of morning: the bacon, the coffee. He'd have his burger for lunch this time.

The sky outside was still dark. Footsteps and voices reached him from the street below. Dmitry was opening to the day, trying to shake off the dreams, something dreary in hushed tones, the weight of his choices pressing down on him in his sleep.

"I'm running late again." Rita sounded surprised. "What's wrong with me?"

After twenty-seven years, he and Rita were comfortable with English, but it was natural to speak Russian at home; both had been in their twenties when they immigrated. Lately, Natasha was more likely to respond in English or miss something if addressed in their native tongue. Soon, they'd have to switch to English around her. Another part of their past, slipping away.

As she zipped past Dmitry, Rita briefly wrapped her arms around his shoulders and kissed his neck. Natasha had settled on the couch with her oversized doll, Mercury, an eerie plastic creature with an unflinching gaze, random blinking, and rigid, submissive arms and legs. Mercury was like a small dead body, and Dmitry couldn't get that image out of his head.

"Pizza for dinner? Sorry, Dimka." Rita used the diminutive version of his name. "Long meetings."

Between his job and Rita's office manager position that sucked endless hours out of their lives, they didn't see each other enough.

"Natasha, say bye to Mama," Dmitry said.

"Bye, Mama." Natasha sounded distant, captivated by her show.

11. Brenda Smith

Brenda woke with a start as if something demanded her immediate attention. But in the first seconds after awakening, nothing urgent came to her as she lay there, staring at the dark window backlight by the moon, which hid somewhere outside the view. The missing body case came back to her, pressing on her with its bizarre puzzle.

She turned to lie on her back— and oh, wow...someone next to her in bed, a head on the pillow. Brenda's brain was still half-full of dreams, but the night before came back to her in a half-focused glimpse. Mary. Brenda felt a smile on her face.

Mary lay half-covered; the moonlight seeping through the window highlighted her left shoulder, breast, and part of her left hip. In this light, she looked impossibly tanned—but Brenda remembered her pale skin, so fascinating and attractive, so different from hers. They'd spent a beautiful night of drinking and laughing, talking, and sex.

For a while, Brenda watched Mary's chest rising and falling. It had been months since she'd been with someone. Then, abruptly, her thoughts returned to the homeless man and his picture, the empty spot on the pavement. She might have dreamed it; it felt more recent than last Friday. How awkward to lie in bed with this beautiful woman as crime scene images rushed through her head. Brenda forced them out, telling herself not to act like the obsessed weirdo she was.

Easier said than done.

This city was so packed with people she would never solve all the murders. She had to solve at least a few, at least this one.

Mary shifted in her sleep, her head rolling onto Brenda's shoulder.

Something incredibly trustful about this gesture, even if it was unconscious—it nearly moved Brenda to tears. She'd missed human touch.

12. Naseem Nazari

The fight with Yasmin bothered him. Naseem wished things hadn't occurred in that order. It was one of those pointless incursions into each other's comfort zones that occasionally crashed their otherwise peaceful coexistence. They were at Yasmin's house. They'd finished dinner. A game of Scrabble was spread on the table between them, one of their favorite ways to spend time together while improving their English.

A strange tension grew in Yasmin's face as she made her word. She used the L in *love* and added five letters to make up *lonely*. A double word score. Still, something unresolved persisted on her face.

Naseem contrasted the two words. "What's wrong?"

"Can we *consider* moving in together?" Yasmin said consider with an emphasis as if giving it a thought would suffice. "I hate spending so much time apart, stuck in our holes. It just doesn't make sense."

"I'm not sure." Naseem loved his time alone: reading, thinking, learning, walking the safe Portland streets, chatting, or playing chess with Igor Pechorin.

"I'd thought you might say that." Yasmin's face with the spark gone out of it. He knew she wanted more of him than he could give. "I'm not getting any younger, you know."

He wasn't sure if he felt like compromising or letting her go.

"This dating business," Yasmin continued. "Seeing each other two or three times a week—who does this? Kids in their twenties? Executives dealing with midlife crises? God! I need someone next to me, someone I can rely on. If I fall and break my leg, I need someone to find me."

"Why do you always pressure me? Things are going so well." Even as Naseem said this, he knew how wrong it sounded, how cliché.

"Well?" Indignation on Yasmin's face. "You think things are going well?"

"Why not?" He was beginning to feel tense. "We have good conversations, good...everything."

"Oh, but that's not enough." Yasmin's arms crossed before her.

"Why ruin something that works?" Naseem could hear annoyance in his voice, and he hated that. Yasmin was right. He wasn't giving her all of himself. He couldn't.

"You're not listening to me, are you? What kind of man are you? I thought you were different."

She was almost yelling now, which always had the effect of shutting Naseem up. He didn't want to be the man who yelled at women, even to defend himself. He'd seen too many such men.

"What?" she kept egging him on. "You have nothing to say?"

"I'm sorry."

"I'm sorry. What good does that do? God! You're just like Ahmed."

In what way, exactly, was Naseem like Yasmin's husband, who'd died four or five years earlier and was a frequent reference point for her opinions about men? It was a hurtful thing. Naseem resented being compared to a dead guy.

"I don't want to think about Ahmed. I've never met him. All I know is what you've told me about him."

"You're hopeless." Yasmine shoved the letters off the Scrabble board, scattering them over the coffee table and the floor.

She stormed upstairs. Naseem knew she'd lock herself up in the bedroom.

And that was the last time he'd seen Yasmin.

13. Brenda Smith

"I love your little place." Mary's voice. "That kitchen is so nice."

Morning light seeped into Brenda's dreams. Slowly, she opened her eyes. "I must have fallen asleep again."

Already, Mary was sliding under the covers with her, and there she was. Her warm body. The touch of skin and muscle under Brenda's fingers, the unabashed hunger in Mary's eyes. They gasped for breath amid their kisses as the cover slid around over their two bodies, finally falling useless on the floor. Temporarily, time let the two of them loose from its grasp.

After, they lay in each other's arms, catching their breath.

"Have you had this from birth?" Brenda sat up to see better.

"What?"

"This birthmark right here." Brenda touched the mark on Mary's knee.

"No one has ever noticed it before." Mary sounded moved.

"Adorable." Brenda cuddled up to her lover, almost offended on Mary's behalf. How could no one have noticed her birthmark? Brenda felt soft from all this bliss.

"Do you have to work today?" Mary asked. "Please say no."

"Oh, sweetie. I'm so sorry."

"What do you do for work again?"

Brenda had dreaded this question. She'd been evasive the night before. Portland was a city of liberals; being a cop was nothing to brag about here. Shit, shit, shit! It was the worst possible moment. Brenda's brain burned as the second stretched into two—still, she was frozen, her chest tight.

"I'm an office manager." She thought of Rita, Dmitry's wife, for no reason she could identify. "You?"

"I'm a vet assistant."

Immediately, Brenda felt terrible. It had been stupid to tell such an absurd lie, especially to a woman she was so into. If they kept dating, it would surely backfire. At work, she dealt with dumb lies like this all day. She was hopeless, completely hopeless. *An office manager.* There it was, said and gone out of her mouth, leaving Brenda stuck in the goo of her lie.

14. The Corrector

The Corrector poured himself some bourbon and sat in his chair, his cigarette in the ashtray smoking away at a steady pace. That's how Marlboros worked. They took care of themselves. It was a good day, time to celebrate. Why did he feel gloomy as shit? Outside, it was still dark. He didn't give a fuck what time it was.

His bedroom was big enough to fit a desk and an office chair. Not that The Corrector used the desk much. He loved the chair most. He'd put the back of the chair against the desk to stretch his legs on his bed.

The whole house was the same: white walls, beige carpets. The only thing different about The Corrector's room was his Megadeth poster plastered above the desk. He planned to add another poster or two, but his mind had been on more important stuff.

Mom was downstairs in her mechanical bed. Hospice. Nothing new; he was used to the idea. His thoughts returned to last week's corrective action. It'd gone well. Dad would be proud of him and offer him a beer. Instead of calling him Junior, Dad would refer to him by his chosen name, The Corrector. They would sit on the porch, watching people walk by.

The warehouse roof the day before had been a nice touch if he did say so himself. It'd taken some work. He'd noted the place a few weeks earlier as he was driving by—not a soul around. He'd made sure of it; he had spent a fair amount of time in his car spying.

He'd tied the ladder to his bike rack. The part about climbing with a load on his shoulders had been hard, but The Corrector wanted it to be. He had to use straps like furniture movers do. He'd challenged himself so that he could be proud later. He was covered with sweat when he was done.

He considered telling his mom about the whole thing. He was dying to share. She'd understand. She felt the same way about politics. But hell, it was better not to rock the boat. His room was dim, with dirty dishes on his old desk. Mom would have given him shit for the mess if she could still walk upstairs. Light seeped through the unwashed window. Rain outside—what else was new? The cigarette smell helped with the stink of all the food leftovers. Two birds with one stone.

So, what was the dread about?

Or was it more like responsibility?

He was on a mission. Too late to stop. The Corrector reaffirmed this in his mind, and just then, something went tweaky in him. He could tell by the way the skin on his neck tightened. Before he knew it, he was sobbing like a baby—just sitting there on his bed and sobbing. It would be embarrassing as hell if anyone had seen him. Dad would have called him a pussy.

Time passed, and The Corrector just sat there as if watching his sobs from a distance, like there was another dude inside there, sobbing his guts out. And all this time, Mom was sleeping downstairs, deep in her medicine dreams. The Muslim man's face came back to The Corrector, the way it had changed when the guy realized he was done for. That bum had almost ruined the whole thing, but things had worked out fine. It was time to send a clear message. The President wasn't afraid to do so, to call a spade a spade.

The Corrector wiped his tears with the back of his hand and got up to pour himself another shot. He hated to admit it to himself, but crying had helped.

The risk felt sweet. No one would find him. No clues to find him by, nothing he'd left behind, absolutely nothing. His corrective action had gone well. Sure, he might've dropped his fucking lighter somewhere along the way, but he'd never been fingerprinted. He had nothing to fear.

15. Sania Jamison

Sania straightened the edge of her hijab. It was just after six, past the time for Maghrib, the evening prayer. She stepped out of Starbucks, her small tray holding two double lattes, one for herself and one for her husband, Atif. Her turn tonight.

It was rainy; the sky hung gloomy and unwelcoming over the sad, dark city. The smell of rotting leaves and mold tinged the air. Sania was grateful for the fabric that kept her hair dry. As she walked, she took in the passersby. Some treated her with indifference; others noted her attire. She was used to it and didn't analyze the reactions. It didn't matter. Eventually, humans would mature and ignore what other humans wore. That time was approaching fast. Living in a place like Portland made it especially easy to believe so.

She wondered how her two children would choose to answer the God question when they were older. Atif and Sania openly discussed other religions and critiques of religion, so the children had a chance to decide.

An old lady walking ahead of Sania dropped her black leather glove. Sania felt bad as the woman struggled to pick it up, her umbrella floating above her, too large for her birdlike frame. The woman must have been in her eighties—lovely and helpless, her paper bag of groceries getting wet on the ground by her feet. Her face, with its heap of gray hair, was strained—she was getting frustrated.

"Here you go." Sania picked up the glove with her free hand.

"Thank you, dear. You're so kind." The smile that bloomed on the woman's face made her look younger.

"You're welcome, Ma'am."

The old woman's smile warmed Sania's heart. It was odd: she'd helped without expecting any payoff, and the exertion had been minimal—and still, she felt better, as if she'd traded a tiny effort for a pearl of happiness. Sania imagined herself at that age. How would it feel to be on the other side of help?

She'd have to wait and see.

16. The Corrector

"What's the best place to go fishing around here?" The dude was Black and middle-aged, his belly hanging before him like a lump of nonsense.

"Fishing?" How in the fuck was The Corrector supposed to know? Fishing wasn't a thing in his family. "Can't tell you."

He was just trying to do his job and get paid. Anyway, the way it kept raining outside, you had to be one crazy motherfucker to go fishing.

"You guys do sell flashlights, don't you?" The asshole was not discouraged.

"Aisle nine." The Corrector pointed.

He inhaled the store smell to settle himself: metal and oil, wood and rubber.

"Thanks." The customer nodded and walked the fuck off.

There it was again, a moment of quiet. Only forty minutes of his shift to go. The Corrector was tired of all the questions. Who wanted to spend the day translating customers' half-ass plans into specific tools and materials? They should all shop at Home fucking Depot. Worse, he had to care for them alone; Daniel was off today.

A few minutes before closing, a kid of eight or nine came in holding a nail. His dad had sent him to pick up a whole box. Easy. The Corrector enjoyed helping the kid find the proper nails. He took the five-dollar bill and gave the change. "Good luck with your remodeling."

"Thank you, sir."

The Corrector was startled when Juan walked out of his office and locked the front door, turning the Closed sign to face the street.

"See you tomorrow." Juan glanced at him.

"See you tomorrow." The Corrector sounded like a fucking parrot. Or one of these newfangled electronic dolls. He'd rather not respond, but the dude was his boss. The Corrector had much bigger fish to fry. Hell! The world would soon know of him but would not soon forget him.

He thought of his mom. He hoped the old bird would still be breathing when he got back.

17. Naseem Nazari

Naseem had had trouble sleeping on the couch. He was thinking about his long life, about Yasmin. Why was he so hesitant about taking the next step with her? He couldn't answer. Minutes turned into hours as he lay there. He would've gone home earlier but missed the last bus.

The sidewalk by Yasmin's house. The man yelled something from the other side of the street. Something about immigrants. Naseem was so preoccupied with the fight that he didn't pay attention at first. The street was dark. Another crazy man shouting on Portland streets; he might as well not get involved.

He was walking away, but the man had already begun crossing the street, approaching at a steady clip. Anxiety rose in Naseem's chest, a wave of heat. He wanted to run, but running would be silly. And the next moment, the man was on him, his hands on Naseem's throat. A white guy, huge, his arms like a wrestler's.

Instinctively, Naseem's hands went up, trying to peel off the man's hands. Any moment, the attacker would let him go. Wouldn't he? Wouldn't he? Naseem tried to kick him with all his might, but the man didn't care. Everything was going red in Naseem's eyes as he tried again to pull the big hands away from his throat. Too tight. His lungs burned, exploding. And the sound—it was his wheezing. He kicked again, his energy fading.

As he lay there on the roof, Naseem could see out of his own eyes, which were open. But somehow, he could also see in other directions. He didn't understand this, but there it was, the world as he remembered it from before death.

Naseem was angry at the man but also perplexed. As if he'd missed something—and now he'd never know what it was. There must have been something wrong with that individual. And the fact that he remained in the world was troubling.

Naseem's anger had worn away after a day or two. Being dead was tolerable, but the memory of Yasmin brought a pang of guilt. He'd failed her. Not because he wasn't around anymore—that wasn't his doing. No, because he hadn't been around in the first place. They'd been together two years, but he couldn't cross that final distance. At times, he still didn't know what to say to her.

That the pains of their past were so similar didn't mean the two of them were. It was difficult to find shared comfort in your sixties. After Ayesha died, Naseem had been prepared to spend the rest of his life alone. He hadn't planned for Yasmin, for any of this.

Still, he thought of Yasmin with tenderness. She'd been there for him; they knew they could rely on each other, be honest. They'd shared many good moments, good hours. He remembered holding her hand as they watched the news, sitting together on the shabby red couch. Her hand, always cold.

His wife, Ayesha, must have also lain inside her body after cancer took her. If so, it must have felt okay: not feeling the pain anymore but still being there. Somehow, knowing this was a relief.

In his mind, Naseem saw Ayesha's inquisitive brown eyes the first time he met her. An arranged marriage had grown into something more. Even now, the place where Naseem's heart used to beat hurt from the memory of her.

The irony wasn't lost on him: to die like this after escaping one of the most dangerous countries in the world. But his friends in Yemen hadn't deserved to die any more than he had. Faisal had been blown up in a terrorist attack, only one leg found after the explosion. Wahid had died from an antibiotic-resistant strain of pneumonia. Already,

Naseem had several years on these friends. In that way, the whole thing seemed fair. What he felt was what Americans called *survivor's guilt*.

In chess, keeping all the pieces in play was impossible. Some had to be sacrificed. He was a piece out of play. The rain had subsided, allowing a few glimpses of blue to penetrate the view before Naseem's eyes. Something about his field of vision didn't make sense, but it wasn't the sky. It was a man's face that popped up over the edge of the roof. The man stopped, taking him in. Naseem felt bad the stranger had to deal with this.

The man looked down, then back at Naseem. He covered his mouth and nose with his gloved hand.

18. Brenda Smith

Brenda lowered her eyes from the rain-smeared windshield to her fists, tight on the wheel, like a first-time driver's. A tightness in her mouth, too, as she thought of the missing body. She hated this waiting.

She was on her way home. The car smelled encouragingly of coffee: the fresh cup she'd brought along, a few used cardboard cups in the back, a spill here and there.

Another thing Brenda noticed about her fists was how small they were. She'd always known she had small hands. The memory of trying to hold a gun at the police academy flashed through her mind. Today, they seemed especially tiny, as if she'd taken an Alice in Wonderland pill made specially for hands. She tried texting Mary to share this observation, but Mary was coming over in an hour or so. The two of them had been calling and texting constantly. It was strange to be so distraught about the case and yet mile-deep in her new love affair. Brenda was exhausted from the lack of sleep.

Mary's face, so different from every angle, kept hovering just outside Brenda's vision, like a small angel: alternately confident and vulnerable but always engaged and engaging. The sexy way Mary's pink hair edged across her neck. Her small nose.

After a day of rain and clouds, the sky had cleared, and a shy glimpse of sun volunteered itself upon the city. As she crossed the Willamette on her way out of downtown, Brenda glanced to the right at the Hawthorne Bridge, its three green handles of steel lattice lazy against the gray sky. The water, too, was gray. She replayed the morning's conversation in her mind, her stupid blabbering about being an office manager. Shit. She might've fucked it all up.

Her phone rang, snapping her back to the present.

Dmitry.

Brenda pressed the button on her steering wheel to accept the call.

"We have the body." Dmitry sounded excited. "I'll text you the address."

Something stood still inside Brenda, and she checked her reaction, worried she felt happier rather than more upset.

"I'll be right there."

She pulled over and sat for a minute or two with her eyes closed, restarting her work brain. She picked up her phone again and texted Mary,

> So sorry something came up at work will
> call when done

Brenda added a bundle of hugs and kisses.

The address was west of town. She'd have to cross the river again. The setting sun's slanted rays ripped at Brenda's winter eyes as she began driving, but she was happy for some brightness after all the rain. She drove carefully, squinting into the world ahead.

She pulled over in front of a warehouse, a peeling gray building with a single small, dull window and vast doors painted a darker shade of gray. The building appeared infrequently used, if not abandoned. The real estate boom that had affected the city had not yet spread to some of the outskirts, but the way things were going, it would very soon. Dmitry stood by the door, talking to a uniformed cop.

"What do we have?" Brenda asked.

"Someone smelled it." Dmitry pointed up. "The body was dumped right on top there."

"Smelled it?" The pieces were coming together in Brenda's head. "Did you look?"

"Yeah." Dmitry gestured toward a tall ladder leaning on the wall.

"I didn't touch anything."

"Was this ladder already here?" she asked.

Dmitry shrugged, looking over at the young cop.

"I had to go get the ladder." For some reason, the uniformed cop looked embarrassed. "We couldn't find one around here."

Brenda began to climb. Heights were not her favorite thing; her dread increased with each step. So did the smell. Five rungs, six, seven, nine—her head reached the roof level. One more rung. The roof was flat; the body lay on its back, about two yards from the edge. A brown jacket, just like in the photo.

With some effort, Brenda pushed herself up onto the roof. She was fit, but so high above the ground, this maneuver felt scary; she didn't look down as she swung her leg over the top of the ladder. The deceased appeared to be in his late sixties or early seventies, although he might have looked younger before decomposition had begun. He was probably Middle Eastern, his hair curly and thick. She put a glove on and pulled the jacket collar away from the victim's neck. Bruises on the throat pointed to strangulation.

Dmitry had climbed up after her.

"Is your phone handy?" she asked.

He held the screen toward her with Michalski's photo on it, the body on the sidewalk. The first responder's head hovered on the ladder just over the roof's edge.

"Granted, it's a shitty picture taken with not enough light." Dmitry shrugged. "But I'm pretty sure it's the same jacket."

Brenda nodded. The color, the shape of the hood—everything seemed to match. She kneeled by the victim and carefully checked his pockets with her gloved hand, not expecting to find anything. No one leaves valuable clues on a dead body. Surprisingly, she felt something firm in the left pants pocket. She reached in. A wallet with a few dollar bills and a bright red business card with nothing on it.

Brenda stared in horrified disbelief.

"Shit," Dmitry said over her shoulder.

She turned the card over. The other side, also blank.

An unsolved murder case from 2018: Maharani Kapoor, an Indian woman from a suburban immigrant community near Beaverton, had had a card just like this stapled to her headscarf. The body was suspended head down from a tree in Oaks Bottom Wildlife Refuge, a thin forest area next to the Willamette.

They had a serial killer on their hands.

Brenda didn't feel well; the smell was getting to her. She placed the red card into a small evidence bag and opened the wallet again.

A driver's license in a small compartment.

"Naseem Nazari," she read. "How did the body get up here?"

"The perp must've climbed with the body on his back." Dmitry scratched his head. "Sounds like a lot of work."

"Sounds about impossible." Brenda considered the body; the man must be at least 160 pounds.

"You think the perp had help?"

"I don't know. That would change the profile, wouldn't it?"

Dmitry didn't reply. Brenda checked all other pockets, hoping to find the victim's phone. No such luck.

Naseem Nazari's face revealed nothing of the horror his last minutes must have been. His expression was calm and curious, as if posing a question Brenda was responsible for answering.

19. Dmitry Volkov

Naseem Nazari's murder had cut into Dmitry in a way he hadn't expected. Dmitry had investigated many murders. Something about the way the body was first missing and then found was as showy as Maharani Kapoor's corpse hung up on a tree. Dmitry's stomach tightened at the thought that Nazari may have died a random death, picked by the killer by sheer accident. Wrong place, wrong time. An immigrant, hoping America was a better place. No part of this seemed fair.

Dmitry parked next to his blue house, noticing, not for the first time, that it could use a paint job sooner rather than later.

"I'm home." He closed the front door behind him.

A wholesome smell of beef permeated the house.

"Hi." Rita's voice from the other room sounded tense.

"What's going on?" Dmitry walked into the living room, and the answer was right before his eyes.

"Brother." Boris rushed toward him. "Long time no see."

It had been a few months. Dmitry tapped his younger brother on the back as they hugged. Boris wore an old pair of jeans, his favorite black Nikes, and a black T-shirt that hung loosely over his tall, skinny body. The smell of Boris's favorite clove cigarettes had penetrated his clothes. That edge, that glimmer in Boris's eyes, was a clear signal: he was running one of his schemes. It could be a minor burglary or a short con of some sort. Oh, Boris.

Rita looked stiff, sitting on the couch in her blue office suit. Dmitry approached her and kissed her quickly.

"Borya, good to see you." Dmitry tried to sound sincere, and he mostly was, even if Rita's energy made it difficult. "When did you get here? I had no idea you were coming."

"Oh, just a few minutes ago. I was talking to your lovely wife."

Rita reacted with a kind of smirk.

Boris was shaky in their mother tongue. Six years Dmitry's junior, Boris, had arrived in the United States as a teenager; he understood Russian when he heard it but no longer felt comfortable speaking it. They spoke English.

"Daddy, I was showing Uncle Borya my new game." The warmth of Natasha's small body as she hugged Dmitry's leg. She looked radiant in her little blue dress.

"Good job, sweetie." Dmitry petted his daughter's head, her curly hair soft and electric under his palm. Tenderness filled his heart.

"Dinner's ready," Rita said.

A platter of beef stroganoff waited in the center of the dining room table, next to a steaming bowl of mashed potatoes. Rita passed around the beef. No one spoke for a minute or two as the plates were filled and silverware clicked against the china. His wife's motivations often puzzled Dmitry. Rita rarely found the time to cook. She was unlikely to make a special effort to honor his brother.

"Looks delicious." The strange gleam remained in Boris's eyes as he shoveled half a cow's worth of beef onto the plate. "Are we going to say grace?"

Dmitry had been expecting something like that. His brother was pushy about his religion.

"We don't say grace." Dmitry picked up a piece of beef with his fork and placed it in his mouth. "But you can say whatever you want to. Be my guest."

Dmitry was more than weary of his family's Jesus-flavored dysfunction. He scooped some mashed potatoes. Yum. The combination melted on his tongue into something deeply comfortable, a taste familiar from his childhood, even if, by the end of the Soviet Union, finding meat in stores had become difficult. He still appreciated the United States, where such luxuries were always available.

"Uncle Borya, why do you always pray?" Natasha's face bore none of the tension, just a beatific smile.

"Because God sees all of us, and we must pay respect."

"Hmm." Natasha looked intrigued.

Boris always had some story or another. God had mysterious ways, or God favored the believers even if they strayed, or some such nonsense. With that half-smile always on his brother's lips, it was difficult to tell if he was serious.

"Daddy, why don't we pray?" Natasha constrained a mischievous look to avoid getting in trouble with her parents, and Dmitry couldn't help but smile. He should've expected her follow-up question.

"Because we don't believe in God."

Rita seemed embarrassed as she chewed mechanically.

Dmitry's and Boris's parents were Baptists; they'd moved to the States in 1992 with the help of a local Christian organization. The family's religious life in the Soviet Union had been secretive; they couldn't be completely open about their faith. If you attended church, someone eventually noticed and reported you to the Communist Party boss at your place of employment; you couldn't hold on to any but the most menial job. College enrollment was effectively out of reach for young people from religious families.

Their parents had held on to their simple employment: a stationery store clerk and a factory worker. No one had expected the communist state to explode. When the USSR broke down, everything was up in the air. There was no stability in the country. They had a chance to get out, and they took it.

Dmitry had given up his religious beliefs decades ago, finding himself more interested in living a simple life than believing in theories no one could prove. He glanced at Boris across the table: a face so familiar yet often perplexing. At this moment, Boris looked smug.

"I didn't know you were in town," Dmitry said to change the topic.

"Always the traveler." Boris laughed. "Just passing through. I thought I'd stay with you guys tonight." That familiar smirk on Boris's face, a sort of mask. "Do you have a problem with that? I can stay at Mom's and Dad's if you do."

A passive-aggressive prick. Why hadn't Boris stayed with their parents, to begin with? He probably needed Dmitry's help with some awful plan.

"Borka, don't be ridiculous." Dmitry did his best to soften his voice. "You know you're always welcome here. You can sleep on the couch."

"Thanks, brother. Rita, hope you don't mind?" This time, Boris's tone was solicitous; Rita had no choice.

"Of course not, Boris." A tight smile on her lips.

"When did you last visit Mom and Dad?" Boris looked up at Dmitry with a challenge in his eyes.

"February or March."

Instead of embracing the advantages of the free life in the U.S., their parents had submerged deeper into religion. They no longer wanted to have friends outside the faith, and Dmitry was tired of their sanctimony.

"They miss you, you know." Boris made a sad face. "I live in L.A. and see them more often than you. Why not stop by once in a while? Just for an hour?"

"You know why." Dmitry glanced at Rita, who looked embarrassed; she avoided eye contact.

"You *have to* visit. Sorry, Rita, no offense, but they're his parents."

"Why shouldn't I be offended?" Rita's eyes gleamed with angry light. "They've plotted against me since Dmitry and I met. Do you know what his mother called me? Do you? *Eta bezbojnaja suka kotoraya ukrala nashevo syna.*" *That godless bitch who stole our son.*

"She didn't mean it," Boris said.

THURSDAY, NOVEMBER 14

20. The Corrector

The Corrector woke abruptly out of blackness. Outside was also dark. His lungs burned, and so did his head. His shirt was soaked with sweat. He sat up in bed and tried to breathe for a while until it came easy again. The Muslim dude's face was stuck in his head, the way he looked when he realized The Corrector was coming after him. A kind of surprise on the man's face. Something about that felt off. As if things hadn't gone the way they should have.

The Corrector pushed this thought far, far down with all his strength. And he was fucking strong.

"Junior...Junior..." His mother's half-cry-half-whisper from downstairs. A surge of panic through him, cold in his arms and legs. Was she about to croak?

"Mom?" He called out.

"Darling!"

Relief flushed through him. The old crow was still talking.

Tonight, or some night like this, he would come downstairs, and there'd she be, cold as a doll. He'd prepared himself for that moment. Hell, he might have to close her eyes. The Corrector rushed down, almost missing a stair.

"Thank you, dear." She looked embarrassed. The Corrector felt bad for her, already knowing from the smell what had happened. "It must be that tuna fish. I wouldn't have woken you, but it's still so long until the morning."

"No worries, Mom." The Corrector glanced at the alarm clock by her bedside, its large red numbers blasting 2:47.

Good thing they'd switched to diapers. He should be able to

change her up in a jiffy. He knew it was a messy one, though, just by the awful smell of it.

21. Sania Jamison

Mom leaned over Sania's prone figure. "Did you check your mail?"

"Mail? What mail?"

"The mail." Her mother's expression was flat, as if she were trying to conceal a mild irritation at Sania's cluelessness. Mother's brown hair was in a tight bun that looked like a baseball.

Immediately, Sania felt guilty; she'd let her mother down somehow, as usual. Mother was biting her lips as she reached for Sania. The touch of her hand on her daughter's shaking shoulder.

Then the hand was Atif's. As Sania awoke, it was her husband leaning over her, and her mother's figure retreated into death. A heart attack had taken her seven years ago.

Sania lingered in the liminal space between sleep and the reality of the encroaching day. Light seeped through her eyelids, warm and welcoming. She had been running ragged for two weeks: all the extra hours covering for a colleague on vacation and another who'd just quit. She was exhausted and overwhelmed by the pressures of the nurse's job. A difficult occupation, but someone had to do it. And anyway, she loved it. She opened her eyelids slightly, letting more light in.

Thump—a small weight on the bed next to her, then another, sending vibrations through the soft mattress. Omar's crooked smile. This boy would need orthodontal help—another expense she and Atif had to plan for. Lidia's high-pitched giggle was contagious. Then, one of their four small feet was on Sania's stomach, and she cried out in pain.

"Ouch, guys. Be careful!"

"Sorry, Mommy." Omar snuggled up to her from her right as Lidia found a spot under her left armpit.

"That's okay, darling."

Sania felt, smelled a child on either side, and for the moment, nothing else was missing in the world. She relaxed into this happy buzz. A sweet moment: all her loved ones, at once.

"Get up, my love." Atif's voice, his broad smile. "Breakfast is ready."

Sania lowered her feet to the floor, feeling for her slippers. A plate of scrambled eggs steamed on the table; the smell hit her nostrils. She'd been too tired to eat last night, and now her belly gurgled with hunger. The rest of her family must have already eaten. They'd let her sleep in. How nice.

Atif used to be Lamar; he'd officially changed his name when they converted to Islam nine years earlier. Secretly, she preferred *Lamar*, with its French sound and reference to the sea. Their conversion had been Lamar's idea, but she'd agreed. Still, getting used to his new name took her a while. He was irritated whenever she relapsed, and she laughed and laughed about it. Sometimes, men were ridiculous like that, stuck in their seriousness. Sania didn't take it personally.

Sania had always been Sania. Lucky her. Her parents had given her a halal name.

She checked her crabby thoughts caused by nothing but the wakening mind's reluctance to click into action—and the fact that she really would have loved her eggs with bacon. Her husband was dear, and she loved him deeply. He was an intensely intelligent, kind man. In any case, these days, it was much better to believe in something than to believe in nothing at all. She got up from the bed and walked to the kitchen.

"Where are the children?"

"Brushing their teeth." Atif pointed toward the bathroom.

"You're looking beautiful this morning." An expression of shy admiration blossomed on his face. If anything, Atif himself was beautiful.

"All done!" Lidia ran to her mother, denying Sania a chance to react fully to her husband's words. Still, they'd warmed something inside her that would remain warm all day.

Lidia embraced Sania's legs and held them tight. Omar's awkward growing body was too short and too tall at the same time. Sania reached out to him to bring him close.

22. Brenda Smith

Brenda had called in advance to make sure Yasmin Haddad would be there. A Palestinian immigrant, no criminal record. Dmitry drove, his profile grim and determined. It was a gray but dry morning, the gloomy sky indifferent to their case.

"Chances are the perp didn't even know the man," Dmitry burst out. "That sucks for us. Normally, there's a reason, a connection to the victim. This time, it could be anyone. We should check the FBI database."

"Could we infiltrate a place where creeps like that meet?" Brenda was thinking, her eyes closed. "What if there's a message board or something? You know, for racists." She paused. She never quite knew where Dmitry stood on race issues; he didn't seem to care. This was unsurprising for someone from another place, especially with his religious background.

"Yeah, Bren. Maybe we could get him to tip his hand. Provoke him, you know?"

"I'll work on that."

Brenda wanted the killer so much she looked forward to searching for him on creepy websites. How twisted.

"And the red card?" she asked. "How can it be that we can't trace it?"

"We've gone over it. Could've been printed at any corner copy shop." Dmitry shrugged. "FedEx, UPS, you name it. Could've printed it at home, for all we know."

"Or it could have been VistaPrint or another big outlet."

"We tried those, didn't we?" Dmitry sounded defensive. "I hate this card business, Bren. It's like the Soviet flag, but I doubt it has anything to do with the Soviet Union."

"I hope not." Brenda smiled at him.

They parked at Oak and 67th, the traffic careful and soft. As they approached the door, Brenda searched her pants pocket for the wrapper to put away her gum. It would be awkward to chew when interviewing a potential witness. She pressed the doorbell button.

They didn't wait long. Yasmin Haddad wore a long purple shawl that covered her body entirely, from shoulders to toes. Exuberant was the word. The fabric looked soft and would feel nice on the skin.

"Ms. Haddad," Brenda said. "Good morning."

"Hi." Haddad sounded worried or tired. "Please come in."

They followed her into the living room, lit by an elegant floor lamp and a desk light opposite it. The space brimmed with shadows and smelled of incense. Brenda was no expert in furniture, but the redwood desk looked expensive. Its curved legs reminded her of ballet, of music. A half-closed blue laptop sat on the desk. The stylish wood chair with a tall back was the opposite of a modern office chair.

The stick of incense Brenda had smelled burned on the desk, next to a black leather-bound journal lying face down.

"Have a seat, please." Haddad pointed at the antique red couch. Dmitry sat, still looking around as if trying to memorize the place; Brenda took the other end of the couch as Haddad perched on the chair by the desk. "How can I help you?"

A row of six masks crafted from light wood hung on the wall above her.

"Is there anything you forgot to tell us last time?" Dmitry asked.

"I'm afraid something may have happened." Haddad frowned. "Someone was over that night. And now, I can't seem to get hold of him. When you stopped by last week, I didn't know if this was related in any way, but now..." She folded her arms on her lap and unfolded them, the fingers of one hand playing with the other.

"Who was it?" Brenda asked.

"My boyfriend." Haddad blushed, her face momentarily helpless, like a little girl's. "And now, *you're* here."

"What's his name, Ms. Haddad?"

"His name is Naseem. Naseem Nazari." Her face hardened with worry. "Did something happen to him?"

"I'm afraid we have sad news." Something inside Brenda broke a little at this point. "Mr. Nazari was murdered. I'm so sorry."

"Murdered?" Haddad's face collapsed.

"I'm afraid so," Brenda said. "I'm sorry, Ma'am."

"Oh, God. Oh, God." Haddad started to cry but controlled herself—instead of sobs, tears came one by one, rolling down her cheeks. "Who would have wanted to kill him? He's the kindest person I've ever met." Her eyes brimmed with questions.

"We don't know," Brenda said. "But we'll find out."

"Where...where is his body?"

"It's at the morgue, Ma'am," Dmitry said softly.

"I want to see him."

"We'll notify you when you can do that," Brenda said. "How long have you known Mr. Nazari?"

"We've been dating for two years or so." Haddad's face had turned pale; her hands remained restless in her lap. "It feels like so much longer."

She'd loved the victim; that was clear. At least he'd had that in his life.

"Do you have a picture of him?" Brenda asked.

"Yes. Sure. Wait." Haddad got up from her seat. She found her phone on one of the shelves in a beautiful redwood bookcase, heavy with books of all shapes and degrees of wear. She fiddled with the phone—then emotions caught up with her; she burst out sobbing. "It's not fair. It's not fair."

With a shaking hand, she passed the phone to Brenda. In the picture, Haddad stood next to Naseem Nazari, both looking solemn, not at all the way Americans pose for photos.

"Thank you," Brenda said.

Haddad just stared, her eyes full of tears. The incense had burned out and lay crumpled, gray bits on the tray.

"When we were here the other day, you seemed worried," Dmitry said. "Did you notice anything?"

"We had a fight, you see. Have I mentioned that?" She looked embarrassed, her cheeks red. "No, I didn't notice anything."

How sad that was, to end on a fight. Brenda didn't know what to say. One of the masks on the wall attracted her attention. Something sinister in the expression of its empty eyeholes, in the wrinkles of its wooden forehead, as if the mask were trying to tell her something indecipherable, all the while mocking her inability to understand it. Brenda made an effort to look elsewhere.

"What time do you think he might have left?" She made sure to sound respectful, not pushy.

"Must have been just before 5 a.m. He usually headed out around 4:45. He had to take a bus to get home. He didn't drive, you see. I got up at 5:17 to use the restroom, and he was already gone." Haddad paused. "He was an early riser. He didn't like to stick around and wait for me to wake up."

"Where did he work?" Dmitry's hands lay folded on his notepad, but his fingers kept twitching. Unusual for Dmitry.

"Carter High. He was a janitor there."

"Did he catch the bus over at Aspen and 65th?" Dmitry pointed in that direction.

"Usually. Unless he wanted a stroll. Then he might walk to the next stop."

"What did you two fight about?" Brenda had to ask.

"Our relationship. Isn't that what everyone fights about?"

It would make no sense to argue or pressure her. Brenda knew that this poor woman bore no share of responsibility for what happened to Nazari.

"How did you two meet?" An irrelevant question. Brenda liked that kind. They made things less formal, often leading to extra information. Besides, memories brought back other details relevant to the case.

"We met by chance at a grocery store." A tortured smile altered Haddad's face; Brenda could tell it was a treasured memory. "We were both looking for halva. Do you know what halva is?" She didn't wait for either detective to answer. "There was something about his face. He looked a bit like my brother, and I looked a little like someone he knew." She was still smiling through tears, seeming a little embarrassed. "We had a lot in common. We both come from religious backgrounds, but neither of us was religious. We shared much of the history, the culture." She stopped speaking and stared into the distance beyond the opposing wall as if Nazari were still listening.

"Where's your family from?" Brenda asked. She already knew but wanted to hear it from the woman herself.

"Palestine. My husband and I immigrated twenty-two years ago."

Husband?

"He died four years ago," Yasmin explained as if sensing the unasked question.

"I'm sorry."

Haddad's mouth moved as if she was going to clarify something.

"We'd like to ask you more about Mr. Nazari's habits," Dmitry said. "Places he went, his routines."

"He worked. He took walks. He read books. He spent time with me. He had one friend, Igor Pechorin. He's a Russian immigrant." Brenda glanced at Dmitry, whose brows went up slightly in acknowledgment. "They met every Saturday afternoon for a chess game. They spoke on the phone now and then. He was crazy about chess."

"Why did you come to the United States?" Brenda asked after a short silence.

"We didn't want to leave, but life became too difficult." For a few seconds, Yasmin Haddad studied their two faces as if hoping for an understanding of the Palestinian conflict. Brenda had a general idea.

"My husband had a business opportunity," Haddad continued. "We packed up everything and came."

"Welcome to the United States," Brenda offered with some delay. Then she felt stupid about saying that, considering how long ago Haddad had arrived here. Not to mention the terrible occasion.

"Did Mr. Nazari seem unusual on the days preceding his death?" Dmitry's face was focused.

"I don't think so." Haddad shook her head. "I didn't notice anything like that."

"Did he mention any troubles or conflicts? Did he have any enemies?"

"What enemies? He was a harmless man." Haddad's brown eyes, set wide apart, deepened with this statement. "But maybe there were things he didn't share with me? Could there be?"

"I don't know, Ma'am," Dmitry said.

"I wish I'd asked more questions. He was a loner." Ms. Haddad shrugged. "He preferred to spend his time quietly. On his own."

"What about the friend, Igor?" Brenda asked. "Do you have his contact information?"

"Yes, I have it written down somewhere. I'll look." Haddad seemed stricken as she dug through her desk, interrupted her search, and pulled up the contact on her phone instead. "Here it is."

"Thank you." Brenda entered the number into her own.

She could only imagine how it would feel to lose someone so abruptly.

23. The Corrector

The Corrector sat in his chair, a glass of bourbon in his hand, his laptop on his lap. Mom would not wake for a while. She'd been on fentanyl lollipops since last night. Those things knock the brain out of you.

He took a sip and looked up what Joey Gibson and his Patriot Prayer were up to. Gibson, smart as a fucking fox and so good at provoking the asshole liberals. Antifa and other clowns jumped in a nano-second, eager to have their cake and fuck it too. Portland was lucky to have a clear-thinking individual like Gibson. Someone had to help keep The Corrector's city from becoming another liberal hotbed like New York or San Fran Fucking Cisco.

He opened Discord. Discord was the real deal, a site so messy and cool that no one cared who posted what. Freedom of speech meant something here. He scrolled through the posts from his pals, Nomber1 and WhysKrak. These two were great; they always backed him up in chats.

The trouble was, as much as he appreciated the camaraderie, people always posted the same shit. *Send the Muslim assholes back where they came from* and all the other good stuff. Fine—but who's going to do all the sending? President Trump was working on it from his end, slowly and steadily. Was everyone else supposed to sit with their arms folded on their chest and wait for better times?

Just then, something caught The Corrector's attention. A new user:

GoodOldBoy74
Heard insider report about the cleanup action in West Hills.

> Congrats to TRUE patriots. Nice touch with the roof. Well
> done.

The news hadn't mentioned his latest action yet. It would, soon.
The Corrector was on his way to becoming a celebrity. His heart
pumped like a crazy beast inside his chest, and his hands and face felt
warm. Someone appreciated what he'd done. He hopped up from the
chair and did a few hops around the room, yelling *Hey, Ho, Hey, Ho*.
Mom wouldn't hear anyway. Maybe she'd get a Christmas dream out
of it.

He stomped, clapped his hands, and said in a TV announcer
voice, "Congratulations to you, sir. Congratulations to you, sir.
Congratulations to you, sir." He felt a smile on his face. He pressed
the Reply button.

> *Thanks man. Just doing my duty is all.*

The Corrector paused to think. Should he let the other guy know
more of what was on his mind?

His mouse pointer hovered over the Post button.

24. Dmitry Volkov

As the landlord let them in, Dmitry kept his hand on his weapon, just in case. Naseem Nazari's studio apartment was tiny. The air smelled stale, a vague mix of old food and neglect.

"What happened?" The landlord's brows tightened around his nose. "Is he okay?"

He wore a wrinkled gray suit, his brown leather shoes covered in mud. Had he gone gravedigging before this? A burly guy in his fifties—or forties, poorly preserved. Dmitry had noticed some years ago that age became more relative around mid-life, striking some folks like a sledgehammer while it left others intact. Dmitry himself hadn't aged very well. He looked about the same age as the other dude.

"He was murdered," Dmitry said, donning a pair of latex gloves.

"Murdered? No way! I can't believe it. A nice man. Always paid on time." The guy paused as if expecting a comment. "Well, I'll be in the car."

The furniture was spare, if not spartan: a bed, a generic office desk, three red Ikea chairs, a small dining table, and a shabby bookshelf with two rows almost filled with books. The closet was nearly empty: two suits—a dark gray one and a dark blue one—two sports jackets, three pairs of sneakers, a pair of brown dress shoes, and a narrow white dresser half-full of socks and underwear.

Dmitry didn't look forward to digging through this place for clues. His intuition told him they'd find nothing. His thoughts were drawn to his own life, his debt.

The tiny kitchenette featured only a sink, a small fridge, and a two-burner gas stove. Brenda opened the refrigerator, but the robust smell of rotting vegetables forced her to slam the door shut. A mini microwave perched on top of the fridge. There was no dishwasher—not even a toaster.

"He didn't know what was coming to him," Dmitry said. "How long has he been in the country?"

"I've requested that information from ICE," Brenda said. "Haven't heard back yet. At least a few years, based on his relationship with Haddad."

Outside the window lay a tiny park with a small playground and a bench, its front board missing. As dusk set in, the park was left abandoned. The scale of this outside space matched the apartment's size, which depressed Dmitry.

"Let's take a look," he said.

He dug into the desk, finding it as sparsely populated as the rest of the apartment. Not a single file in the lower, file cabinet section, a few receipts and two pens in the top drawer, a thin stack of letters in the middle. Just the letters themselves, in a language that looked like Arabic. An envelope or two would've helped to get hold of relatives and friends.

"We'll have to have them translated." Dmitry showed Brenda the letters before packing them in a plastic evidence bag.

Also in the middle drawer, a good-looking pair of brown leather gloves and a metal cup adorned with ornaments, impractical for drinking. A relic of some kind. Next to it, a copy of *Moby Dick*, with a bookmark on page 39. Nazari hadn't gotten far.

An old Mac laptop sat closed on the desk's surface. Dmitry opened it, pressed the button, and waited for the screen to come up. The computer was not password-protected. The desktop came up, with the background of a foreign city: yellow buildings clustered together organically, a mosque or two and plenty of shadowy passages, endless stairways crisscrossing the picture. *I could get lost there for a year or two*, Dmitry thought as he stared. The city was beautiful, and its otherness was immensely intriguing. But it also had a threatening edge, after all the Christian stuff he'd had to deal with in his family.

He took a cursory look at the files. Nothing unusual. A folder named Immigration and another named Letters, both words in English. A test file under Videos. Nothing notable under Recent Files. Dmitry clicked the email icon on the desktop and was taken to a login page.

"Not much so far," he reported to Brenda, who was busy taking pictures. "I can't get into his email without a password; we'll have to contact the provider. Can you look into his social media accounts? Maybe the killer tracked him online first."

"Why don't *you* look into his social media accounts?" Brenda grinned. "I already spent last night impersonating a right-winger to trap this asshole."

"I know, Bren, I know." Dmitry gave her his most charming smile. "But you're so much better at all this computer stuff."

"I don't know about that." She laughed.

On their way out, they found the landlord in his beige Volvo, typing away at his phone as if his life depended on it. Dmitry knocked with his knuckles on the window, and the man rolled it down.

"We're all done here," Dmitry said. "When was the last time you saw Mr. Nazari?"

"Not for a few months. I don't come out here very often."

"Give us a call if anything comes to mind." Dmitry handed the man his card.

He and Brenda walked over to their unmarked car, a black Ford. It was beginning to drizzle.

25. The Corrector

The Corrector's head fell on his chest. He must have dozed off. The smell of spices from the Styrofoam container of Chinese food he hadn't finished reached him from the desk where he'd left it. He considered finishing it up, but he wasn't hungry.

The laptop before him lit up from his movements. The Corrector squinted to read, his eyes still adjusting. Ah, the response he'd typed:

> Thanks man. Just doing my duty is all.

He'd been about to post it, but now he was worried. Who the fuck was GoodOldBoy74? Could be anyone. The Corrector smelled a rat. Could be a well-meaning stranger, could be a fucking trap. Shit! He had to be careful. Something about the post screamed: COPS. How else would they know about his corrective action?

No way, sir. The Corrector wouldn't be fooled so easily. He slammed the laptop shut.

This bullshit set his mind on edge. And the pain in his left foot didn't help either. In no time, his glass was empty. The bottle of bourbon was right there on the desk; he didn't even have to get out of his chair to pour himself more. The spicy deep-brown liquid burned his mouth in a life-affirming way; the good medicine smell calmed him down. Whoever invented bourbon had been the first fucking genius ever to grace the face of this sad planet. The Corrector downed the second glass in one go, impatient for the sharp edge of anger to dull in his head, clearing room for thinking and planning. As the last drops ran down his throat, he considered checking on Mom. Then again, he checked on her every hour or so. Always the same story, except things kept getting worse. The Corrector's knees were tired from the stairs.

He tried to imagine himself in Mom's shoes, knowing that death was already knocking on his door. The Corrector couldn't imagine it. He was too full of energy. He still had so much work to do for his country. There would come a day when America was free again, and those who'd worked for that future would be applauded.

He looked out the window. Outside was like a big muddy puddle of nothing. The Corrector poured another drink. Now, he had to take it slowly, or he would be worthless in the thinking department. He had to be ready to act if Mom finally kicked the bucket. He hopped up from his seat and jumped around just a little, screaming *Fuck! Fuck! Fuck!* to settle his nerves a bit. He was a little unsteady but balanced enough to catch himself from wiping out. That made him feel hilarious as fuck, warmth radiating from inside to the edges of his being. He had a good laugh imagining what apartment neighbors would have thought if he and Mom didn't own a house. Fucking neighbors! He almost wished he had someone living upstairs, downstairs, and all around so he could annoy them with his stomping and heavy metal.

He thought back to the days before. His second time...and it had come out well. The Muslim asshole deserved it. Instead of going slow as he'd intended, The Corrector downed the fucking drink and poured another. Who cared anymore? Going slow was for pussies. The Corrector was a different kind of person, a new kind. He had to go fast to go at all.

As the sweet warmth spread through his body, his mind kept warming up, too. Now, he was happy. His steps a little more unsteady, he walked over to the stereo. Cannibal Corpse, there to indulge. With the first hard riffs filling the room, joy pushed through the air into The Corrector's pores, sweeping him into a dance. Here he was, celebrating, bouncing back and forth to the rhythm, his clenched fists in the air. Now and then, his knees buckled under him from the drink, and he dropped like a turd on the soft carpet. That was funny like hell, and he laughed. Then he pushed himself up and kept dancing. He could feel a happy grin on his face. The pounding feet, the fists, the music, the screaming. *Fuck, fuck, fuck!* His mother was downstairs, oblivious to all this noise. Life was to enjoy, to be happy. *Murder, hatred,* the lyrics flowed into him, and The Corrector danced, yelling the lyrics to the fucking heaven above.

26. Dmitry Volkov

Dmitry slumped on the living room couch, feeling old. Tired, saggy, caved in like an old pumpkin, a vegetable they loved in this country. His eyes were glued to the TV without fully registering it. On the screen, ugly, colorful animals chased one another, screaming in high-pitched human voices. Dmitry had never appreciated animation, even as a kid in the USSR. Natasha sat beside him on the couch, giggling at the nonsensical action. At least she was enjoying it. Mercury the doll sat on Natasha's other side, dead as ever.

Natasha wore her tiny blue jeans and a hoodie, the hood pulled over her head. Dmitry smiled at his daughter and petted her on the head. At her age, his life had been different—no Cheerios, no sodas, no jeans.

Dmitry's heart lay deeper than the bottom of the ocean. Last night's poker game was going so well. Winning and winning until his luck abandoned him. The thing was, when Dmitry got nervous, his skill for the game began to wane. Increasingly, he realized he was a so-so poker player. The adrenaline took over; his mind retreated.

He'd walked out with another seventeen hundred in debt. The total approached thirty grand between his credit cards and what he owed Misha. The rain had poured down Dmitry's neck as he stood on the street corner, wishing to disappear, the water on his face cool and tender, like Rita's fingers.

His life was unraveling, his thoughts out of sequence. Yet, at this moment, sitting next to Natasha, he felt he would find a solution. That was a part of him, the senseless Soviet optimism. No matter how unlikely, things would be okay in the end.

And Natasha? She didn't deserve a father like him. So what if he was born in a shithole country. Not an excuse for losing his way in his new life.

They'd just finished dinner; the smell of lasagna hung in the air. The frozen kind, from a box, which didn't make it any less delicious, at least to their Russian immigrant tastes. Back in the USSR, his family had been able to get noodles occasionally, but tomato sauce, sausage, or Ricotta cheese were a pipe dream if one could find a pipe. The noodles had gone well with hot dogs or bologna if Mom managed to find either.

His thoughts returned to his present worries. Misha. Dmitry rued the day he met the guy and agreed to play a game.

Rita stood in the doorway, measuring him with a concerned look, her brows scrunched up. She was so beautiful in her blue sweatshirt. At that moment, he loved her more than ever.

"What's up?" Dmitry forced his lips into a smile.

"You okay?"

"Yes, baby. I'm fine."

His heart hurt at the thought of concealing his debt from Rita—but he couldn't bring himself to tell her the truth. They took turns on the mortgage, and after last night's loss, he no longer had the cash. He'd never sunk so deep. Before, it'd been just pocket money. He'd always caught up on the bills, but his credit card debt grew. Too bad he couldn't pay the mortgage with a credit card.

The pressure was on. He had to sort it out before the December statement arrived.

27. Brenda Smith

Mary rented a small, well-appointed studio close to the Central Library. Beautiful hardwood floors, soaring ceilings, surprising angles, a cute bedroom loft with a door and a landing, and an exquisite spiral stairway leading up to it.

"Wow." Brenda took it all in.

Even the air smelled unique and intriguing. It was like flowers but subdued and had much more to do with the body than flowers.

"You like?" Mary laughed.

"This must cost a fortune."

It was much more elegant than Brenda's functional but regular, slightly shabby place.

"It would cost a fortune if I signed the lease now. I've been here for seven years. Fortunately, my landlord is a friend. He's barely raised the rent at all."

"No shit!"

They kissed right by the door, and Mary closed it behind them.

"I missed you," Brenda whispered. "Been thinking about you all day."

Still kissing, they made it to the bedroom and collapsed on the bed, bouncing from the extra-springy mattress. They both laughed as they continued kissing until there was no more room for laughter in the kiss. For a moment, Brenda thought about Jessica and felt a sense of glee at knowing that, finally, something else was happening in her life. Jessica was fading away forever in Brenda's heart, in her rapid pulse.

For the first time in what seemed like years, Brenda felt happy, relaxed—and free. Her body warmed up, tingling—and the dead body on the warehouse roof retreated, disappearing beyond a gray Portland horizon in her mind. Mary's breath smelled of beer most endearingly, her warm hands electric on Brenda's skin, neurons firing in neon glee. It was enough to feel—to feel herself, Mary, this.

28. Dmitry Volkov

Misha sat in a vast black leather chair, his face severe and smug. This guy could have Portland's police chief whacked if he wanted to. He looked misplaced in a striped wool sweater full of gray, red, and green horizontal lines, the colors too joyful for his personality. Dmitry had already been frisked by two unsmiling dudes who kept watch by the door.

The small windowless room featured a table with two chairs, a bookcase, and a floor light. A large Salvador Dali print dominated one of the walls, a pomegranate biting a fish biting a tiger. A vase stuffed with too many red roses sat in the middle of the table. Still, the room smelled of male sweat.

"Dima!" A huge grin animated Misha's face, something animal about it, like baring his teeth for a kill. The teeth, too, were animal-like, yellow, and uncared-for, with a gap in the bottom row. A gold tooth shone on the other side of Misha's mouth, reflecting the light from the floor lamp. Without getting up, Misha offered his hand. His palm looked small, his skin unusually well-groomed for a man.

"Misha."

Misha's handshake was energetic and brief. "Good to see you, old friend," Misha said in Russian.

"You too, Misha, you too," Dmitry replied in their native tongue.

"Will you drink some vodka with me? Lesha, pour us some vodka." Misha nodded at one of the bodyguards, who took no time to pull a bottle from the mini bar hidden in the bottom shelf of the bookcase. Who would have thought? There were only a few books on the upper shelves, and a clock running an hour and twenty minutes behind, its chessboard face a color match for the bookcase. Was this an actual design choice?

Two shot glasses full of vodka arrived in their hands; they clinked. Both exhaled and downed the drink.

"Phew. You like my vodka?" That scary smile was back on Misha's face.

"Yes, Misha. It's great." It tasted just like regular vodka to Dmitry.

Misha leaped from his chair, his smile replaced by a look of disgust and contempt, his wild face escaping its contours. He was a fire-breathing demon. The transformation had taken no more than a second.

"You like my vodka! Ha! *Chuvak. Ty okhyel!*" With every Russian word, he pounded the small table with his fist. The slang meant Dude, you're penisified and somehow sounded even worse in Russian. The two empty shot glasses hopped up and landed on the table again with a slight clatter. "*Gde moi dengi?*"

Where is my money? Right. Dmitry had expected this question.

"I'll pay you back soon, I promise." He felt awful saying this, realizing the statement was more of an intention than a certainty. "You know I'm good for it."

"When? When will you pay me back?" Misha's muscular figure towered over the small table, over Dmitry, his blue eyes focused intensely on the detective's face. "I hear you've been playing more and losing more instead of considering your responsibility to your old pal, Misha. Tell me it's not so."

So, Misha already knew about yesterday's game. Dmitry sighed. Of course, Misha knew. He knew everything he wanted to know in this city.

"You're right. I've looked it up. Gambling. It's a disease." Dmitry became uncomfortable being the only guy sitting; he rose and stood awkwardly between his chair and the table. "I'll stop, but I need a little more time to pay you back."

"Disease? Disease! A little more time? A little more time?" Misha muttered to himself as he strolled back and forth along the back wall, stooped, his hands playing with each other. Thinking, performing, a little of both? Dmitry was tired of all the theater, but he had no choice but to watch. "Fuck me!" Misha screamed as if answering Dmitry's request. "Why does everyone think I have more time? Every fucking fuck tells me they need a little more time. Do I look like a guy who pulls time out of his ass? Do I?"

The image of Misha pulling time out of his ass was so preposterous Dmitry struggled not to laugh. Misha stopped, his arms folded on his chest, as if expecting an answer. Then, he gave a casual nod to one of the bodyguards. Before Dmitry had time to consider this, the man stepped up, and a fist slammed into Dmitry's abs, so unexpected that he had no time to move or flex against the punch. All the breath went out of him in a choked gasp, and he hunched over as if hovering over the floor.

"You think because you're a cop, you can fuck with me?" Misha's voice was edgy but controlled. "You can't. Don't even think about it."

"I know," Dmitry wheezed. "I'd never do that, Misha. You'll have your money back, I promise. Give me another month."

"You have two weeks. Only because we go back, you understand? If we didn't..." Misha dragged his index finger across his throat.

At that, all passion went out of Misha's face. Where was the guy, and where was the act? Dmitry knew the conversation was over. Misha rose and walked out, followed by the bodyguards. Abruptly, the room was empty of everyone but Dmitry. The door stood open. He was free to go.

FRIDAY, NOVEMBER 15

29. Dmitry Volkov

Brenda was already at the office, poring over a stack of papers. The powerful, acidic coffee aroma permeated the room, welcoming him. The office looked gray; the rain outside was not subsiding.

"The victim's phone records." A Brenda kind of greeting.

"Anything interesting?" He walked over to the coffee machine and filled his tall, light blue mug with a handle shaped like a human ear, a present from Rita.

"Doesn't look like it. Mostly brief calls. Pizza orders. He called Yasmin Haddad almost every day, and she called him. Once or twice a week, he talked to his Russian friend, Igor Pechorin. Long conversations."

"We should talk to that Pechorin, shouldn't we?" Dmitry hated speaking to one more Russian, but work was work. "What do we have from ICE?"

"Not much." She shrugged. "He's Yemeni, but we already knew that. A refugee. Became a U.S. Citizen in 2015. No family in the States. Finding relatives back home will take some time if they're still alive. Things don't look good back there. There's a civil war and a cholera outbreak."

"Cholera? You're serious?" Dmitry's head went abuzz with that piece of information. "I didn't think cholera existed anymore, anywhere in the world."

"I guess it does. Oh, and I've posted on this site called Discord. Pretending to be a right-wing extremist, you know. We'll see if the perp tips his hand."

"Nice." Dmitry was embarrassed. Brenda had already done so

much on this hopeless case while he'd been losing money and dealing with his growing Misha problem. Poor Bren, she didn't deserve it. She didn't deserve *him*. "Thanks for all the good work."

Brenda just shrugged, still typing away at her keyboard.

"Do you have any friends?" Dmitry asked, surprising himself.

Brenda was silent for a moment.

"Not really."

"Me neither. Rita has friends, and they're my friends, in a sense. But if not for her, they wouldn't spend time with me. I don't mean other cops. I'm friendly with them like you are—we go out for drinks, right? But it's not friendship. Camaraderie. Is that the word? So many cops are assholes. I come from a different culture. I'm not one of them. I'm not one of anything, you know."

"I understand how that feels." Brenda swiveled in her chair and listened with full attention.

"I act tough. Play the role." Dmitry paused for a second to consider himself. Which part was him, and which was his role? "You know, the jokes, the bravado. I don't let my guard down."

"No." Brenda's face went distant, reflective. She held her mug with both hands as if for reassurance. It was hard to tell what she was thinking. "Do you ever wonder how your life would have been if you stayed back in Russia?"

"Sometimes. But it's been so long, you know."

"Don't you miss it?" Brenda paused as if looking for the right words. "The country? The culture?"

"Honestly, there's not much to miss."

Brenda stared at him incredulously. "Don't you miss the language?"

"Rita and I still speak it at home. I miss being in a place where no one questioned my right to be. Know what I mean? I was just one of the people in a place that was fucked up, but being fucked up was normal. Oh, I don't know what I'm saying."

"It makes sense."

If he hadn't come from that dysfunctional communist world, he would've made a better life. He would've been another person.

"You're my only friend," he said. "How about that?"

"Here in Portland, it's hard to get a social life if you're a cop." Brenda cracked up. "And I can't blame the place. Let's get some breakfast."

As they walked down the long corridor to the exit, the unsettling gray light from the large windows dominated the space. A ceiling tile was damaged; water drops dribbled into a large blue canister on the floor. Each splash rang like a small bell from a fake church.

Their favorite table at Linda's was ready and waiting for them.

"When you and Rita met, did you know right away she was the right one?" Brenda asked as they sat down.

"I did." Dmitry nodded. "Or I hoped so. She was so...you know."

"So what?"

"So *Rita*. So bright and shining. And I don't just mean her looks."

Dmitry closed his eyes, remembering. They'd been so young. Endlessly naive, their worldview handicapped by hardcore faith. Back then, it had been easy to make decisions. Now that he was middle-aged, everything was so much more complicated.

"No doubts at all?" Brenda asked.

"There's always doubt. Why do you ask? You met someone, no?" Dmitry pointed his index finger at her, grinning.

"Yeah." Brenda's face lit up.

"It must be going well then?"

Dmitry had always known Brenda would meet someone, a woman smart enough and brave enough to be with her. He hoped this was the one.

Brenda considered for a second. "Really well. But it's all so new I can't tell what's what. Am I right for her? I don't know, I don't know."

"I'm sure you are, Detective," Dmitry said in his Russian-sounding British accent. "How are you finding your hamburger?"

30. Brenda Smith

Carter High School was a gray, nondescript two-story building on the outskirts. The school's community service officer welcomed them into the lobby, all granite floors and giant windows with rivers of fading green carpets. Brenda racked her brain for the officer's name but couldn't remember it.

"Detectives." He nodded. "I'll take you to the head office."

He looked tired, something about his movements slowed, as if he were conserving energy.

"Sorry we're a few minutes late," Brenda said.

As they walked down the corridor, a smell of stale sweat and something sweet from the cafeteria assaulted Brenda's nostrils. She wasn't good at math, but it was twenty years and counting since high school, like another life. These memories were freaking her out. Not a pit, but a boulder in her stomach as she remembered her high school experience.

They'd arrived during class; low voices echoed through the building, augmented by a higher pitch here, a burst of laughter there. With no one in sight, the place was especially eerie. Brenda felt distinctly the queer girl inside. The smell brought back the boys' faces, their lusty ogling, and the awkwardness she had felt early on at their advances. Locker room mentality. The pushy girls from well-to-do families were yet another thing.

Two people waited in the office: a stout middle-aged lady in a dark gray pantsuit and a man in his sixties dressed in jeans and a white t-shirt. The woman rose and offered her hand.

"Principal Bartholomew."

Brenda's fear of principals hadn't gone away in all these years. Their bland faces and ability to make it her fault always got to her. She did her best to suppress these feelings. "Thank you for taking the time to talk to us."

"This is Rod Aldridge, our maintenance supervisor. I invited him because you said this matter was related to Naseem Nazari."

Aldridge had a mole on his nose, making it difficult not to look.

"Did something happen to Naseem?" Concern or irritation on the principal's face?

"He hasn't been to work all this week." Aldridge shrugged. "I was worried about him. Had to move my team around to cover for him."

"He was murdered." Dmitry looked sad, almost apologetic.

"Murdered?" The principal's face dropped. "Oh, no."

"Do you know anyone who might have wanted to harm him?" Brenda asked.

"Harm him? Can't think of anyone, anyone at all. He seemed like a good man. We've talked just a few times. A smart guy. Very well informed."

Aldridge kept nodding in agreement.

"Well-informed about what?" Brenda asked.

"Society, politics, you name it." The principal looked sad. "He was concerned about the state of affairs in the world. Not so long ago, he was cleaning up after a meeting, and I asked him how he liked it here in America. He said, *You Americans are so lucky to be able to vote.* He told me about the situation back in Yemen. He was good at explaining a political dilemma in just a few sentences. But as I said, we've only had a chance to talk a few times. I'm sorry, though." She did look sincere.

"Did he belong to any political groups?" Dmitry asked.

"Not that I know of." Bartholomew seemed rattled by the question.

"Who did he hang out with here at work?" Dmitry was playing with his pen, his notepad in the other hand. He hadn't made any notes yet.

Aldridge's brow tightened in thought. "No one, really. Custodians work mostly on separate tasks. It's not a social job. I've seen him talk to others here and there, sure, but only on occasion."

"Who was on the same shift with him?"

"I printed a copy of his schedule for you." Aldridge handed Dmitry a thin pile of sheets.

"Thank you." Dmitry began scanning the pages.

"What else can you tell us about Mr. Nazari?" Brenda would give her pinky for something more substantial, but nothing seemed to be coming.

"He's been employed here for about two years. I'll get the records. He was always on time, always did an excellent job." A defeated expression on the principal's face.

"Did he ever talk about his activities outside work?"

"He liked to read. He was working on his English."

The image of the just-started copy of *Moby Dick* in the desk drawer flashed in Brenda's mind. Something sad about it. "When was he at work last?"

"Let me see." The principal consulted her screen. "Thursday, November 7th. I don't think I saw him at all last week. It's all in that printout, isn't it, Rod?" Her smile was a sort of anti-smile: sad, anxious. She clicked some buttons on her desktop, her face looking older than just a few minutes ago.

"Please give us a call if you think of anything else." Brenda handed Bartholomew her business card.

The principal turned her face to Brenda. "I hope you find whoever did it." Her eyes looked kind.

Her request was reasonable. They owed Naseem Nazari as much.

31. The Corrector

Time pressed down on The Corrector like two thousand fucking pounds of nothingness. He was losing that feeling of usefulness like he'd done something important. And that meant he had to do more. His country demanded it. The Corrector had to deliver.

It was tough not being able to share what he'd done. After the trap on Discord, he'd decided to stop posting. Wouldn't want to lead the cops to himself. But the fucking secret pushed at him from inside; it had to come out sooner rather than later. Again, he considered telling his mom. Mom would understand. Before too long, the old crow wouldn't be able to converse much. He wanted her to know, really *know*. He wanted her to be proud of him.

He opened a jar of applesauce and scooped some out into a dish. Lately, Mom had been so-so at chewing. It was easier to feed her mushy stuff like this. As he puttered about in the kitchen, he could see the edge of her high-tech bed in the living room, her legs covered with a gray blanket. The rest of the house was as much of a mess as the kitchen. He should pay someone to clean up. But he didn't have the time to do all the looking. He'd deal with the mess once Mom was dead.

She was awake. Good. More often than not, he had to wake her for her meals. It felt wrong, jerking her out of her rest and back into her pain so that she could spend a little longer on this shithole of a planet.

"Ready for some lunch?"

"Yes, Junior." He knew his mom would do her best to eat, poor thing. They'd been through this too many times.

"Here we go." He brought a teaspoon of pale mush to her lips, and she carefully sucked it in, her eyes on him. Almost spooky.

"Thank you, son." She looked real meaningful and intense. "Thank you for everything."

"No worries, Mom. What're you going on about?"

"I mean it, Junior. Thank you for letting me die in peace. Here, at home. It would suck to die at some shitshow hospital—no, thank you." A grimace on her face.

"Yes, Mom. I know." He didn't want to explain that hospital was not an option; people didn't just get parked there until they died. She got the same deal as other folks. He was okay with that.

The Corrector scooped up another spoonful. He was used to the smell of his mother's dying. The faint, fresh apple smell cut through it, reminding him of his childhood. An image flashed before him: Mom's smile from those days. Her face with a spark, her prominent cheekbones. That day, they'd brought a kite to the Oregon Coast. Dad had stayed home. The wind blew and blew. The Corrector could still see the red kite, with the ocean foaming nearby. Mom must have been in her early thirties. Hell. He wouldn't mind returning to that place and starting again.

"It won't be long now." Her voice was almost a whisper.

"Come on, Mom. Don't go there."

"Screw it." A scoff, a crooked grin on her old face. "I'm telling it like it is."

"I know." The Corrector wanted to deny the whole business of her dying, but Mom wouldn't allow such bullshit.

Another spoonful. And her slow chewing, as if applesauce was something to chew. The pressure of his secret was coming up in his mouth, overflowing. It was like throwing up, something he couldn't stop.

"Mom, I've got to tell you something."

32. Azar Bayat

Azar opened her eyes. Here she was, on her bed in her Portland dorm room. How shocking that still felt after three months in the United States. Like a brand new, better world she'd read about. Better, but still so flawed. She hadn't expected so many homeless people.

The street hum bathed her ears in an inscrutable mix of voices and vehicles, a different combination of sounds than at home, although she couldn't explain why. Common messages in English like *Hey, dude, Thank you* and *What's up* cut through the mass of sound. She'd fallen asleep after a late lunch following a challenging sociology class. In her dream, an elderly woman had faced her with a stern, unreadable expression. Azar kept saying, *I want some soup, I want some soup,* but no soup was around. She still felt the awkwardness of that perplexing moment, goose pimples on her skin.

In real life, Azar was the opposite of hungry. Her lunch, a beef burrito, still sat heavily on her stomach. She'd have to get out of bed and drink some water. Her roommate, Rose, had been out since the day before, probably spending time off campus with her boyfriend. It was good to have some solitude.

The old woman in the dream had held Azar's hand in her small, wrinkled palms. Strange that she was someone Azar didn't know, instead of her grandma, Maman Feri, who was eighty-four and so frail that Azar dreaded the possibility of never seeing her again. After too many encounters with medical professionals, most of Maman Feri's body still functioned as intended, but no one knew how long this fragile balance would last.

With a pang of guilt, Azar remembered saying, "I will be back to visit before you know it, Maman Feri. I promise."

But once Azar had finally done her research and discovered the cost of everything, it became clear: she didn't have the money to pay for her flight to Iran and back. Everything pointed to spending her winter break in Portland. Azar had mixed feelings about that: nostalgia for home, excitement about the winter holidays here in the United States, and the freedom to control her life. She felt so much more grown-up than ever before, so much more real.

She looked forward to her coffee date with Becki. The two of them had hit it off in literature class, debating whether the works of disgraced artists should be viewed independently of their creators' ethical choices.

"No one is about to defend the Woody Allens of the art world," Bruce had said, and a few students mumbled something or shrugged, a mixed reaction. "But what about artists from underrepresented groups, like Junot Díaz or Sherman Alexie?"

For a moment, there was no answer. The silence pushed at Azar's throat: a demand, an opportunity.

"For every supported voice, a similar or stronger underrepresented voice exists that never gets the attention. There's not enough attention out there for all the deserving voices." As she spoke, Azar heard well-formed English flowing from her mouth without having to translate any words from Persian. A shocking and marvelous experience, as if English was about to let her in.

"Not considering the author's moral choices is a privilege," Becki said. "Would you feel the same way if you were one of their victims? Or a person who's faced similar damage? Or someone who looks the same?"

That thought had surprised Azar. Was ignoring the immorality of others a privilege? After the class, she and Becki had started talking, and there seemed to be no end to meaningful things to discuss.

33. The Corrector

"What is it, son?" The Corrector's mother looked more tired than curious.

"Remember how President Trump said, *These aren't people, these are animals?* The aliens, you know." The Corrector expected his mom to react, but she kept silent, listening. He felt like he needed to explain a little better. "They're ruining our country, you know. I decided to do something about it."

"You're going into politics?" A puzzled look on her wrinkled face.

"No, Mom. I took the matter into my own hands, that's all." The Corrector felt proud and apprehensive, his heart fast from adrenalin. Surely, Mom would share his joy.

"What?" She stared blankly, a thin line of applesauce dripping down her chin.

Something sunk in him; he was like a dog expecting a kick. A mistake to tell her. But no backing out now. He'd already started.

"I took care of a couple of them, you know." She often had the TV on, but The Corrector wasn't sure how much of it she watched. She muted the sound most of the time. "You may have seen it in the news."

Mom stared, her eyes firmer than they'd been in recent weeks. A frown settled on her face.

"Shh...hm..." What was she mumbling? Then, her voice cleared a bit. "Junior, what the fuck are you saying?"

"The aliens. They got what they deserved. I put them out of their misery."

She stared again uncomprehendingly. She must be out of it. The whole thing put The Corrector on edge. Hell. Bitterness seeped through his body, from the sore foot to his face on fire. His mother kept staring, her face contorted like she was having a stroke. The Corrector felt the pressure to keep talking.

"Hell, Mom! They're like invaders. Like pests. They take regular people's jobs and won't even learn English. I don't know where to start. When you have pests, what do you do?" He waited a few seconds for an answer, but Mom remained mute as a fish. He felt like a kid, begging her for something and getting no response. "You call the exterminator, just like we did at the old house when we got cockroaches. Isn't this what Dad would've wanted to do? He didn't have the balls to do it himself, did he? He was better at knocking us around." The Corrector loved his dad, admired him, but facts were facts. He remembered the blows, and he remembered the bruises on his mother's face and his own in the mirror.

"You're fucking with me, Junior," his mother finally said, her eyes sharp as if she was about to drill a hole in The Corrector's head.

"Mom! I wouldn't fuck with you." He stared her in the face. "I did it."

"Bullshit. You wish you did." That hateful glare in his mother's eyes. That, too, had been a part of his childhood. He'd almost forgotten. "Oh, Junior..." His mother's face sagged all at once, a tear in her right eye—and she looked like a sick person again, a stick figure on white sheets. Her old, wrinkled hand reached for one of her fentanyl lollipops on the bedside table.

"What, Mom?" The Corrector didn't know what else to do or say. Embarrassment spilled over him; he felt nothing except a dull sense of betrayal. "You don't believe me?"

She just lay there, a shadow under a gray blanket.

The Corrector stilled himself. He'd wait for her to pass and get on with his mission.

34. Sania Jamison

Sania's shift had ended, and she sat in the locker room, unwinding. She was exhausted from her four 12-hour days: extra hours to fill in for Jason, who was on vacation. She loved her job as an ER nurse, but there were days when the relentless nature of her profession caught up with her and the hard edge of humanity felt particularly close.

The room was small, with two rows of lockers and a long bench. The pungent odor of medication, illness, and disinfection permeated the air in a way that had become deeply familiar—the same air, continuously circulating. The smells from patients long gone might still be meandering in these rooms.

Sania looked at her phone. A voicemail from Aunt Barbara. Sania didn't have the energy to call back right now. Today, among the standard fare of acute migraines, heart problems, and minor cuts, they had a gunshot wound. Those were the worst. Just a kid, a twelve-year-old. A drive-by shooting. Two cops hung about, but Sania was used to cops and paid them no attention. Her job was to take care of the victims.

The kid was Korean: skinny, athletic, with an abdominal wound that had caused a fair amount of bleeding. The ambulance brought him in at a near-capacity time; some visitors had to sit on the edge of the small flowerbed in the center of the waiting room. Two people sat on the floor, their backs to the wall.

The boy's mother had perched on the windowsill, crying, mascara smeared over her cheeks, a crumpled tissue clutched in her hand. She wore sweatpants and a gray T-shirt. The woman shivered whenever the entry door let a gust of cool autumn air in, a grimace of pain passing across her face.

The next time Sania had run into the mother was at the cafeteria a few hours later. The woman sat at one of the small tables, a ham and cheese sandwich on the plate before her barely touched. She produced a curved smile when her hollow eyes picked out Sania.

Sania approached. "What happened?"

"The bullet scraped his spine. He may never walk again."

"Oh, God. I'm so sorry."

"He's only twelve." The mother was crying again.

Her face was still before Sania's eyes all these hours later.

"Girl, you should go home." Betsy's voice drew Sania out of her reverie. Betsy was older and soft in behavior and appearance. She was among the few long-term employees in this place that saw significant turnover. Betsy was always even-tempered, as if in possession of a secret recipe for attending to pain without taking on too much of its weight. How did she do it? It was only Sania's third year, and there were moments when she felt she'd already had enough.

"I'm just catching my breath." Sania sighed.

Betsy laughed her soft, unobtrusive laugh. "A tough day?"

"Yes. But no deaths." Sania removed the light gray hijab she'd used at work and replaced it with the bright purple one she'd worn on her way here. It was her ritual, even though she wasn't sure it made sense.

"There you go. And now, out of here with you, dear." Betsy waved her hand toward the door.

"Goodnight, Betsy."

"Goodnight, sweetheart."

Sania walked swiftly across the tiled linoleum floor, the obedient automatic door sliding open to let her out. It was already dark, the moon hanging precariously over the roofs.

35. The Corrector

The pressure in his brain pushed The Corrector outside. Fuck! He zipped his dark blue jacket against the cold and headed down Fulton Street, looking for something to occupy his attention. His eyes took in every detail.

Most people he saw at this hour were regular white folks. Some Black people, sure, but what could one do about that after all the generations come and gone? A burly white guy in a dark blue tracksuit passed The Corrector, glancing curiously at him. What the fuck? But he didn't want to bother with the dude. Something about the body posture and the big shoulders reminded him of Dad.

Dad was restless as fuck in the same way The Corrector was right now. The restlessness that men felt. When Dad was like that, it was safer not to bug him. He was liable to snap you if you asked the wrong question or just happened to be standing before him.

He remembered that one time when Dad was really at the end of his rope, in the worst way. It must have been Mom's fault. She'd always bugged Dad about all kinds of nonsense: the bourbon, the beer, the cigarettes. The everything. Dad broke Mom's cheekbone, and she had to say she'd fallen off the stairs and ate through the straw for weeks. The Corrector had to hide under his bed some nights. Later, when he was eleven or twelve, he started spending evenings elsewhere, hanging around with his pals, with all the beers and joints and the stupid kid talk.

As The Corrector approached, the smell from Killer Burger down the street grew stronger until he felt his mouth water. But the place looked too crowded.

Dad had said—and The Corrector remembered this very well:

Now and then, a man must explode without worrying about what might happen. That's how the world worked, how it had worked since the beginning of time. Who was he to question that? He wanted to dance around and stomp his feet, but he had to restrain himself, what with all the people around.

As he passed the Starbucks on the corner, The Corrector winced from that stupid pain in his left foot. The pain seemed to explode from nowhere these last few weeks. It came and went like a fucking thief. But compared to what his mom was dealing with, he had to be okay with it.

It'd started a year earlier, soon after that Maharani woman. First, a vague ache, then a burning. He'd gone to see a doctor, but of course, he had no symptoms when he was there. And nothing on the X-ray. The damn charlatans were making money hand over fist and couldn't even figure out a stupid foot pain. The doctor's name was Zuckerman. Of course, he was going to be a con artist.

The Corrector limped because the damn foot hurt so much when he put his weight on it. But in an hour or two, he'd feel nothing again—like the pain had never happened. He wasn't crazy: there must be a fucking reason. He needed another drink to dull the pain.

That Muslim woman coming out of Starbucks looked familiar—it wasn't the first or the second time The Corrector had seen her smug face and her stupid coffee cups in a cardboard holder. Her whole appearance, not giving two fucks about anything else, a dumb headscarf over her head like they were in Afghanistan or something. Like America was there for her kind to take over.

Someone had to do something about this bullshit.

He waited for her to walk half a block, then followed her at a safe distance, with plenty of pedestrians between them. She'd suspect nothing, even if she decided to turn her hijabed head around and look. Which she wouldn't. A sense of safety oozed from her as she walked, her chin up. It started to drizzle.

36. Dmitry Volkov

Dmitry was tired, but Nazari's Russian friend *might* know something. Work was work. They had to check him out, assuming the DMV had the correct address. Dmitry didn't trust Russians. They came from a dark place without morals, making them more susceptible to corruption.

"What exactly does this guy do to afford this place?" he asked as they pulled up by one of the new luxury three-story buildings on Division. The first floor was all ice cream and toys and tourist stuff. Portland was changing right under his nose. It was exciting, somehow.

"I have no idea." Brenda checked the rearview mirror and slid the car into a parking spot. A lucky find at this hour.

The glass front door was locked. Brenda fidgeted with the keypad next to it. They waited. A car honked around the corner. A woman laughed in the distance.

"Who is it?" The male voice was gruff.

"Police," Brenda said into the security box. We need to ask you a few questions."

"Questions?"

The door clicked. Dmitry pulled on the handle, letting Brenda in first. They rode the elevator to the second floor, taking in the posh modern setup. No. 24 was to the right of the elevator lobby. They knocked, and the door opened without delay. Out of habit, Dmitry's hand was on his weapon under the jacket.

"Police?" The man asked with an open expression, as if he, of all people, had no reason to fear the cops. And perhaps he didn't.

"Are you Igor Pechorin?" Brenda asked.

"Ee-gor."

Dmitry couldn't help laughing. As Brenda introduced them, Dmitry wondered if he could read a former *tovarish*, comrade, as folks in the Soviet Union had referred to one another, a form of address gone with the country that had coined it. Pechorin looked calm and unthreatening in his bright red bathrobe and slippers. The wall-sized windows overlooked the street.

"We're here to talk about..."

"Don't tell me," Pechorin cut in, his long, thin hand covering his eyes theatrically. "I already know, and I don't want to find out. My dear friend Naseem. He missed our weekly chess game. I've been calling him for days." He waved Dmitry and Brenda into the apartment; they followed him through a broad kitchen area and into the living room four times the size of Rita's and Dmitry's. "Sit down, sit down."

Pechorin was blond and had a slight build. No taller than five-eight. Light and athletic, in his mid-to-late forties, and probably fast on his feet. With some displeasure at himself, Dmitry realized that he was unlikely to chase this man down if things ever came to that.

"Tell me, tell me, Detectives. Why all this suspense?" Pechorin's accent was typical for a Russian immigrant; the *th* transformed into something closer to a *z*. Instantly, Dmitry felt superior. His accent remained, but at least he had mostly conquered that challenge.

"*Vi govorite po Russki?*" Pechorin threw at him as if reading his thoughts.

"*Da.* But we'll stick to English tonight. My partner here doesn't speak Russian."

"Sorry." Brenda smiled. Sometimes, she was way too polite.

"Where were you on the night between November 7th and 8th?" Dmitry stared Pechorin squarely in the face. Wasn't there an old novel with such a character?

"Let me see." Pechorin scratched his hairy chest. "What day was that?"

"Last Thursday and Friday."

"I...I was in Chicago for a few days." The guy looked hesitant, as if uncomfortable with the question. "And now that we're done with this preliminary conversation, this small talk, if you will, what happened to my dear friend Naseem?"

Dmitry softened his voice. "He was murdered."

"I knew he was gone." Pechorin's face crumbled; tears rolled down his eyes. For a few moments, he struggled to recover his composure. "A drink? To my friend, Naseem Nazari, the most beautiful man I've ever had a chance to meet." Moving about nervously and abruptly, Pechorin grabbed an oversized bottle of Stolichnaya from the coffee table. "Russian vodka, you understand."

"No, thanks," Dmitry said. "We're on duty."

Igor winked at him, already filling a shot glass; the wink felt entirely wrong for the circumstances. Igor exhaled and downed the liquid in one gulp. His face strained as he grabbed a pickle from the small dish on the table and tossed it into his mouth, chewing with vigorous abandon. "Indeed. You better believe it. He was beautiful, body and soul. I don't mean as a lover, Detectives, you understand—just as a human being. But a lover—that would be an honor." He'd already poured a second shot. "To Naseem, who..."

"Let's stick to our questions," Dmitry said. "So, he was your lover?"

"No, man. Just saying that I loved the guy."

"What was your reason for traveling to Chicago?" Dmitry was tired of hearing about Nazari's charms; he was more interested in finding his killer.

"Business." Pechorin's face had gone pink from the quick infusion of alcohol. "I'm in the import business, you see. I do all kinds of deals. Chemicals and stuff."

"Chemicals and *stuff*?" Brenda's brows went up.

"Nothing illegal, Detective," Pechorin grinned. "Have some vodka, you'll relax." Now, his face had changed: his expression seemed sincere, not at all mocking. "Pickles? I make my own, you see. You have to use less salt. They don't know how here in the States. You'll agree, won't you?" He used the pickle in his hand to point at Dmitry.

"I don't care for pickles," Dmitry said.

At this moment, a naked woman much taller than Pechorin emerged from the bedroom. "Igor, what's going on?" She stood in the doorway, paying as much attention to Dmitry and Brenda as if the two detectives were transparent. Dmitry couldn't believe his eyes. She was attractive as hell; he felt embarrassed. His bullshit Christian kid self still hid somewhere inside him.

"Sweetheart, just wait for me," Pechorin pleaded, stripped of his air of confidence. "This is important. Go back to bed. I'll be there in a moment."

"Fuck you, Igor," the naked girl said as she walked out. At least she knew how to say his name correctly.

"So, you trade chemicals with other countries. Did I get that right?" Dmitry didn't like the guy. Something smug about him.

"You got it! I facilitate business between several American companies and my employers in Moscow." Pechorin smiled briefly. "What do you think of Putin?" He scrutinized Dmitry and Brenda intensely as if his life depended on their answers.

"Hmm...pretty strict?" Brenda sounded hesitant. "I don't know much about politics."

"Strict? You're right. Russia wants *strict*, or at least it thinks so, but it will never be free until it's rid of that man. Do you remember the USSR?"

"Never mind the USSR." Dmitry was getting impatient. The murderer's red business card was enough USSR for the week. "I'm assuming you have tickets or reservations you can show us? For your trip to Chicago?"

"Indeed, Detective." Pechorin didn't move to provide any of this information, but Dmitry let it slide. He and Brenda could get back to it later if they still felt any suspicion about the guy.

"Do you know anyone who might have wanted to harm him?" The question was becoming tired; it felt wrong in Dmitry's mouth, a formality.

"No, most emphatically not. He was the loveliest man in the world. He'd argue with you till dawn but wash your dishes after you went to bed. He'd let you talk as long as you wanted and ask you all about yourself. A rare, rare soul. I've never felt as comfortable talking to another human being."

"We think the crime may have been racially motivated," Dmitry said grimly.

"I see." Pechorin sat down, looking deflated. "In this country, in 2019, I'm not surprised." He pursed his lips in a childish grimace. "Don't get me wrong: I love America and Americans. Most Americans. Russia is even worse. You must understand me, Detectives?"

Brenda nodded; Dmitry said nothing. Most Americans were okay, but in their job, they dealt with too many who were not. Brenda might say it was a bag full of stones, and you needed only one stone to kill someone. Or some such thing. Who was he to judge, anyway? He'd fucked up more than he'd done right in his own life.

37. The Corrector

The Corrector shadowed the Muslim woman for a few blocks until she took a left on 12th, heading into a residential area. He stopped under the awning of some pastry shop and pulled a cigarette out of the pack in his pocket so he wouldn't seem suspicious if she happened to turn around.

He watched her out of the corner of his eye as she walked down half the next block and approached one of the houses. The Corrector's foot throbbed, but he did his best to tune the fucking thing out. Bigger fish to fry. The cigarette tasted great, helping him think. He was about done with it when the rain started, huge raindrops slamming into the ground. Good timing. Already, small puddles were forming on the pavement. He thought about his mom back at home, how she'd never go outside again and feel the rain.

When the Muslim woman disappeared into the house, The Corrector felt something coming up in him, like he might get to sobbing again. That wouldn't do. It would be embarrassing as hell—and surely someone would remember a grown-ass dude crying on the corner. That wasn't correct procedure. He headed to the bar two blocks down.

The bar stood nearly empty. Old counter, dark wood. He didn't come often, but the place was okay, not one of those newfangled shitholes full of lights. The Corrector hated places like that.

A carpet cleaner scent merged with the smell of burger grease from the kitchen—a good old American smell. A dude at one end of the counter was nodding his bald head, dozing off with his drink. A young couple in a booth along the wall went about like it was their first fucking date: happy and laughing. And good for them.

Usually, The Corrector preferred to drink at home. There, he could play his music as loud as he wanted and do any fucking thing he liked: yell, stomp around, swear at the walls, scream along with the music. Mom's hearing hadn't been at its best even before fentanyl. As long as he showed up to care for her, everything else was fine. Since the time he'd tried to talk to her about his corrective actions, there'd been few words between them.

Not much he could do. Living long wasn't the thing. Cirrhosis of the fucking liver had gotten Dad's ass years ago, and The Corrector had no ambition for a long life either. Helping clean up this country—that was a worthy goal. Gavin McInnes of Proud Boys had it right when he said that Muslims had a problem with inbreeding. Who cared if they did it in their own shit countries, but it was not okay here, in the United States of America.

The Corrector's foot still throbbed, but he decided to pay no attention. Fuck it. He had to live with it. He'd looked it up online, but how was he supposed to pick one from all the different options? Tendinitis. Neuropathy. Damned if he understood what these ten-dollar words even meant. The Fucked Up Foot syndrome.

The bartender approached with a dumb smile like it was Christmas. The dude was tall and skinny and had a small mustache.

"Hi. How's it going?"

"Bourbon, neat," The Corrector said.

SATURDAY, NOVEMBER 16

38. Brenda Smith

Brenda's dreams were disconnected, full of dread and longing. Jessica was there, but then she became a different, faceless woman to whom Brenda was inextricably connected. Even in the dream, Brenda was tired of her. Bodies, dead and alive, piled up. Sexy female bodies turned up lifeless. Angry male faces.

Brenda woke sweaty and scared. She wished Mary were there and then remembered that she was. Relief washed through Brenda as she exhaled.

She turned around to look at her lover, curled up and immeasurably cute in sleep. How delightful that felt. Brenda suppressed laughter.

She sat on the edge of the bed for a while, reflecting on the fear that had woken her. Lights from the passing cars moved in circles on the ceiling, settled down, and leaped into motion again. The never-ceasing city life, patterns concluding and starting again, repetition upon repetition. But people were not repeatable. Every person meant something to themselves, to someone else, to the world.

Mary whimpered in her sleep.

Then, it was light outside; Brenda had fallen back asleep. Her head was off the pillow. She could see Mary puttering about in the kitchen, Brenda's old gray T-shirt loose on Mary's skinny body. The street was louder now; the light had spread through the room.

Brenda sniffed the air. Pancakes—and coffee, definitely coffee. It had been years since anyone had cooked her breakfast. Brenda was so moved she almost cried. As she relished the moment, her eyes grew heavy again. She resisted; the morning was off to an exciting start, not a minute to waste.

"Ta-da. Breakfast is ready." A huge grin on Mary's face, a match for the brief interlude of the sun outside. "Get up, sleepy head."

Brenda felt her face turn on its light, a smile bursting from inside her. "Thank you, M."

"It's not the first time you've called me that, beauty queen. What's up with the M business?" From her lover's flirtatious tone, Brenda knew Mary didn't mind.

"Something about that name of yours. I'd rather not think of you as the mother of Christ." Brenda guffawed to make sure Mary knew she was joking. Still, she tensed, afraid she'd crossed a boundary.

But Mary burst out laughing. "Call me anything you want, as long as you get your ass out of bed this moment. The pancakes will get cold."

As if swept into a happy current, Brenda sat up in bed, her feet firmly inside this new, promising day. She rose and stretched on her way to the kitchen. "You took care of everything." Lingonberry jam, strawberry jam, and butter were already on the table, making Brenda's mouth water. "Thank you, baby." Her heart was a swirl of feelings. A bite, a sip. "Hmm..." That bittersweet taste, the mix of coffee, jam, and pancake in her mouth. She chewed it slowly, savoring.

Mary plopped on the kitchen stool across the table from Brenda and watched her with—what was it? Curiosity? Admiration? Maybe both. It felt good to be stared at in this way. It'd been a long time. With a half-smile on her lips, Mary's dimples were especially prominent. What a perfect face. Her pink hair was like a fire around it.

"What do you do at the office?" Mary asked.

Shit. Brenda was still waiting for the caffeine to kick in. What should she say? She was mad as fuck at herself. She'd known this was coming, but she wasn't ready. She didn't have it in her to make up some coverup, some office schedule, some bullshit story.

The moment stared her squarely in the face.

"I must tell you something, M. Please don't be mad."

"What?" Mary's face tensed.

"I'm not an office manager."

"You're not?" Mary stared uncomprehendingly.

"No. I'm a cop. I'm so sorry I lied to you."

"A cop?" Mary looked at her blankly. "You've gotta be kidding me."

"I panicked. I didn't know how to tell you. It's Portland, you know. I'm not an asshole like some cops are, I'm a homicide detective, but still..."

"I know it's Portland." Mary nodded, a contemptuous grimace on her face. "Many of us move here to live an honest life. Play straight with ourselves and others."

"I'm sorry." Brenda wished she'd waited another day for her confession.

"That's bullshit." Mary's bag was already in her hands, her coat over her arm as if she'd practiced instant leaving.

"Wait, wait. Can't we talk about it?" Brenda hopped off her stool. "Wait a minute."

But Mary just breezed past on her way out, a severe expression on her face, her disappointment radiating through the room. The slammed door hit Brenda's ears like a final verdict.

39. The Corrector

The Corrector felt so fucking pumped he could barely breathe. He was in his car, watching. Rain slid down the windshield, a good helper. Blood rushed through his head with a loud whoosh. The car smelled of cigarettes, as usual.

He'd been watching her house for a couple of days now. Couldn't help it. A cute thing, two stories, dark blue, almost black in the dark. And in a lot better shape than his own house. How was it fair that these Muslims had a better life than his? Even the tiny patch of flowers and greenery in the front yard looked happy. Shit.

He was too close to home. This wasn't correct procedure. Sure, his dark blue 2012 Ford was nothing special. Still, someone might notice. He should have picked his next target in a different part of town.

But the truth was, The Corrector had been hooked the moment he first saw her. His blood had boiled so hard he couldn't keep himself in check. It wasn't his fault she'd tempted him with her coffee cups and her proud look like she was the queen of the world.

40. Dmitry Volkov

As Dmitry unlocked the door of his house, he knew. His brother's smell, the stupid clove cigarettes he favored. Boris smoked so many of them that the scent followed him like a ghost. He had a spare key and never bothered to call or text. This wasn't always convenient, but family was family.

The truth was that Boris did what his passions dictated, and others were forced to cover for him. Dmitry was relieved that Rita and Natasha were away for the weekend visiting Rita's sister in Sacramento. Natasha was a small wonder that didn't belong amid the heavy Russian past Boris still carried in this new country.

Dmitry entered his elongated living room, the window at the other end half-constrained by the white curtains on either side. Just then, Boris bent over the coffee table and snorted a long line of coke off the electric bill that Rita must have left there. He was setting up for another line when he saw Dmitry.

"Dimka! Shit. You startled me. Want a line?"

"Why not?" Dmitry could use an energy boost, especially now that the working day was on the wane and fatigue began creeping in.

"Now we're talking." Boris got out of the way, positioning himself at the end of the couch.

Dmitry sat in his brother's spot. He exhaled the stale air, then leaned over the coffee table for a big woosh of a line. The coke kicked his body into gear, his face cracking open into a smile. He picked up the electric bill, with OVERDUE printed in red letters. When Rita was back, he'd have to explain.

"A drink?" Dmitry asked.

"Yeah, a drink." Boris stretched, the tips of his long fingers reaching for the ceiling.

Dmitry fetched vodka and orange juice, which he divided between two glasses without much concern about the proportions. He avoided eye contact as he handed a glass to his brother.

"Thank you, sir," Boris drawled mockingly. He brought the drink to his lips and took a quick sip. "Hmm...Delicious." An idiot grin lit his face.

They sat there for a few minutes, not talking, and Dmitry thought back on their childhood, the way he'd bullied Boris during some of those years and protected him during others. That one time when he stole Boris's birthday cake. He'd meant it as a joke. When their parents weren't looking, he removed the cake from the fridge and left it on the stairway windowsill two stories up. Dmitry assumed the cake would still be there; he'd return it once he'd had a chance to enjoy everyone's puzzlement. But as the dinner went on, he began feeling nervous. What if things didn't go as planned? He snuck out to check; to his horror, the cake was gone. He never made up the courage to tell anyone.

He and Boris had had good times, too: studying together and plotting against their parents. Since then, their shared years had collapsed into the occasional shared hours.

"I need your help," Boris looked serious, his large, wide-open eyes aspiring to sincerity.

"What help?"

"This dude I buy from when I'm in town." Boris pointed at the small coke baggie on the coffee table. "He's mentioned a job. A jewelry store. I think we can do this, no problem. You being a cop helps."

"Doesn't God have issues with such things anymore?" Dmitry didn't even want to ask how being a cop helped in the petty crime his brother was contemplating.

"God is more forgiving than we think." A half-smirk on Boris's broad face.

"No way. I'm not doing it." Dmitry couldn't trust his brother and his plans. Not because he didn't love Boris. Boris was unreliable. Flaky by nature.

"Won't you even let me tell you about it?"

"Borya, give me a fucking break." Dmitry raised his glass. "To you."

As they clinked, the sun's glint between two aggressive clouds slid off Dmitry's glass and into his eyes, momentarily blinding him.

41. The Corrector

As hours passed, The Corrector got bored, his legs stiff in the cramped space. She wasn't going out again, not tonight. Not on a night like this. No one had walked by in half an hour. The Corrector considered all the water running down the street. What the fuck? He thought of his dad. Dad hadn't done much all his life. The Corrector wouldn't make the same mistake. Here he was, doing something.

More time passed as The Corrector smoked a few cigarettes. Jittery from hope but annoyed about the delay, he desperately wanted a drink. He'd had a couple earlier to get himself straight, but he'd been postponing the next one to keep his head clear.

He needed it soon. It was time to give up for the day.

And what do you know? That's when she came out. Right around seven, with darkness all settled. She stepped down the porch stairs, looking at her phone and frowning, her face framed by the stupid hijab. She shrugged and put the phone away into her small beige purse, a silly thing that wouldn't even fit a bottle of bourbon.

And then she headed down the street in the direction of his Ford, her hijab swaying in the wind like a fucking pirate flag.

The Corrector knew he might never get another chance like this. It took him half a second to decide. No one would notice him in this rain. Not a soul was around, everyone keeping dry in their stupid holes.

42. Sania Jamison

Sania was annoyed as she pushed the door open. Annoyed and resigned. Fresh air smelling of rain rushed by her face. With Jason still on vacation, every staff member mattered. And now, Betsy had come down with the flu or something nasty, and here Sania was, returning to work on her day off. They'd planned to take the kids out for a movie, but now, Atif would have to take them.

Her family would be fine, but knowing that wasn't the same as being there with them. Sure, Sania loved the occasional time away from the children, but she felt the opposite today. A puncture wound, a fractured skull, two fingers cut off by a saw: it had been a hard week. The pressure of these damaged bodies she wished she could fix all at once with a magic trick.

There was no magic in her profession. She began walking toward her car, wishing to God Betsy would not end up stuck at home for days. Sania couldn't manage this on her own; she simply couldn't. They needed to hire more help. This chronic understaffing was infuriating, considering nurses did most of the medical care work. She walked briskly, aware of her hijab's propensity to absorb water, looking down to make sure she didn't step on a pile of dog shit.

They, too, had a dog. Atif and Sania hadn't found a reason good enough to deny the children this pleasure. Sania smiled as she thought of Omar and Lidia. It hadn't taken her long to fall in love with Helen, their golden retriever. Being loved unconditionally had its bonuses.

She was startled when something touched her shoulder. A hand, like a spider, but worse. Sania twisted her body, turning her head to look. A man, tall, broad shoulders. He'd knocked her hijab loose, and it fluttered around her head, making it difficult to see. All the while, the hand's grip on her shoulder was growing firmer. Only then did Sania remember: SCREAM!

She inhaled, but already, an elbow was around her neck. The man's body hung over her, the stale smell of alcohol and cigarettes and sweat. She grabbed his arm with both hands, but it wouldn't budge. It wouldn't budge. Her hands shook as her body desperately swallowed the last of the oxygen.

Everything went white.

43. The Corrector

The Corrector smiled as he pulled his prisoner's phone out of her beige purse and turned it off. That way, it wouldn't be traced to his location. He knew she'd be out for only a minute or two. He started the car and turned the music on, just in case. Iron Maiden felt right for the moment. *I just want to see your blood.* The whole thing had been seamless.

The Corrector drove, making sure not to swerve or speed as he kept an eye on her in the rearview mirror. Soon, she stirred, panic on her face. No wonder, with that duct tape over her mouth. Her hands went up to her face; then she saw what an excellent job he'd done tying her up, both her arms and her legs. She squirmed a bit, then settled. Sensible. She wasn't going anywhere. He was in complete control, and she fucking knew it.

The Corrector pulled in and closed the garage door behind him. No one would hear them now. Not even his mom, who spent her days checked out in the living room.

He reached back to remove the duct tape from the Muslim woman's mouth. It was awkward, stretching like that. Her eyes were on him, full of hate and fear. Mom's eyes had looked like that when Dad beat her. Except, Dad must have cared about Mom, even if he beat her. When The Corrector was a kid, it'd been hard to tell.

The woman gasped for breath, her eyes darting around the car and then back at his face. "What do you want with me?" She cleared her throat.

It was like a splash of icy water had hit The Corrector's chest. She had no accent he could hear.

No accent at all.

He'd thought she was from the Middle East or whatever. But she sounded like a regular person.

"I don't have much money, but I can get more." She was trying now.

"Just shut up." The Corrector needed to think.

Again, her brown eyes darted around. He got out and opened the back door. Trying not to pay attention to her tense, sweaty body in wrinkled scrubs, he grabbed her beige purse where he'd dropped it behind the driver's seat. The purple hijab had come off her head but was still wrapped around her shoulders. The Corrector's hands were shaking. He needed a drink bad.

He rifled through the purse. Too much crap: lipstick, eyeliner, a little pink powder box. A vial of yellow perfume, a few tickets, receipts, and pens. Too much of every damn thing. Floss, napkins, keys. And in the side pocket, her driver's license.

Sania Jamison.

Even the name sounded American. What the fuck was going on? He couldn't just let her go, not after she'd seen his face, his car, his garage, everything. For what seemed like ever, he stood there next to his car, his thoughts going over and over the situation. He should let her go. No, he couldn't let her go.

He felt like crying. But it wouldn't do to show weakness like that. This whole crying thing was beginning to get on his nerves. He got out of the car and opened the back door, leaning in uncomfortably to untie her ankles. The prisoner's eyes were firm on him, but she said nothing.

44. Sania Jamison

Sania had never been so terrified in her life. Her hands were shaking, her armpits soaked, her throat sore from struggling to breathe with the duct tape over her mouth. The man was deranged. His gray eyes shone with a devilish glow, and the smell of alcohol was overpowering.

"Get out." The voice was flat, inhuman. Something collapsed in Sania at the sound of it. "Come with me."

The man was at least six-two, broad in the shoulders, his face glistening with stupidity. The face was not memorable, but Sania knew she'd remember it for the rest of her life. She crawled out of the car and desperately looked around. The garage door was shut, separating her from the rest of the world. If she weren't so scared, she'd be angry and humiliated. All she could see were shelves packed tight with boxes, old shoes, and lamps, stuff you'd expect in any garage. Sania's abdominal muscles burned; her extremities buzzed with a dull ache. Still, she realized she was upset at herself for not finding the time to call Aunt Barbara back.

"Why are you doing this?" Sania's voice came out lower than his. Her throat hurt. She closed the car door behind her and stood by the car, not knowing what to do next.

For a moment, the man just stared at her without speaking. Feverishly, Sania wished Atif were there to protect her. The faces of her children came, and she pushed them away. She couldn't think of them now. They didn't belong in this dreadful place.

"You sound like an American girl." Incredulity on the man's face. His ugly, drunk face. "Then why are you wearing a fucking headscarf?"

For a while, she said nothing. The man was pacing about in the space between the car and the door to the house. His face was tight, his eyes unfocused. Then he slammed the wall with his fist. "Answer me, goddamnit."

That sent Sania shaking. "I...well..." She didn't know. The ends of thoughts ran away from her before she could recapture them. She couldn't think straight, couldn't explain it. "My husband decided to adopt Islam." Her teeth chattered.

"Why the fuck would he want to do that?" Now, the man looked offended.

It had taken Atif years to convince her. Conversations that must have added up to hundreds of hours. How could she answer this crazy man in just one sentence?

"I wanted to support him." Sania shrugged. "It didn't seem important at the time. Is this why you brought me here?"

She already knew the answer.

45. The Corrector

It *was* fucking important, now. The Corrector's skin went all goose pimples.

"If you let me go, I won't tell anyone." Her eyes were like any person's. The Corrector didn't want to look.

I won't tell anyone. Right! People always say that. Fat chance! She'd run to the fucking cops the moment he let her go. But something had gone wrong now that he'd talked to her. His hands were shaking, and there was zero fucking energy in any of his muscles. Talking was softening him up in a way he hated as if he was less sure about everything.

He would need to keep drinking to keep his nerves in check. Luckily, he'd refreshed his supply of bourbon the day before. He kept some of it in the garage, some in his room, and a bottle or two in the kitchen. There were no glasses, but a few coffee mugs sat on the rough wood shelf by the door. The Corrector picked one of them and poured himself a hefty dose.

"Can I have one?" Sania Jamison looked straight at him, shivering.

"I thought you Muslims weren't supposed to."

"It's a special case." She tried to smile as if it was a joke.

She was trying to make him like her, that's all. But what the hell? He poured her some into another mug and untied her hands. She was harmless, her ankles still tied. She leaned on the car and sipped it without talking. The Corrector didn't want to watch her. He closed his eyes. His head was throbbing.

What are you going to do? Dad's voice in his head, with his southern drawl and all.

"Nothing. Still thinking."

"Thinking?" The woman said.

The Corrector must have spoken out loud. And who cared at this point? He had to put an end to this nonsense. He took one more drink, then one more. She stared, worry in her eyes.

"What are you doing?" Her voice cracked.

He didn't answer. Things had grown soft and warm in his body and his thoughts. The bottle was still half-full. He raised it over his head.

46. *Azar Bayat*

World Cup Coffee buzzed with the egalitarian hipness Azar had expected from Portland. The smell of coffee and baked goods was sublime and invigorating.

"What are you going to get?" Becki's round, freckled face bore a grin that made her look serious and amused at the same time.

"What do you call those things with apples inside?" Azar pointed at the pastry display case. "The bagels?"

Becki's face screwed into incomprehension.

"Donuts?" Azar tried again.

She was appalled at her wooden attempts at English. Now and then, the best she could do was to stack the words one at a time, expending endless brain cycles to produce a simple sentence. This was after years of weekly English lessons. She was upset at herself for not studying harder, but she was also hopeful.

She was already fluent in French. Since childhood, her parents had taught Azar and her sister, Bahar, by speaking only French on the weekends. French rather than English had been offered in Irani schools years before Azar was born; many of the older generation were comfortable with it.

"Hmm...Bear claws?" Becki's brows went up.

"Yes, bear claws!"

Cinnamon, too. That was part of the smell. Through the window, Azar noticed the hasty pedestrians, many dressed in blue and black puffy coats. While she and Becki waited in line, Azar threw furtive glances at the other customers, watching their postures. Especially the women. She admired American women. They must feel so free, and one day, Azar hoped to learn to feel that way. She and Becki placed their order and took a small table by the window.

"How was it, growing up in America?"

"Oh." Becki shrugged. "It was no big deal for me. It depends on your childhood. Mine was pretty average. Middle class in the Midwest, you know." Becki gave her a curious glance, apparently trying to gauge whether the notion of middle class in America made sense to Azar.

"Yes, I understand." Azar nodded a few too many times. Midwest? Where was that? She had no idea but was afraid to say so for fear of offending her friend. She liked Becki, who seemed sincere and unpretentious among the student crowd that wasn't always warm to everyone.

"I've been dying to ask about you." Becki's bright blue eyes drilled into Azar, but not in an unfriendly way. "Your life must have been difficult. Or has it? I don't mean to sound presumptuous." Becki placed both palms on her chest, a touching gesture.

Becki was a generous person; she really was. In her eyes, Azar saw the kindness of security, the kind Iranian youth didn't usually experience, not with all the hatred and unrest around.

"Not my personal life. I'm luckier than some." Azar didn't know where to start. "It's the society in general. Women especially. Men, they can get away with anything. They can say anything to you. As a woman, you have no recourse. My mom was arrested once because some drunk didn't like how she wore her headscarf. *Too much hair.*"

"Arrested?" Becki looked incredulous. "Why?"

"The Guidance Patrol, they're like religious police." Azar's hands trembled as she spoke; this was the closest she'd gotten to sharing her feelings about the home country with any American. "They accused her of a disturbance."

She grabbed her water glass and took a few gulps, her heart beating fast. "Sorry. It still activates me. You wouldn't believe it, but in an Islamic court, you need three female witnesses to overrule a man's claim."

"I didn't know that. I'm sorry." Becki did look sorry, her brows furrowed, her lips pursed. "What happened to your mom?"

"They let her go the next day. Phew."

"Shit." Becki looked offended on behalf of Azar's mom. "This must have been nerve-wracking."

"Yes." Azar remembered the evening of phone calls and the sleepless night at the police headquarters.

"After you get your degree, will you have to return?"

Azar thought about this for a moment. Her boyfriend Soroush assumed she would. Soroush, Soroush, Soroush. A pretty name that came with a cute face. Azar liked him quite a bit, but she wished she loved and missed him more.

"I don't think so."

Becki nodded without digging deeper into this subject as if sensing how raw it still was for Azar.

The barista called their names, and they got up to collect their drinks. Azar scanned the space again. Seeing more of other women's bodies in public was another new experience.

Back at the table, she closed her eyes briefly, enjoying the first few sips of her drink. The bitterness connected her not only to her background in Tehran, where alcohol was forbidden and coffee and tea were drinks of choice for social gatherings, but to the greater world of freedom and creativity she'd longed to explore. She thought of Proust in his cork-lined room, with his love of silence and good coffee. She, too, had been stuck in a room like that: a small room of censorship where ancient culture and fundamentalism collided. Her real life would begin here, now.

47. Dmitry Volkov

Dmitry nervously broke off and chewed small pieces of heavy dark bread on the plate before him. He felt out of place at Kachka, a quintessential and crazy expensive Russian restaurant overcrowded with happy, laughing people who had no reference for his worried soul. He felt invisible, but this was for the best. Usually, he couldn't afford to eat here.

The mix of smells in the dining room featured many undertones of the Russian cuisine familiar to Dmitry from birth: butter, onion, chocolate, sour cream. Elegant wood panels adorned the walls, and a stairway ascended to a loft packed with customers. Blue-patterned tablecloths overflowed with concentric circles. Dmitry's green, casual chair would be comfortable if he could settle into comfort. An industrial-looking ventilation duct ran along the ceiling, featuring several speakers. The sound of Russian pop, more recent than Dmitry's emigration in 1992, made him feel like he was behind the looking glass in the world of the dead.

He was sweating as he prepared to deal with more shit from Misha.

Meet me at Kachka at 7. Life and Death :)

Death was capitalized in Misha's text. Whose life? Whose death? He used a smiley face again. Motherfucker. At least his bodyguards wouldn't be throwing punches at a public place.

Dmitry had never seen Misha without bodyguards; he'd asked for a table for four. His throat was warm from the shot of vodka he'd just downed. Americans wouldn't place an order before their friends arrived, but Russian hospitality required appetizers, *zakuski*. He'd opted for a cheese plate, which took forever to arrive while tables around him were being served. He could barely hear the waiter or his thoughts over the chaos of animated conversations in Russian and English competing in loudness with the boisterous music.

Dmitry picked a small piece of cheese off the delicate plate. A blue pattern of concentric circles was pierced by arches that looked three-dimensional, the plates matching the tablecloth. Hesitantly, Dmitry placed the cheese on a piece of bread. Normally, he would have loved it, but tonight, the food tasted like cardboard; he had trouble swallowing. Even finishing the first bite was a struggle. He had to drink half a glass of water to get it down. He parked the unfinished mini sandwich on a saucer with a simpler set of curving blue lines. No one had had such refined dishes back in the USSR, except for thieves and party *apparatchiks*.

It was 7:25 when Misha and two guys finally rolled in. Misha wore a pair of tight-fitting jeans and a striped tee, red and black. Wasn't he cold? An exuberant pair of leather shoes completed his attire, the two thin stripes crossing the front of each shoe adorned with copper buttons that seemed purely decorative. Extra bits of leather hung off the front of each shoe as if the shoemaker had been determined to use all the available material.

Misha beamed like they were best friends. "Dima, *braht!*" *Brother.*

Dmitry rose from his seat, and the two of them hugged. A shorter man, Misha felt small in Dmitry's arms, but Dmitry could tell that every bit of Misha's body was muscle. An evil machine ready for action, Misha was imposing despite his size.

"*Privet, braht,*" Dmitry replied into Misha's ear. This response sounded tentative even to him.

By contrast, Misha's companions were massive. They wore sports jackets, a formal step up from Misha's, and their attire looked more comfortable in this weather.

"A drink?" Dmitry sat down as Misha slipped his compact body into the opposite chair.

"Yes, of course." Misha beamed. "Why not?"

They continued speaking in Russian; it seemed natural under the circumstances.

"You two, sit down." Misha moved his palms up and down as if leading a helicopter to a landing. His stone-faced bodyguards settled their broad frames in green chairs.

Dmitry poured for Misha and reached over to one of the bodyguards' glasses, but Misha extended his hand like a karate move. His palm covered the man's glass.

"No drinking for these two." Misha's eyes were on Dmitry. "They're working."

The bodyguard muttered something under his breath, making eye contact with his companion. It didn't seem like a demonstrative gesture, but instantly, Misha's eyes changed, shifting to the man. Misha's face was different, too: the sharp angle of his jaw or the way his brows went up, two small curves. His skin looked too tight on his face as he wrinkled his eyes at the bodyguard. Dmitry felt cold inside.

"Sorry, Misha," the man mumbled.

Dmitry poured a shot for himself and put down the carafe. His hands shook a little, and the glass clinked against the table. Self-consciously, Dmitry withdrew his hand.

"To us." Misha raised his glass, completely relaxed now, his attention on Dmitry.

Which *us*? For a moment, Dmitry saw himself from outside: a formerly Christian immigrant from Russia, a cop, now mingling with a criminal who was also a former victim of the Soviet Union's personality destruction machine. It was a crazy equation he couldn't solve.

"To us." They clinked.

48. Azar Bayat

"I don't think we Americans know what it's like to be from a place like that," Becki said. "No matter how many books we read."

Azar admired Becki for trying to understand and see things from the other person's perspective. "Maybe. I'm glad you don't have to face some of these hardships here."

Azar bit into her bear claw, the odd mix of flavors alive in her mouth. She could do this for the rest of her life. Coffee and bear claws.

"I've been meaning to ask." Azar looked around and lowered her voice, aware that her question may be challenging. "Why are there so few Black people here in Portland?"

"Oh." Becki sighed. "I wondered, too, so I looked it up. It's the history of racism here. Oregon used to exclude Blacks altogether. It even was a haven for the KKK. The state is trying to put all this behind, but you still see plenty of problematic views. Especially if you drive an hour or two from Portland." Becki spoke quietly as well. "Hell, even here in town, there are probably still plenty of racists."

"I see." Azar didn't have a more insightful comment.

"Why come to America, of all places? Isn't it dangerous for you, especially now?" Becki pointed her index finger up as if this were where *now* perched each moment.

"Dangerous?"

"I mean, right-wing violence, Trump, *make-America-great-again*, all that."

"Oh. Well, this exists everywhere in the world. Europe, too. A lot depends on what you compare it to. Iran is extremely volatile; most other countries are safer and more democratic. Besides, I have family here."

"Family?"

"My aunt and uncle live in Lake Oswego. They left decades ago, in the '90s."

"I see." Becki nodded. "By the way, have you heard about that immigrant who was killed a week or two ago?" A frown on Becki's face. "A Yemeni man?"

"What? No, I haven't."

Becki fiddled with her phone and produced the article. *Yemeni Immigrant Killed in Possible Hate Crime.*

"Wow. Elderly male..." Azar scrolled with her index finger as she read. *"The way the body was positioned made me feel we may be dealing with the worst here,"* the detective assigned to the case said.

"All sorts of crazy people out there." Becki's face scrunched up in disgust. "You have to be careful."

"I will." Azar was a little uneasy about being careful in some abstract way she didn't quite understand.

"Anyway...Do you miss anything about your country?"

It was an infinitely easy question and endlessly tricky. Of course, she missed things. But she was relieved about the absence of others. "My boyfriend. My sister. My parents. Maman Feri...how do you say it? Grandma. Friends." Azar checked her heart for things she missed. "Certain foods. I could find most of them here in Portland, but they're too expensive for my budget."

Azar looked out the window. It had begun raining. Her eyes fell upon a Trump-Pence bumper sticker on an old Ford pickup truck. The irony, escaping a totalitarian regime only to find herself in an America at war with itself and headed toward a police state. Still, somehow, Azar couldn't help liking it here. Speaking freely and expressing her opinions as she wished was exhilarating.

"What's your boyfriend's name?" Becki asked.

"Soroush."

The thought of Soroush squeezed at Azar's heart: his deep brown eyes, the fact that she might never see him again. Not unless he came here. When she thought of that possibility, she felt ambivalent. Soroush belonged to the old world. Azar craved new opportunities and new connections. She was out of prison. She breathed slowly, letting this epiphany sink in. She could finally be herself, as conceived by herself. Herself, separate from everything else, including her history.

"I still don't understand why you have to study abroad," Soroush had complained the last time they'd talked. "You can get a great education here. You know everyone. You can lead your private life any way you choose. It's not like you must check in at the mosque daily."

"Live any way I choose? Really? Easy for you to say. You're a man. You have all the opportunities. You don't have to wear a hijab because of a religion you don't even believe in."

Soroush had blushed but said nothing. He was too much of a man, an Iranian man. In any case, he was so young; she was too. They'd met too early in life to be a real thing.

"So-roush," Becki repeated slowly as if holding the sound on her tongue. "What a lovely name."

"It means *happiness*."

"Happiness," Becki said dreamily. "You must miss him like hell."

"Oh. Sure." Azar didn't want to dwell on Soroush anymore. "You know, back at home, we were always fed the narrative that America was evil." She smirked, recalling the simplistic propaganda. "Many people still hold that belief. My family and their friends know better." She was acutely aware of her privilege as she spoke. "What was your upbringing like? What does it mean, *a typical Midwestern family*? Isn't that what you said?"

"Two brothers, two sisters. Enough food for everyone, a house, you know. No luxury, but a comfortable life."

Becki described her family dynamics, siblings' ages, and how they'd treated one another when they were young. Azar listened carefully, trying to hold the details in her memory. Overall, Becki's story sounded like something that could happen anywhere. Not an American life, just a life.

49. Dmitry Volkov

Misha was a known entity here. A server was already at their table with an extravagant tray of appetizers. Next to caviar and lox waited a plate packed with strips of steaming sirloin steak, not even on the menu. A small bowl of herring perched on the other side of the tray next to beets, a vegetable Dmitry absolutely hated. The inevitable pickles winked from the other side of the herring.

Misha was already stuffing his mouth with a cracker and a sizable helping of lox. "How's life? Tell me everything." Misha downed his vodka and quickly poured another shot while still chewing. Somehow, his enunciation didn't suffer at all. He acted as if they hadn't had a conversation the other day. As if he hadn't threatened Dmitry.

As if this were a separate reality.

"Good," Dmitry tried.

His life wasn't good. It was as far from good as it had ever been.

"Let's have some boiled potatoes, too." Misha used English to address the waiter, who still hovered nearby.

"Coming right up, sir." The waiter spoke with no trace of a Russian accent.

"Listen, Dmitry, do you think I'd ever fuck with you?" Misha's eyes were right on Dmitry's now, any trace of a smile gone from Misha's face. Everything inside Dmitry tensed up.

"Would you fuck with me?" Dmitry repeated. The question sounded like a trap, a puzzle. "No, why?"

"Would I fuck with him?" Misha asked the two bodyguards, and both stopped chewing and shook their heads. "I wouldn't fuck with you. So, I'll tell you straight." Misha handed Dmitry a blue post-it note with nothing but a number. "Here's what I need from you."

"What is it?" Dmitry stared at the number, something familiar about its shape.

"That's a Portland Police Department case. I need the evidence."

"The evidence?"

"Don't worry, it's not drugs or anything. Just some spreadsheets. Bring it to me by..."

The end of Misha's comment was drowned out by a deafening chorus of yet another optimistic song from their hopeless former homeland. Or was it the inebriated group to Dmitry's right, so loud they could be heard from Moscow? It was a wrong moment to ask Misha to repeat himself.

"What?"

"I'll knock ten grand off your debt." Misha sounded as patient as ever.

"Ten grand?" Dmitry was offended. "Too dangerous. I'd be committing a serious crime and still owe most of what I owe now."

"Life is dangerous, my friend." Misha looked excited, proud of his exceptional wisdom. It was uncanny how quickly his expression changed from happiness to disdain and back to merriment.

"I can't do it." Now, it was Dmitry's turn to shake his head. "I just can't. I'll find another way to pay you back."

"Yeah? How long has it been now?"

Dmitry didn't answer. It *had* been a long time, much longer than Dmitry had expected to be in debt, especially to someone like Misha.

"That daughter of yours, she's so cute. Someone showed me a picture." Misha picked up a pickle from one of the plates and crunched off half of it. "What's her name now?"

Dmitry's body seized. Was this really happening? Blood rushed to his face.

"Oh, I remember now," Misha's menacing smile returned.

"Natasha. What a lovely name."

"Thank you." Dmitry's hands were shaking; he hid them under the table and tried taking deep breaths without being conspicuous.

"Dima, I need your help with this. Help me, and I'll help you. I'll be nice and knock off half of what you owe me. A final offer. You have to understand: if you don't help me, I'll find another way. You're the one who has everything to lose."

Everything? A gigantic void opened in Dmitry's mind. His head felt cotton-packed; he couldn't think straight or make decisions. He was no longer sure what was at stake, what was mere words, and what meant more. *Life and death?*

"Spreadsheets? Aren't there digital copies?"

"That's the thing." Misha's face brightened as if he appreciated Dmitry's keen insight. "The original hard drives were destroyed. All that's left is this printout this guy made. A big mistake if you ask me. The dude didn't know who he was dealing with."

Obviously not. Dmitry didn't want to find out what happened.

"Didn't they get scanned?" he asked, cluelessly.

"Not necessarily. It's a small case, comparatively." Misha sounded confident. He seemed to know more about the police procedure than he should. More than Dmitry. "Too much paper to scan everything. Even if they did, making the case with copies is more difficult. Signatures, you know." He winked.

Dmitry didn't know enough about financial crime to have an opinion.

Misha crunched into another pale pickle. "These *ogurchiki* are something else. My favorite. Anyway, Dimka, the less you know, the better." The potatoes arrived in what couldn't have been more than three minutes, but to Dmitry, it felt like half a day. "Now we're talking." Misha placed two steaming tubers next to the other bits and pieces on his plate. "Dima, you're not eating. Eat something."

"I'm not hungry." Dmitry's mouth was dry; he could barely speak, much less eat.

Silence reigned for a minute or two as Misha and his men munched while Dmitry awkwardly picked at his potato. What exactly had Misha said about Natasha? Dmitry was so stressed he couldn't remember the exact words, but the threat was unmistakable.

"Okay, *braht*." Misha picked up the carafe and poured an equal amount of vodka into each shot glass. "To friendship." A huge grin returned to his face, like an accessory he could activate at will.

Dmitry raised his glass, and they clinked. The two of them emptied their glasses in unison, bottoms up. Anything less would seem insincere. The two bodyguards looked on with longing.

Misha's grin just sat on his face, his eyes both severe and ominous. "I wouldn't fuck with you."

SUNDAY, NOVEMBER 17

50. Sania Jamison

It was a shock to find herself like this, in her body, but unable to feel it. Sania focused on pushing away the fear that was quick to invade her. She wasn't unconscious. The opposite of that: Sania was utterly aware of her surroundings.

She expected her heart to race like a frightened horse, but it was silent.

Then she understood. So, this is what being dead meant? After everything she'd read and thought about it.

How ironic to find herself in this state. Muhammed said a soul that dies loses sight, yet Sania could see clearly. There was no way to explain it. Not only could she see in front of her, but her vision also extended in all directions. Still, she had to focus; she couldn't take it all in simultaneously. She wasn't an omniscient godlike creature; she was her same old self.

As she lay there on the grass, she knew it was impossible to settle for this outcome, yet there was no energy, no movement in her body to refuse it, like being paralyzed. A river whispered next to her. Now and then, a car passed on the nearby road.

It was dark, but it had already been dark when she left the house. Was her shift over by now? If so, her family might be worried. Atif may have assumed she'd had to stay at work even longer. Soon, he'd text or call. Where was her phone? She didn't see it anywhere near her. Then she remembered: it must still be in her purse. And the purse was nowhere around.

She was worried about Omar and Lidia. She couldn't imagine what her two babies would have to go through. She pictured their beautiful eyes and small bodies.

Sania was mad now, furious. The whole experience buzzed through her synapses: the way the killer had grabbed her as if he'd practiced. She'd always planned to hit, bite if such a thing ever happened—and she'd landed in the backseat of his car, completely powerless. She had no time to react.

The rest was crumpled in her memory, from finding herself in the guy's creepy garage to a few phrases they'd exchanged. The last thing she remembered was sipping bourbon from a coffee mug. She still didn't know why she'd asked for it. The killer had raised the half-empty bottle over his head, his face blank, like a mask.

Sania would give anything to punch, strike, or hit him until he expired. But he wasn't here. And she couldn't move. She knew she'd never move again. She wanted to cry about it, but no tears came out.

51. Brenda Smith

Brenda sat in her kitchen, thinking about the case. What a mess. She didn't know what to consider next. Minutes ticked away without a solution.

Her phone startled her. Mary? Brenda felt a smile emerging on her face.

It was Dmitry. She picked it up.

"We have another victim."

"What?" Brenda could feel her face tense. "How do you know it's our killer?"

"The red card."

"Shit."

"I'm headed to the crime scene," Dmitry said. "Want me to pick you up?"

"Sure." Brenda rubbed her eyes. She'd only just gotten out of bed; she'd stayed up late the night before, obsessing about Mary's lack of response to the apologetic calls and texts following the cop vs. office manager fiasco.

She finished her coffee. There was no hope. Her life was gloom, uninterrupted. Naseem Nazari was dead; nothing was going to bring him back; his murder had left no traces. She hoped the new crime would be messier, so it would lead them to the killer.

Brenda rinsed her coffee cup, locked the door behind her, and came downstairs. In the bright patch of an unusually sunny day, she waited a minute or two for Dmitry's car to pull up.

"A cop just stumbled upon the body," he said instead of a greeting as Brenda got into the car.

"A cop?" Brenda couldn't quite see the relevance.

"Yes." Dmitry looked excited. "The perp dumped the body by the river, a few miles out of town. Right by Klein Point."

Brenda's head still buzzed from last night's drinking. Every fiber inside her felt tense. Buildings blinked outside the car window as she sat in the passenger seat, trying to focus. Natasha's car seat was in the back, surrounded by crumbs, a rubber duck, a notepad, and a small pink T-shirt. Brenda couldn't help smiling at the thought of Dmitry's kid. Natasha and Brenda had a special bond.

"What do you think of that Russian asshole, Igor Pechorin?" Dmitry asked. "He's been on my mind all night."

"Over the top, wasn't he?" Brenda admired something about Pechorin's dramatic presentation, his professed love for Nazari. She didn't know how to explain this.

Dmitry shrugged, acute displeasure on his face. "I wouldn't be surprised if he killed his friend over a chess game."

Brenda felt her eyebrows go up. "You know he didn't."

"I don't like Russians."

Brenda smiled at him, but Dmitry either didn't notice or didn't acknowledge her reaction.

A police officer waited on the side of the road. Dmitry pulled over. They took in the scene. Just twenty yards off, the Willamette River curved elegantly around a clump of willows, their loosely hanging branches still wet after months of rain. The sun sat on the top of a nearby birch tree.

"What a spot." A spark in Dmitry's eye, as if he was struck by this contrast of beauty and murder the same way Brenda was.

They followed the officer down a narrow path through waist-level grass. The meadow next to the river looked swampy, and the air smelled of moisture and rot.

The victim was white, in her thirties. Skinny and thin, her long brown hair a halo around her head as she lay there, face up, her head toward the water. The blood matted in her hair seemed to be from a wound to the temple caused by blunt force. She wore blue nurse's scrubs; a purple shawl must have fallen off her head and lay crumpled next to her right shoulder. The arms pointed at strange angles from the body—a matchstick figure, broken. A bright red business card between two fingers of the right hand was impossible to miss.

"How did you find her?" Brenda asked the cop.

"I was just driving to work. Had a few minutes to spare. Thought I'd stop and look at the river. I love this spot."

"What time was it?" Brenda asked.

"8:27."

"Thanks, Sergeant," Dmitry said. "Forensics should be here any minute. Make sure they process your shoes. We'll be doing footprint analysis."

"No worries. But..."

"But?"

"How will I drive without shoes?"

"Don't worry, they'll need them only for a few minutes," Dmitry said.

As if on cue, the white forensics van appeared around McLaughlin Boulevard's wooded curve. The river was dark gray, except where the mud swirled in brown eddies. The song of insects filled the air— Brenda was surprised she hadn't noticed until now. She donned latex gloves and bent over the body, checking the pockets. There it was: a small, brightly colored wallet with a driver's license. She hated to look.

She looked.

"Sania Jamison." Brenda frowned. "Sounds like an American name."

Nothing else was in the wallet; Brenda placed it into a small evidence bag.

"It's like the motherfucker is mocking us." Dmitry's clenched fists were ready to punch the killer—and Brenda wanted to be there too, punching the life out of him. She wasn't as sure as Dmitry that the killer cared about them. What he seemed to care about were his victims.

She carefully held Sania Jamison's hand and pulled out the red card. It was blank, identical to the other two. Who was this Sania Jamison? Brenda couldn't get over the feeling of personal grief, as though the victim was a family member rather than someone she'd never met before.

Matching the tire tracks would be hopeless. Too many cars stopped at this spot. The river, the grass, the dead body. It must have been heavy on the killer's back. Or not, considering how he'd dispatched Naseem Nazari's.

Even at night, cars were frequent on this road. This pointed to a killer under pressure, too stressed to think of a better option. Or just careless. Brenda looked down, examining every inch of the path and next to it. She felt her jaws jam together from stress and made an effort to relax them. And then, between two blades of grass, she saw it—a button. Dark gray, almost black.

Brenda's heart was beating fast. *Slow down,* she told her heart and her mind. This button could have been here for months, years. But something inside her insisted: no, the button was new, an artifact of the crime. Brenda got out her phone again and took a picture. Then she carefully picked up the button, placing it in a small evidence bag.

"What do you have?" Dmitry yelled from the riverbank.

She explained, and Dmitry saluted with his thumb up in the air.

"We're going to get him," he yelled back.

But they needed more than a button. It wasn't even big enough for a fingerprint. What good was a button if they lacked the garment? More a taunt than a clue. Again, Brenda had to tell her mind to slow down and wait for more information. Waiting was becoming increasingly difficult.

The forensics team was setting up their gear, impatient to take over. Jim Lundstrom stood twenty yards away, looking around as if trying to decide what to include in the crime scene. The river glistened around the willow cluster. It would be nice if they could interrogate the water, ask the willows a few questions, interview the sky.

52. Dmitry Volkov

"What sha-hll we do, Detective?" Dmitry asked in his inadequate British accent, but this game already seemed wrong for the kind of case they were on and for his mood. For some reason, Stalin came to mind. Born in Georgia, Stalin spoke Russian with a strong accent yet dominated the country and killed millions of people.

They sat at their favorite table at Linda's, inhaling the lovely greasy smells—but Dmitry's mind was not on the food. His Misha problem wasn't going away on its own. He could shoot Misha one night, but let's face it, he wasn't a killer. Besides, the dude was better guarded than most. Could he turn Misha in in exchange for witness protection? But Dmitry didn't have anything concrete on Misha. Nothing he could prove. His colleagues would laugh at him. Even if he wore a wire, he'd get nothing from Misha. The dude was smooth. He never said anything he couldn't account for.

Brenda was done with her burger and played with the three remaining French fries. If Dmitry were in Narcotics, it would be easier to get hold of something he could turn into cash. Dead bodies were the worst; they were of no value. So, he'd had to scramble with the spreadsheets. He hoped he'd left no trace when he stole them from the evidence storage.

"How are things with that girl you met?" he asked. "What was her name?"

"Mary." Brenda twisted her mouth into a pained scowl in a way that made Dmitry's heart sink a little. "Not good."

"Shit. What happened?"

"I think I blew it."

"What on earth did you do?" Dmitry finished his burger and dabbed his face with a napkin. His damn beard and mustache always ended up greasy. He'd been dying to shave them off, but Rita claimed that the facial hair looked sexy on him. With all the other things in play, Dmitry wasn't about to disturb the power dynamics by changing his looks.

"I lied about my job. Told her I was an office manager. Like Rita. The stupidest thing I've ever done. I told her the truth a few days later, but it may've been too late." Brenda shrugged. "I get it; it's freaky when someone lies to you on the first date. Especially if that someone is a cop. Especially in Portland."

"Shit, Bren, I'm sorry. Just explain it to her."

"I tried. Left half a dozen messages."

"That's tough." Dmitry wasn't sure what else to say.

"I'm just hopeless, that's all." Brenda sighed.

"No, you're not. You're fine." It was awkward to have to reassure her. He didn't know much about Brenda's personal life.

"Anyway, what are you doing for Thanksgiving?"

"Russians don't do Thanksgiving, you know." He shrugged. "It's an American thing. You?"

"Not sure yet. I'm not big on Thanksgiving either."

"Don't you envy London cops?" Dmitry asked.

"London cops? Why?"

"All the security cameras."

"Oh, that." Brenda thought for a second. "A mountain of footage to go through, and we don't even know who we're looking for."

"Don't they have software to scan for patterns?"

"They must." She grinned. "But here in Portland, we have to do it on our own."

53. The Corrector

The Corrector had just rung up another customer with a set of flashlights, from tiny to a unit bigger than a horse's dick. What was it with all the flashlights these days? The dude had looked serious about it, like the purchase would solve all his household problems. A white guy but weak-looking. Not a fighter for the future by any stretch.

The air had its usual hardware store smell: grease, metal, wood. Reassuring. The Corrector's coffee was bitter; it had sat in the coffeemaker all day. Still, he didn't feel like the effort of brewing more. He was still tired from last night's adrenaline and stress and all the drinking he'd done after he disposed of the body.

The door opened again just as he was about to step out for a cigarette. The Corrector looked, and his skin went all Girl Scout goosebumpy. It was the Muslim woman he'd taken down, dressed in all black.

What the fuck? What the fuck? What the fuck?

She approached like a ghost. Already, her voice rang in his ears, *Please let me go.* The shock of her having no accent at all.

"Sorry, sir. Do you have rechargeable batteries?" Now he could see. The face was slightly different: the nose longer, the eyes farther apart.

"What batteries?" The Corrector was still on edge, struggling to control himself.

"A. A. A." She said each *A* separate like that.

"Of course we do, lady. Just because the shithole you're from doesn't have batteries don't mean we don't have them here in America." The Corrector was almost surprised at himself; the words had just poured out. Dangerous territory. He cut himself off and stomped off toward aisle 4, where a shitload of batteries sat on display.

He assumed she'd follow, but she just stood there, staring. Clearly, her English was no good. There was no end to them, and they were going to be the death of America. Should he apologize anyway, just for the sake of his job?

She walked out without another word before he was done thinking about it.

MONDAY, NOVEMBER 18

54. Brenda Smith

The lab was soaked in light from the overhead lamps. Too much light.

"The footprints," Jim Lundstrom said. "The hiking shoes are common. Columbia Sportswear. But there's something about the wear pattern. I'd say the perp was limping."

Jim squinted at Brenda as if she'd brought even more light with her. The slight chemical smell that always hung in the lab was familiar and comforting.

"Limping?" Brenda held her breath.

Finally, something concrete about the killer, apart from the fact that he was a big guy, used a lighter, and had buttons on his clothes.

"Yep."

"But remember, he was carrying a body. More weight may have been on one side. Couldn't it be that?" She stared at Jim, desperately hoping he would reject this theory.

"It's hard to be completely sure, but with a load on your shoulders, you'd put more weight on the heels of your feet, not on the side of one foot. Also, the other footprint would've been affected differently. It's just a feeling I have." Jim shrugged. "We'll need to run some tests to be sure."

"That's good, very good."

"Glad I could be of service." A friendly smile. Jim was like the dad Brenda had never had.

She felt overwhelmed as she walked back to her desk. Not enough information. Medical records, witnesses, shoe stores. What to check first? She might be happier as a preschool teacher or a grocery store clerk. Or a fucking office manager.

Dmitry had left more than an hour ago. Where in the world was he?

Brenda printed out Sania Jamison's phone records. She wanted to compare them to Nazari's to get this off her list. She didn't expect to find any cross-references.

She looked around for Nazari's records. They didn't seem to be anywhere in her possession. She walked over and pulled open the top drawer of Dmitry's desk.

Nothing but pens. She pushed the drawer shut and opened the next one. All sorts of junk, including tons of paperwork.

And a manilla envelope of an evidence bag.

It didn't look familiar. Brenda read the label: not a homicide case. What was it doing in Dmitry's desk? Brenda couldn't help looking inside. Financial documents, from what it looked like. Spreadsheets.

It was a shock. Brenda's chest and shoulders felt frozen with contradicting emotions. Just in case, she took a picture on her phone. Proof, in case something went wrong. But there must be a reasonable explanation. She'd ask Dmitry and clear it up. Nazari's phone records were in the same drawer. She pulled them out and pushed the drawer in with too much force.

It didn't take Brenda more than a few minutes to confirm that the two victims had no numbers in common in their call history. She thought of Maharani Kapoor. Months had passed. Phone records would lead her nowhere. There was no point in this line of investigation. No point at all.

55. Dmitry Volkov

Sania Jamison's husband, Atif Jamison, sat in a chair across from the two detectives. He was a Black man in his late thirties—early forties, his face crossed with grief and his hair disheveled. Dmitry felt terrible for the guy.

"I can't believe it. She just went to work—and now..." Jamison paused as if uncertain how to finish his thought.

"I'm so sorry," Dmitry said. "When was that?"

"Saturday night..." Jamison hesitated. "Yes, Saturday night, around seven. Sorry, I haven't had any sleep."

"That's okay, sir. We understand. Does she always work nights?" Brenda asked.

Dmitry noted her choice of *does* instead of *did*. A softer touch. Brenda was good at this.

"Not usually. It was her day off, but someone on the night shift called in sick. She's a nurse. She wanted to help out." Tears in Jamison's eyes. "If she hadn't, she would...she'd be alive now."

"She couldn't have known." Dmitry was no stranger to regrets, the what-ifs. "Where did she work?"

"St. Martin's Hospital. The emergency room."

"Did you see or hear anything unusual last night when she was leaving?" Brenda asked.

"No."

"Did she usually drive to work?"

"Yes, but her car—you see, it's still here. It's parked around the corner. I hadn't noticed until yesterday morning." Atif Jamison's hand rubbed away the tears.

"So, it looks like she never went anywhere?" Dmitry asked.

Jamison just stared in response.

"Thank you, sir. We won't hold you anymore." Brenda handed him a card. "Please call if you remember anything else. I'm so sorry."

"Thank you." The guy just stayed there, not realizing the interview was over.

The Jamisons had two children under the age of ten. Dmitry thought of Natasha and how she might feel if he disappeared from her life.

"I'll escort you out," Brenda said.

While she was gone, Dmitry sat there, thinking of the broken families they saw in their work. What was that expression Brenda had used? A bag full of stones. Two birds with one bag full of stones. Two bags in a stone. His thoughts were getting loopy.

Brenda walked in, shaking her head in dismay.

"So, the woman never made it to her car? Careless to strike so close to her house. Our perp must be spinning out of control."

"Or just getting confident."

"Let's go back over what we know," Brenda said. "Sania Jamison was picked up next to her house. It's a residential area. I'm thinking the killer might live nearby."

"He might've been just driving through."

"Possibly." Brenda considered. "But I don't think so. The victim led a regular life. The perp must have been watching, waiting for the right moment. He wouldn't have driven across the city for this. It was more like a crime of passion. He'd noticed her before, and he didn't like her hijab. She was the right target for him. He tracked her."

"What about Nazari? He lived on the other side of town. Maharani Kapoor lived in Northwest, but her body was dropped off in Southeast, where fewer immigrants live. There's no rhyme or reason to any of it, Bren."

"The first two murders seem better planned. He did his research. This last one was more like an improvisation if you can call it that."

Brenda maintained that the killer was becoming more careless. She might have a point. Dmitry trusted his partner's intuition.

"You're probably right." Dmitry shrugged, unsure where to go next with the scarce information they had—and at an even greater loss about fixing his own life.

56. Azar Bayat

Azar lay in her dorm bed. No classes till 11 today; she'd slept in. From the opposing wall, a print of Bahar Sabzevari's self-portrait stared back at Azar with confidence and hope for the future of Irani women. As an Irani-American who'd emigrated in 2003 and now lived in New York, Sabzevari had been among Azar's favorites since she'd become interested in modern art. Ominous, vaguely human shapes rendered in bright colors congregated around Bahar. Whether they were demons or clerics was open to interpretation. Yet, the optimism of Bahar's face prevailed. It felt strange and meaningful that the artist had the same first name as Azar's sister.

Azar rose from her bed, her bare feet feeling the dust on the floor. She filled the electric tea kettle and pressed the button, her heart aching for her family. They were intolerably far, even with the convenience of FaceTime and WhatsApp. The difference of eleven and a half hours made conversations logistically tricky; the half-hour annoyed Azar to no end. It felt like an unnecessary time control measure from a regime stuck two thousand years back on time's axis.

She glanced at her smartphone. Three calls from Soroush. Of course. At the thought of Soroush, Azar felt bored. For every three books she had read, he was familiar with one. To every five interesting ideas she had, he answered with one. A less than auspicious ratio for a long-term relationship. She hated herself for not finding the right words to break up with him sooner. Then again, she hadn't been as clear about her disappointment until she came to Portland.

Azar was tempted to call back, but the vast difference in time, in addition to being an annoyance, was a good excuse. Weekends made it easier to fit her life into the lives of those back in Iran. She promised herself to call Soroush on Saturday, and she already knew she might not have time for it. There were too many papers to write and things to discover in this exciting, unfamiliar city. Hours and days slipped away from her, packed with new experiences.

Instead of responding to Soroush's pleas for attention, she opened WhatsApp and found the thread with her sister, Bahar. Using Farsi-English, Finglish, the SMS-friendly variant of Farsi expressed with Latin characters, she wrote,

> *studying too much. miss my little sister.*

She thought for a while but couldn't muster the inspiration for anything more substantial. She pressed Send.

The fall semester was ending, and Azar was behind on her sociology paper. She was writing about power dynamics in a totalitarian society, and the Islamic Republic sounded remarkably similar to what she knew of the communist regimes and other nefarious political projects of recent decades.

"Communism and Iran...hmm," her professor had pondered when she first mentioned the topic. "Aren't you comparing apples and oranges?"

Azar had already heard that expression.

"Not really," she said. "It's about the triumph of ideology over... how do you say it...humanity. The type of ideology is secondary. The propaganda, the *great* leaders, the secret police." Sure, most such regimes had ended by the time she became interested in them, but her family still talked about the 1970s and '80s as if they were ongoing.

The professor scratched his cheek, thinking. "Okay then. Sounds promising. I'm curious what you'll do with it."

Azar poured herself a cup of tea and dipped a corner of a sugar cube in. She brought the softened edge to her mouth; it melted on her tongue, and as she sipped the tea, the bittersweet mix spread through her mouth. She remembered Maman Feri, the tea ceremonies in their Tehran garden, the hours they'd spend talking under the light breeze of slow summer days. It seemed like another life. Even Azar felt like a different person.

57. The Corrector

The Corrector felt unsettled, to put it fucking mildly. He was changing his mom; she kept drifting off even as he completed the task. The stink, acrid and deathly, was so familiar by now that it didn't bother him anymore. But the change in her attitude was a fucked-up thing. She'd been different since his big reveal. Too bad.

The Corrector regretted bringing up the whole thing. He tossed the dirty wipe into the stinky trash can and pulled a new diaper from the bag in one of the shelves built into the high-tech bed. The move was familiar now, and his mom barely weighed anything. Poor thing. She was like a doll as he moved her around—just as brittle.

At least she'd had some juice and a few crackers; she'd sucked on them instead of chewing. Sure, she was being annoying like hell with her disapproval, but still, he didn't want to watch his mother starve. The Corrector left her in her boat of a bed and came upstairs. He stretched in his chair, bourbon in hand. Even the gray window needed washing. Fuck!

Dad's voice spoke in The Corrector's head. "How could you fuck up that bad?"

"What?"

"You know what I'm talking about, Junior. Don't fuck with me."

"Get out of here," The Corrector begged.

Dad had always been a prick. Over the years, his image had grown soft and fuzzy in The Corrector's mind, but somehow, the bastard had come into sharp focus over these last couple of weeks.

"What have I told you?" Dad's voice. "You can't control yourself, can you? You and your fucking mother, two peas in a pod, hopeless."

"Shut up! Shut up!" The Corrector screamed. He popped in Slayer's *Hell Awaits*, near full volume. The floor shook from the bass, but still, he couldn't chase Dad's voice out of his head. Mom was so out of it the music wouldn't bother her.

"You better get hold of yourself, Junior. That was fucking risky. What if someone saw you through a window or some shit?"

"No one saw me," The Corrector said out loud. Then he felt even more creeped out because no one was listening. He felt the sobs coming on. No way. He just sat there on the bed, crying, beating the bed with his fists as the music screamed at him and the whole fucking world.

"Fuck! Fuck! Fuck!" He heard himself yelling through the tears.

Then he remembered a day—he must have been seven or eight. Mom and Dad whispered over the kitchen table like they did when they didn't want him to hear. Dad's anger rose suddenly; he jumped out of his seat like there was a spring built into it. With a move so quick no one had time to react to, he smacked Mom on the face. "You fucking bitch."

She began crying, covering her face; Dad stormed out. The whole thing took five or ten seconds. These things didn't take long in their family. At least Dad would be gone for a while, out for a drink or two or three at the bar.

"Your fucking father!" Now that Dad was gone, Mom screamed at The Corrector, a little boy. "Why didn't you defend me? You both hate me! You fucking men." Tears ran down her face, and she grabbed her hair and began tearing at it like she did on the worst of days.

"I love you, Mom," he'd had to say. "I do." But as he said it, he didn't know if it was true. After all these years, it was still difficult to know about such things. He'd never been trained in love; that's what it was.

Later that night, Mom had sat there with a growing bruise on her cheek. "Something in your dad is broken. In all of us."

Strange how these memories were coming back today, of all days.

58. Brenda Smith

Since getting home, Brenda kept drifting around, unable to settle in any one spot. She sat on the couch, but her legs felt restless after a minute or two. She got up, walked over to the window, stood there for a while watching the gray sky with its medley of fast clouds and the intermittent rain, then moved to her bedroom and stretched on the bed, only to get up a minute later for a glass of water. She was intensely uncomfortable, body and soul. A familiar feeling, one she remembered from earlier cases, one she got when random clues had been collected and vague possibilities had presented themselves. Still, nothing was clear enough to act decisively. Except, this time was worse. Even the smell in her apartment was annoying, more of an absence of smell than anything concrete. She returned to the window and cracked it open; the fall air rushed in like a wet tongue.

Brenda opened her laptop and loaded KATU.com, Portland's news station. Her hands trembled a little as she typed the letters into the browser. *Two Local Murders May Be Connected*, read one of the more prominent headlines on the home page. Leaked information that wasn't going to help anyone.

Brenda clicked on the link and read the brief article. It was accurate enough as to what had happened. *How long will the murders of minorities be tolerated in Portland?* The enthusiastic writer's conclusion didn't do anything to improve Brenda's mood.

The evidence bag in Dmitry's desk came back to her. The more she tried, the less she could get it out of her mind. She liked Dmitry, even if she couldn't claim to understand him. So often, his good-looking face seemed opaque. She couldn't imagine his life in the Soviet

Union, but it must have been harsh.

Her phone chimed. Mother. Brenda was grateful for this distraction, ready to hear another person's voice. She stretched on the couch and pressed the green button.

"Mom."

"Honey, I'm afraid I have some bad news." Her mother's mouth must have been too close to the microphone; the sound came out all puffy. "It's your dad."

"What about Dad?"

Her parents had moved to Florida many years ago, right before their breakup, which was unsurprising after two decades of squabbling. Sometimes, Brenda wondered if they'd stayed together for so long just for her sake. When she was nine or ten, she had become aware of her father's affairs. His drinking had not been particularly endearing either. These days, she had little interest in her dad, and yet there it was, a pang of anxiety at her mother's remark. A compression belt around her chest.

"He's sick. You should give him a call."

"Sick?"

There was a slight pause.

"Pancreatic cancer. He just found out."

"Oh, God! That's the bad one, isn't it?"

"Yeah."

"How long does he have?"

"A few months."

The anxiety persisted, but Brenda felt no reaction of grief—or hadn't had time to develop one. She would've been worried, even crushed in another version of her life—but the news was merely stressful. Brenda took a breath.

"How are you taking it?"

"Well, we're not best friends anymore, as you know. God, Bren, I don't even know what I think. Weird. He'll be gone, and I get to stick around. We're the same age."

Brenda stared out the window as she listened. A minute earlier, a glimpse of the sun had made its way through the gray pudding, but now the gray was back. What did it all mean? What did it mean that her dad was dying?

"I guess I'll have to call him," Brenda said. "It's been a few years."

"I know, baby. I know." Her mother's voice was full of concern. Momentarily, Brenda felt an overflow of appreciation. Mom had done so much for her; she'd been on Brenda's side in the pointless wars for control over her own identity that her father had waged during her teenage years. Mom had accepted her as a queer person without debates or reservations, while Dad had pouted and kept asking if it might be a passing phase.

It took time to stop hurting in response to his attitude. Time, distance, and much help from other people. Dad had never entirely made peace with her sexual orientation; he kept throwing around cheap hints about God's lack of tolerance. Who needed such a narrow-minded god, anyway? Or such a narrow-minded dad?

"How's he taking it?" Brenda asked.

"I don't know, sweetie. All I got was an email from him. Very brief."

"Is he still with Ruth?"

"No, they broke up about a year ago. Good for her, I suppose."

"Yeah..." Brenda didn't know what to say.

"How are you doing otherwise, darling?"

"Not bad. Got a nasty case right now. I don't even want to talk about it."

Brenda felt impatient as they said their goodbyes. Should she have made more of an effort to know her dad, no matter how ugly his views? Too late; he was as good as dead. The two of them had zero chance to recover from years of distance. She longed to rid herself of this latest information, to return to a simpler world where it didn't apply. She wasn't ready to think about this.

Brenda headed to the kitchen to make herself a drink, but a second phone call caught her halfway. She'd left her phone in the bedroom. She ran to pick it up and pressed the green button without reading the caller ID.

"Mom?"

"It's me." Mary's voice.

Silence.

Brenda waited, breathless.

"I've been thinking of you," Mary said. "Maybe we could give it another try?"

Brenda was shellshocked, delirious, delighted. She wanted to respond, but her voice would not obey her.

TUESDAY, NOVEMBER 19

59. Dmitry Volkov

Dmitry woke in the middle of the night, startled by a dream he couldn't remember when he was out of it. Rita lay on her side, breathing evenly, her back covered by her favorite blue nightshirt, gray in this light. Something tightened in his chest at this familiar sight.

Outside, cars rolled by with casual irregularity. The moon hung in the corner of their bedroom window, nearly full and vaguely menacing with its thin missing section. Dmitry knew he wouldn't be able to go back to sleep. He had allowed real life to penetrate his thoughts, and now there was no way to stop them from spinning around. Again, he imagined tracking Misha down, finding a vulnerable place and time. But could he kill another person, even as vile as Misha? So far, he'd only fired his gun in the line of duty, aiming at the legs.

He could leave Portland and start his life from scratch. He'd done this when he was a kid, barely twenty-two. But now, in middle age, he felt unprepared for such extremes. Besides, there was no telling about the impact such a move would have on his family.

His brother was cooking up something, but so far, Dmitry had resisted the temptation to ask what it was. Yesterday's headline still hovered in his mind: *Two Local Murders May Be Connected.* Shit. He didn't want any extra attention on the case, on him. Wrong time for that.

Rita turned onto her back, her fingers on the covers twitching now and then in the moonlight. Her fingers were slightly spooky if he stared at them, but her face was beautiful and calm. Dmitry felt utterly lonely at that moment, so close to his wife and hopelessly distanced by the problems he had created.

He got out of bed and tip-toed out of the room. In the dark kitchen, he poured himself a glass of water. He wasn't thirsty—but the urge to do something pressed on him.

Natasha's door was ajar, as she preferred. It creaked a little as Dmitry opened it all the way. There was no chance he'd wake her. A hammer or an electric saw—and she would keep sleeping undisturbed.

Dmitry walked over to his daughter's bed. He winced in pain as his bare foot landed on something sharp. He picked it up: one of Natasha's Lego structures, three blocks joined in an angular arc. Natasha lay on her belly, her arms spread wide as if she were flying in her dreams. Maybe she was. Mercury was crammed into the corner next to Natasha's head, the doll's too-long leg sticking out from under the pillow. Dmitry just stood there, watching his daughter's motionless little body, her breath steady like a good locomotive's.

He noticed that his fingers were still playing with the Lego piece. He placed it against one of the legs of Natasha's bed instead of bothering to bring it over to the part of the room where toys were supposed to sleep, as Rita would've.

Leaning over his daughter's bed again, Dmitry listened to her breathing. If he ended up in jail or killed by Misha's henchmen, Natasha would still be here. He placed his hand on her back, warm and clammy with sweat. His hand was as wide as her entire back.

60. Naseem Nazari

By now, Naseem was used to immobility. This aspect of his condition no longer bothered him. This epiphany would have surprised him before, but lying in a morgue freezer was no different than lying on a warehouse roof. Somehow, the things he had been able to see were still before his eyes.

The box around him was wide enough for a body; that was all the space Naseem needed. He didn't feel constrained; he wasn't about to move. No matter what he wished for, his shoulders would never touch the sides; an inch or two of distance would always remain as long as he was in this state. He had no idea how long that might be.

What upset him was the young woman a row down and a few slots to the left. She was tall and athletic; she had a kind face. Her eyes were wide open, examining the world. Naseem knew that she was a victim of the same killer. Her pain and anger filled the space around them.

Long ago, the choice of cruelty had ceased to surprise him. If he could talk to the young woman, what would he say? Nothing about his calm would make sense to her.

As time passed, Naseem noticed his recent past fading in his mind, information slipping from him without being replaced by new impressions. He still remembered all the facts, but it was getting harder to recall Yasmin's face, her voice, her hands. He didn't try to hold on. It would be impossible; that much was clear.

By contrast, his earlier memories remained as sharp as ever. His childhood: the poverty, the struggle, the way the villagers helped one another. The rats. He remembered the rats. Later, Aisha's eyes. How giddy they looked in their good moments together after they'd learned they were in love, even with the challenges of their arranged marriage. These recollections grew increasingly vivid as if inviting him to wherever he was destined after this intermediate period was over.

The man's hands on his throat; this detail still bothered Naseem. But he'd made it through. And now, he felt optimistic as he watched the young woman in the row below. The two of them had more future on their side than their killer did. The murderer would be held responsible. They would all see to it.

Out there, Naseem's killer was digging himself deeper into his insanity. Naseem could see him drinking and stomping about in his room like an ape from hell. Two detectives were trying to solve their case. One, a man in his early fifties, was preoccupied with other matters. Naseem focused on sending every bit of information to the female detective. She was in her forties, tired, honest. She was in love. He didn't know how this worked but felt the intuitive energy flowing out.

61. Brenda Smith

Brenda woke from a movement next to her, blissfully aware of Mary's body before she remembered the rest of her life. The most delightful smell in the world, coffee, hit her nostrils.

"Got an early shift." Mary sent her an air kiss. She was sitting at the foot of the bed, her pink hair a delicious mess. "Don't get up."

Brenda wanted to disobey: to jump out of bed, kiss those sexy lips, tell Mary once again how happy she was to have her back. She knew better. Mary needed neither drama nor exuberance in these early hours.

It was such a relief to be forgiven. Brenda didn't take it lightly.

"Mary," she said the name slowly, holding it in her mouth. "I'll never lie to you again." To think that she'd used to call her M. Now, the name *Mary* was sweet on Brenda's tongue.

"I know you won't." Mary sounded matter-of-fact, as if she took for granted that Brenda would not be such an idiot twice. And she wouldn't.

Abruptly, Dad's condition came back to Brenda. His distant dying. Whenever she'd considered calling him, it seemed like anything would be too little and too late. What a mess that man had made of his life, with his half dozen or more women, his charm, his inability to follow through on anything, his right-wing views, his homophobia.

She pushed these thoughts out of her mind before they could spoil her bliss. Mary rushed about, collecting her things, already dressed in her work scrubs. So fluid, so purposeful. She sat down on the bed, leaned over, and planted a long kiss on Brenda's lips. "See you tonight, sleepy head."

"See you." Brenda's voice came out broken, a whisper.

The apartment door clicked, and the emptiness was different, a hopeful kind. Brenda lay there, remembering Mary's body next to her: her long legs, her pale, translucent skin. The physical pull Mary's body had on Brenda's desire. A big grin came to her face as she thought of these things. She especially cherished Mary's freckles and the way Mary would occasionally look at Brenda with astonishment, as if something Brenda had said was unique or unexpected. But her thoughts and habits were familiar and routine, while Mary's comments and mannerisms were endlessly charming. Her sense of humor, the little faces she made, the grins, the quips, the intense eyes. Brenda moved over in bed so her head was on Mary's pillow. Mary's smell.

"I love that you're so serious," Mary had said. Shocking. Brenda had assumed that her obsessive pursuit of her job and inability to relax were bound to annoy anyone. That's what had happened with Jessica, or at least so it had been said in their attempts at analyzing their unfolding breakup. Mary, too, might come to hate Brenda's grim dedication, but it was better not to focus on such hopeless outcomes.

The case weighed on Brenda's soul. She hopped out of bed in one energetic move, surprising even herself. Thankfully, enough coffee remained in the coffeemaker. She poured herself a cup and sat in the kitchen. The day's first taste of coffee was incomparable.

Brenda rubbed her eyes, trying to focus on her goals for the day. Two cops had been dispatched to canvass the neighborhood, but interviewing Sania's neighbors had yielded little information, apart from an elderly lady who had noticed a blue car parked across the street for a few hours. What surprised the woman was that the driver had stayed inside the car all that time. But she didn't know the make or the model and hadn't gotten a good look at the man. Information like that teased without helping.

Brenda rose and walked over to the window. Portland lay there, its many bright lights already awake to the day. The sound of rain outside had persisted through the night. Any number of people may have seen the killer. This was the most frustrating part. Those individuals had been merely walking by; there was no way to track them. In any case, they would not have noticed much of value. She had to find another way.

Her conviction that the murderer lived in the vicinity of the third victim's house was based on nothing. Trust yourself, Brenda thought. Stick to your intuition. The killer may have been going about his own business when he saw the woman. He may have been sitting at a cafe or, more likely, a bar. Brenda grabbed her phone from the bed table and pulled up the area on Google Maps. There were three bars in the area.

62. Azar Bayat

The Proud Boys assembled in a large, menacing group at the side of Pioneer Courthouse Square, all red brick and symmetry. A gloomy gray sky loomed over Portland, preparing to strike any moment. *Make America Great Again, Lock Her Up,* and other neo-fascist slogans screamed from signs and shirts. Many right-wingers wore military-looking outfits; Azar couldn't tell if they were the actual US Army uniforms.

Becki grabbed Azar's hand and nearly dragged her toward the opposite side of the square, where the signs read *Hate Not Welcome Here, FCK PRDBYZ, Black Lives Matter,* and *Power to the People.* It was a mixed, informally dressed crowd with nothing consistent about their appearances.

"Those fuckers are acting cool because they know they're not welcome here," Becki yelled into Azar's ear.

"Of course, they're not." Azar's voice was drowned in the swirl of noise.

Portland was a progressive city, but shouldn't these clowns with their Trump signs and empty eyes have the right to demonstrate? Azar struggled to understand. She'd learned that Americans were liable to hate other Americans more than they hated anyone else. But she didn't hate anyone in America. She hated only the people who would shove religion down your throat. And historical figures, of course: Hitler, Stalin, Mao Zedong—that kind. She felt optimistic about the States no matter what. Things in Iran may not change during her life, but here, in America, they would improve.

"Let's get a little closer." Becki grabbed Azar's hand again and began making her way through the crowd, pulling Azar along. Azar kept nearly bumping into people, apologizing, and feeling awkward. The smell of cannabis and human bodies was mixed with that dusty, clean scent of a city after rain.

Azar's heart raced as she remembered participating in the recent protests in Iran. Even today, thousands marched back home, demanding the end of the clerics' power. Although oppression hadn't ended, the modern era had made it impossible for the regime to block information or to keep young people ignorant. The internet had made a difference, but it was difficult to predict when this difference might turn into political change. It could happen anytime, as in the Soviet Union. Or it might not happen for another half-century. Today in Iran, people died, and over five hundred were in prison for their wish for democracy.

Here in Pioneer Courthouse Square, tension percolated, palpable in the sounds the two sides made, the many *Fuck you's* and *Get out of Portland's* mixed with *Make America Great Again* and again and again. Hatred simmered in the way the two groups eyed each other, faces stern and unwelcoming.

"What are these Proud Boys trying to achieve?" Azar yelled.

Becki shook her head and pointed to her ear; she hadn't heard through all the noise. Azar had been meaning to look up the white supremacist group, but she'd stayed up working on an essay until nearly 3 a.m. She could easily imagine the kind of nonsense these Boys might believe.

"Never mind!" she yelled back.

Fifteen or twenty cops in riot gear gathered at critical points throughout the square. They stomped around in their positions and talked among themselves and on their walkie-talkies. Occasionally, they exchanged a joke with the nearby Proud Boys.

As if reacting to the smell of pot thick in the air, Becki, too, pulled out a joint, lit it up, and puffed. She offered it to Azar, who accepted and took a small puff, then another. It had been a while. The drug reached into her brain like a telescope, rendering all objects four-dimensional, infinitely fascinating. Like a crazy fist, her heart pounded at the walls of its enclosure.

Becki measured her with a curious glance, and Azar was embarrassed to realize she still held the joint in her fingers. After the lenient cannabis laws in Iran, it was good to be in a state that had legalized marijuana. From what she'd heard, Portlanders weren't supposed to smoke in public spaces, but it seemed as if everyone in the square was doing just that.

"Thank you," she yelled, and Becki responded with a huge grin.

They passed the joint back and forth until the buzz in Azar's head and the beating of her heart became so loud they overpowered the crowd.

One of the Proud Boys held up a megaphone and began speaking, but Azar couldn't parse the speech in the square's scattered acoustics. It must have been her lack of experience with spoken English because others around her seemed to be reacting with expressions of disdain and anger.

"...won't allow...America...dent Trump...we must..." The onslaught of words continued. It was too much: trying to understand, to process it all. Azar reminded herself to breathe.

The people in front of her were taller; most Americans were. Azar had to move from side to side and tilt her head this way and that to see. But not much was happening. She grew distracted, her thoughts jumping from her family to her sociology paper to her sad country of birth.

Then, all at once, the sounds around her changed. They grew angrier, more urgent. The crowd shifted, and Azar saw two men fighting. The square expelled a sigh of tension, or was it her own sigh? She squinted to see better.

The fighting men were both white; one wore a MAGA shirt. Bigger and stronger, he was beating a skinny young man who stumbled, his face a bloody mess. Before she knew it, Azar was running toward the wounded man. Even as her feet fell before her, she was surprised at herself. How could she help? If she just ran fast and pushed the attacker with all her momentum, he would surely lose his balance. The police officers would assist her.

She was two or three yards away when a sharp pain burned her back, knocking the breath out of her. She collapsed, gasping. As she raised her eyes, an angry cop's face looked down on her, a baton ready to strike again raised over his head. Azar shivered, an image in her eyes: an Islamic police soldier slamming a metal baseball bat into a protester's head. How the poor man's body had sagged. But it was unthinkable that this should happen here, in a free country. Then, the cop seemed to lose interest in her and scurried off.

Becki was leaning over her. "Azar! Are you okay?"

The pain in Azar's back was intense, but she could breathe again. "I think so."

Her body seemed to function correctly as she rose. Sirens blared, joining the red and white flashes of the police cars. The screaming continued.

"Let's go," Becki yelled, taking Azar's hand.

63. The Corrector

The Corrector pushed the door open and entered Straight Nail Hardware, ready for his four hours of torture. He could do it; he'd done it before. Bobby, the morning dude, waved to him, already on his way out the door. The Corrector's shift started at 1 p.m. He assessed the situation to see how many customers there were, hoping for none.

Just then, Juan appeared at the office door, his eyes straight on. Uh-oh. The dude must have been waiting for him.

"I need to talk to you." Juan was all serious, like a rooster. What was that about? The asshole extended his thin arm to gesture The Corrector in. Reluctantly, The Corrector followed Juan into the office.

"Take a seat." Juan sat in his chair, grim like a fucking storm cloud. Didn't even close the door behind them. "We've received a complaint." His face was firm like a fist. No wonder. The motherfucker must have hated The Corrector's guts because The Corrector was a patriot, not some brown guy from someplace else.

"What complaint?"

"A customer complaint." Juan stared at him with smug certainty. "Frankly, I'm not surprised."

"Not surprised?" The Corrector felt his juices heating up. It must have been that Muslim woman. Shit. He should've known. He remembered Dad, his face red from anger. He was his father's son. "What do you mean not surprised?"

"I've heard the stuff you and Daniel go on about in the back room. At least he keeps it under lock and key with the customers. That's the least we can ask of our employees."

"So, what're you saying?" The Corrector may have slightly raised his voice; he wasn't sure anymore.

"We're letting you go." Juan kept nodding like a fucking doll.

"What?" Every fiber burned inside The Corrector. He longed to explode, strangle this puny fuck right here and now. "Can you give me another chance?" He said instead, feeling miserable for stooping this low. He still needed the money.

"Sorry, the decision is not up to me. I'm just letting you know."

Shit. Just for a moment, The Corrector was speechless. Already, Juan was out of his seat. The anger in The Corrector's heart was growing immense like the fucking sky. He had to work to constrain himself from smashing the asshole's head. He needed another corrective action soon.

64. Azar Bayat

Azar's heart still raced from her dangerous encounter with the cop. The sky was gray but dry, and the equally gray Willamette River rushed in the opposite direction as they walked south along the embankment. The air smelled of water: thick, organic, promising.

"How's your back?" Becki turned her head. "We're going to sue for this," she continued without giving Azar a chance to reply. "Fucking cops."

"Sue?"

"Yes, file a lawsuit. He hit you smack on the back, motherfucker. We need to let some journalists know, as well."

"It will heal." The notion that people could sue the police was still new to Azar. She shrugged, then winced from the pain caused by this motion. The pain in her back had spread, now centered around her shoulders.

"Heal? I sure hope so. But we need to get attention to this."

"I don't know, Becki." Azar wasn't sure how to politely curtail her classmate's initiative. "It was...how do you say...a scuffle. Maybe the cop didn't mean to hit me. And as a legal alien, I could get into trouble if things go wrong."

Becki cast a sideways glance at Azar and nodded.

The esplanade was full of people: young and old, walking and running, many on bikes and motorized scooters. It was a free-feeling place. So close to where the extremists were trying to make a stand, there was no sign of them, no trace of their influence. Still, the encounter had left a sense of threat in Azar's heart.

"Are the cops on the side of the Proud Boys?" She tried to read the reaction on Becki's face. "Why?"

"Most cops are rightwing. Think about it. Who'd want to control what other people do? Especially based on some laws that others may have invented for political reasons. How's it in Iran?"

"It's the same." Azar was beginning to feel loopy from the pain but proud that she'd done something worthwhile, or at least tried to. "The clerics are the ones who want to control everybody, and they are as rightwing as it gets. Then there are the Basij, the religious police. But why are these Proud Boys even here? It's clear no one wants them."

"It's a provocation."

"What about those immigrant murders here in Portland? Are they connected to the Proud Boys in any way?"

"Hmm…It's hard to tell. I hope they catch the bastard soon."

As the river dragged its gray and brown mass back north, Azar could see three elegant bridges crossing its broad flow. The water returned the shimmering outlines of reflections, revealing a second, hidden city.

65. Brenda Smith

Brenda sat opposite Dmitry at their table at Linda's. The smell of food was intense and optimistic, the scents of burgers, fries, and pies blending into a harmonious whole. Brenda felt like a flexed muscle from knowing that the murderer out there was planning his next move. Outside, the rain had just stopped and was ready to begin again, judging by the angry storm clouds taking over the sky to the east. Dmitry studied the menu, his face as grim as Brenda felt.

"Trying something new this time?" She forced herself to act cheerful.

Dmitry could be moody sometimes, but he was a good partner. Brenda had come to appreciate his broad, confident face. But now, with the evidence bag in his desk, what did she know? She wasn't ready to ask him, not yet.

"I think I'll have a burger." A grin on Dmitry's face.

"Great idea. Me too."

Liz, their favorite server, half-smiled in her charming and slightly distant way as she approached.

"How's your day, Detectives?"

White, in her forties and a single mom, Liz seemed a bit worse for wear, with wrinkles and black circles around her eyes. But she was fit and claimed to go to the gym four times a week. Brenda liked to chat with her when she came alone.

Once they placed their order, Brenda got up and made her way down the aisle between tables, doing her best not to study the faces of other diners. She used the restroom and carefully washed her hands, examining her reflection in the mirror. She was so tired of this face:

neither ugly nor gorgeous, just the average face she'd been born with. She wasn't getting any younger. But Mary kept telling her she was beautiful, and that was good to hear.

With a quick move, Brenda tore off the minor afterthought of a paper towel already hanging from the dispenser. So much effort to dry all these hands when, in the end, they would have dried on their own in a matter of seconds. She walked out.

"Okay. Imagine you're the killer." She plopped down in her seat across from Dmitry. "What's your next move?"

Dmitry finished chewing, his brow tight in thought. "I'm happy with how well everything worked. Intoxicated by killing. Tempted to try it again."

"So, how do you go about it?"

Dmitry scratched his cheek. "I might watch the places where people congregate and single out someone I don't like. Pick a vulnerable one."

"Like lions and buffalos?"

"Something like that."

Liz approached to refill their cups, a busy expression on her face.

"Thank you." As distressed as she felt, Brenda made sure to smile. She took a big sip and was forced to swoop the hot liquid from side to side in her burning mouth. She'd barely managed not to spit it out. "Ouch," she said when she could speak again. "Anyway, if you're him, where do you go?"

"A mosque. A community center. A restaurant."

"Should we warn them?" Brenda knew their range of potential targets was too broad but wanted Dmitry to confirm this.

"Can't get the whole city panicked just in case the guy strikes again."

"Right." Brenda moved her coffee cup from the right side of her plate to the left in a decisive move, as if this would help solve the case.

It was frustrating, guessing like this. More than frustrating. It was hopeless. Darkness was settling in Brenda's mind, but Dmitry made her feel less desperate. And there was Mary out there somewhere, in the bigger world she would reenter when the workday was over. If only she could get the case out of her head.

"Too bad we don't have security cameras like they do in London." Dmitry grinned. "We'd have our killer by tomorrow."

"You're obsessed with those cameras, Detective," Brenda said in her British voice.

"Have I mentioned them before?"

66. Dmitry Volkov

Dmitry parked down the block from his house. He needed a private moment. He closed his eyes and just sat there, breathing.

He thought of his youth in the USSR. The propaganda. He'd never imagined he'd be driving a car, living in this functional new place. His life had improved so much—then why had it gone so wrong? He'd already handed the stolen evidence to Misha's guy and still owed Misha over fifteen thousand.

Dmitry sat there for a while, trying to clear his head. Then he started the car again and drove the remaining block.

As he entered the house, the smell of baking hit his nostrils. A pie? Rita must be back from work early. Dmitry felt a moment of joy, but as he reached the kitchen, one look at Rita made his insides sink. She sat at the kitchen table, her stern face signaling a grave problem.

"What's up?" Dmitry tried to sound jovial.

"We've gotta talk."

Dmitry took in the situation. Natasha was watching one of her kids shows; she paid no attention to Dmitry's arrival. The pie steamed on the stovetop.

"About what?" Dmitry sat across from his wife, feeling an emptiness inside.

"About your brother. What is it with him stopping by every other day?"

"It's not every other day." Dmitry bristled at the exaggeration.

"How would you know?" Rita stared meaningfully, her brows converged. "You weren't even here for some of his visits."

"I can't tell my own brother not to come by, can I?" Emotions boiled inside Dmitry, not as much from Rita's challenge as from the rotten couple of days.

"You're supposed to protect your wife and daughter from your creepy brother." Rita's voice was growing in volume. "Can I be any blunter? You're a cop; you shouldn't have trouble understanding this." Dmitry hoped Natasha wouldn't hear their argument from her spot in the living room. Only about seven yards and the TV volume separated them.

It went downhill from there. As Dmitry tried to explain, Rita brought up other issues. He was supposed to clean the closet, the this, the that. He had trouble focusing on her tirade.

"Shit, Rita. I'm not in the mood for this. I've had a bad day." Dmitry's energy was draining fast.

"To hell with your day!" Rita was yelling by now. "What do I care about your day?"

Too loud. Dmitry turned to check if Natasha had noticed, but his daughter's face remained glued to the screen.

WEDNESDAY, NOVEMBER 20

67. Brenda Smith

Brenda had been preparing for this. Still, she walked into the office feeling so stressed that her hands shook. Interrogating her partner would not be the same as interviewing a random person, but she couldn't postpone this conversation any longer.

Dmitry swiveled in his chair, a happy grin on his face. His open expression made the whole thing worse. Brenda forced herself to get straight to the point.

"We have to talk."

She closed the office door behind them. Just the two of them.

"Uh-oh. Ominous." Dmitry's grin could mean anything.

Already, Brenda was less sure about what she had to say.

"I found a piece of evidence in your desk," she mumbled. "I was looking for Nazari's phone's records."

"Evidence?" Dmitry's voice had turned neutral, his face almost expressionless. The kind of face criminals adopted when they tried to conceal their emotions. Brenda didn't like it at all. She walked to the coffee machine and poured herself a cup, her heart working overtime against her chest.

"Why did you have it in your desk?" She turned around to face him.

"I don't know what you're talking about." Dmitry's face remained neutral and unreadable as he sat in his chair, his arms folded on his chest. Bad news. If he had nothing to hide, he wouldn't need this mask. His usual grin would be there, his large, crooked teeth. She'd chased that grin away.

She pulled out her phone and thumbed through the photos.

"This."

"You took a picture of the inside of my desk drawer?" Dmitry stared at her phone, pretending to be dumbfounded. "That's fucked up, Bren."

"Come on, Dmitry. Don't fuck with me." She kept eye contact. "We've been partners too long."

For a while, Dmitry said nothing as Brenda waited, her breath uneven. He was probably buying time, trying to think of a good answer.

"Fuck, Dmitry." She was yelling now. "Tell me."

"There's nothing to tell." He stared squarely at her as he said that. This wasn't going to work.

"Nothing? Really?"

"Shh..." Dmitry looked around. "Okay, I'll tell you, just no yelling." The indifferent mask was gone; his lips curved as if weighed down by the gravity of his mistake.

"Fair enough." Brenda's fists were clenched tight against the awkwardness of this scene. She'd rather be anywhere else, but she couldn't. She had to face this. She forced herself to sit and gulped from her coffee cup.

"Shit, Bren. I'm in trouble. I owe money to some bad people."

"What people?"

"It's best you don't know. I've got a gambling problem, you see. I've been reading about it." Dmitry's bushy brows rose and fell with his nervous speech. "I'm going to make things right."

"Make things right?" Brenda wasn't sure what to do.

"I know this looks bad." Dmitry nodded.

"*Looks* bad? It *is* bad." Brenda repeated the word softly, more to herself than Dmitry. Bad was not nearly enough for this.

"I know, I know. But I'd never do anything to hurt a real case."

"What the fuck do you mean by a real case?"

"One that matters." Dmitry sat there with his head buried in his hands. He looked up and made eye contact. "This was just a few spreadsheets, that's all. I'm sorry, Bren."

"Just a few spreadsheets?" A constraint in her chest. Anger. Yes, she was angry but also empty from this deception. "So, you disappeared them?"

Dmitry just stared, an edgy gleam in his eye. Brenda blew her nose with a tissue from a box on her desk to buy a moment to think. But no thoughts came, nothing to wash the dirt away.

"You need to turn yourself in."

"No, Bren. I can't. Think of Natasha. She needs her father."

"No kid needs a criminal father.

Dmitry just stared, his eyes like coal pits.

"Fuck you, Dmitry." The coffee cup in her hand—her favorite cup. Lukewarm. The next moment, it flew, hitting Dmitry smack on the chest. Coffee splashed over his shirt, a brown stain that would've been a wound if coffee were blood. With a delay, the cup fell to the floor and shattered.

68. The Corrector

The Corrector sat next to his mother's mechanical bed, trying to figure out if she wanted juice or something. Mom was going down quickly, poor thing. That was the truth, and he had to stare it square in the face. His mother barely took any food anymore. She just lay there with her eyes closed. Was she sleeping? She'd hardly spoken to him since that last fucked up conversation. Who would have known the old bird would disapprove? Oh well. It was too late to worry about that.

He held her sipping bottle to her lips, and she must have felt it. She opened her mouth and moved her lips over the nipple, her eyes fixed on him. Every few seconds, her throat shuddered as she swallowed. Was her mind still here or not?

"Mom," he said. "Won't you talk to me?"

She kept staring. After some delay, she moved her lips, but no sound came out.

After a while, she grew tired of sipping, and he put the bottle on the side table attached to the bed. It swiveled around and made the whole thing so fucking handy. The only relief about her not eating and barely drinking was that The Corrector didn't have to change her very often. But he would keep changing her forever if he had to.

The Corrector rose from the bedside chair and headed back upstairs. The sun through the dirty window played with the specks of dust over the stairs. It made him feel something, but he didn't know what it was. For some reason, he thought of the American girl he'd killed. What a fucking mistake.

The bottle was right there, on the floor by his bed. Good old bourbon. He gulped out of the bottle, feeling the warm relief spread through his body. He poured a fair amount into a dirty glass, smiling from knowing he had it to rely on.

He popped in a Megadeth CD and stretched on his chair, his legs propped up on his bed as he sipped the spicy brown liquid. He leaned this way and that and repositioned his legs, but no matter what he tried, he was uncomfortable. His mission wasn't over; now, he had to consider the next steps. But his mind wouldn't cooperate; thoughts hid behind one another instead of standing up in order.

The fucking bourbon was barely working anymore. Troublesome. That's how it had been with Dad for a long time until his liver must have given out because even a small drink would get him from sober to gone. The Corrector remembered it so well only because it was so fucked up. The minute his father had downed a shot, his words slurred, and he had trouble with balance. The Corrector had been just a boy then. Back then, he couldn't understand the instant change. It was scary, that's what it was. Fearing his dad as a kid wasn't so bad. It had made a man out of him, made him ready for his mission.

Then he remembered what a pussy he'd been with Juan firing him the other day. Instead of punching that asshole or at least giving him a piece of his mind, The Corrector had just mumbled something stupid. Luckily, Dad hadn't been there to see it. But it was all good in the long run. Once Mom finally croaked, God rest her soul, his expenses would go down a bunch. He wouldn't need the job. Fuck it. Good riddance. More time to plan his next corrective action.

He grabbed his phone and googled "murders in Portland." The third listing was about him. No shit. *Serial killer targets Muslims and minorities.* Fair enough. He scanned the piece: nothing but the basic facts. The names, this and that. It would be nice if his name could be printed next to those other names. But there was no such luck in this line of work.

Still, it felt good to be mentioned in the media. Everything else may have been fake news, but this wasn't. The Corrector was the real thing.

69. Dmitry Volkov

"Daddy, can I watch TV until Mommy gets back?"

"Sure, honey."

"Yay!" Natasha ran over and settled on the couch, her small hands already on the remote. The images and the sounds filled the living room.

Dmitry ordered a pizza and sat in the kitchen thinking, waiting for Rita to get home. He hadn't had a chance to talk to her since their fight the night before. The morning had been rushed, as usual. They both knew better than to start arguing during those scarce early minutes.

A huge grin grew on his face as he remembered picking up Natasha earlier. Today had been his turn. His daughter in the flow of students, her red jacket, her face bright like a small sun. She was more beautiful, more animated than all the other kids. Picking her up was his favorite part of the day. These five or seven minutes with his daughter, her stories. *Daddy, Martha brought her hedgehog to class. Daddy, I got a gold badge.* Even when they didn't talk on the way home, he enjoyed every minute of it.

He owed Rita an answer concerning Boris, but there wasn't a good one. He couldn't bring himself to turn his brother away. Her request didn't seem fair. Too much to ask. His brother had never done them any tangible harm. But it was a difficult matter to talk about. And did Dmitry even have the right to bring it up after what he had done?

He had to tell her about the debt. He'd looked up the symptoms on the Mayo Clinic website:

- *Being preoccupied with gambling, such as constantly planning how to get more gambling money*
- *Needing to gamble with increasing amounts of money to get the same thrill*
- *Trying to control, cut back, or stop gambling without success*
- *Feeling restless or irritable when you try to cut down on gambling*

Everything matched. He'd stopped reading after half the list; he needed more time to think about it. He was on an overload. No choice but to tell Rita about it, but how would he explain getting so far into debt behind her back? How would he explain Misha?

He couldn't.

Something in him knew it was too late. The debt was too huge. Unfathomable. His heart beat with an empty sound, his chest hollow as if his insides had been removed.

The pizza arrived. Pineapple and pepperoni, Rita's favorite. The smell from the box, spicy and sweet, filled the kitchen. The pineapple part didn't make sense to Dmitry: to add something sweet to a pizza was, quite simply, a wrong move. But Natasha shared her mother's preference; they couldn't just order half and half. Dmitry didn't mind picking the pineapples off his slices. Pizza was like magic, unavailable back in the USSR. He'd been twenty-three the first time he'd tried it, here in Portland.

What a great husband he was, Dmitry scoffed at himself. So tolerant about pizza choices. Meanwhile, his life choices would destroy the family. Outside, the rain had slowed to a drizzle. Lazy drops slid down the dark window.

The sound of the key in the lock; Dmitry felt a tightness in his sternum, a premonition of something going off track very soon, something he'd have to hold on to with all his might. Rita entered the kitchen, the smell of fresh air on her coat. Her brows went up as she saw him.

"Hi." Dmitry's voice came out husky; he cleared his throat.

"Hi." An embarrassed smile on his wife's face.

So, she wasn't mad at him anymore? But he still had to tell her about his problem.

"Dimka, I'm sorry. I've been thinking about it all day." Rita threw her purse on the counter, and it slid along the granite surface and smacked against the backsplash. The metal lock clicked softly against the blue tile, a warning. "No matter how weird Boris is, he's your brother. It's not fair of me to ask you not to invite him here. This is your house, too."

Dmitry felt detached from the moment, one conversation replaced by another. "I ordered pizza."

As if it wasn't already obvious.

"Thank you, baby." Rita walked into the living room, turned down the volume on the TV, and sat next to Natasha, who snuggled up to her mother without taking her eyes off the screen. Mother and daughter seemed infinitely comfortable together. A sort of joy glimmered in Dmitry's heart as he watched. They were so lovely, but he, Dmitry, was no longer clean enough to be with them.

After a few minutes, Rita kissed Natasha on the forehead and returned to the kitchen, her face radiating calm. She removed three dinner plates from the cupboard and brought them to the dining room table. She was such a good person that Dmitry's heart ached from what he was about to reveal. He exhaled, then inhaled. He felt shivery. If he didn't say it now, he'd never say it.

"Rita, I'm in debt. I have a gambling problem. I owe someone a lot of money."

"What?" Rita's smile faded, her glaring eyes two planets in another solar system. "What money? Who do you owe it to?"

"A Russian dude you don't know. But I'll fix it."

"Dmitry!" Rita's voice grew in tension with each syllable. "That's terrible. How much do you owe?"

Dmitry's face felt hotter with every second. He couldn't keep eye contact.

"Ten thousand." He didn't have it in him to reveal the actual number.

"Holy shit. And you've never told me?" Her face crumpled in what looked like dismay, disgust, or both.

"I'm sorry. I'll sort it out, don't worry."

"You'll sort it out? You need help. We could lose everything."

"No, no. I'll think of something." Dmitry tried to infuse his statement with a confidence that he didn't feel. Despair clutched at him from inside, every muscle in his chest tight. His hands were shaking. Boris. He should call Boris for advice.

"What kind of something?" Rita's eyes grew with every word; they brimmed with tears. "You've been lying to me for...for how long?" She turned her head toward the living room. Dmitry looked, too, but Natasha seemed immersed in her TV show. "Fuck, Dmitry. All those nights you told me you were working on the case, you were gambling?" She shook her head. "Is this why we never have any extra money?"

As he listened, Dmitry was puzzled, too. This was not what he had expected his life to become. He couldn't believe that even here, in the wonderful United States, his life had turned into a poisonous snake, spiraling out of control.

70. Sania Jamison

Days passed, and Sania remained dead. To her surprise, she was still around. After the police officer had discovered her on the riverbank, more people had examined her body before and after transporting her to the morgue. Sania didn't mind. Usually, she would've been embarrassed, but she wasn't. She no longer had access to embarrassment.

Finally, they'd left her alone. Rows of freezers lined up the opposite wall, a mirror of this one. She took stock of the other slots, most of them empty. She'd never imagined being able to feel and see this. It might have been scary, but it wasn't.

Sania thought of her family. Atif, Omar, Lydia. These names brought a smile to her lips; she could feel it even if she couldn't actually smile. She could see them, sense them out there in the world, but without precision, as if in low resolution. They floated warmly without quite touching her. She knew she'd have to let them go. They would be okay. They were okay. She wasn't irreplaceable.

Sania felt warm thinking about the last thing Atif had said to her before she stepped out of the house that night: *I love you.* If ever there was a message to send her off, that was the one. She felt loved, even as she lay there in the morgue, motionless. Not every dead person was as fortunate.

With a particular clarity, Sania saw an older man on an upper shelf several slots to the side. Somehow, she knew he was another victim of her murderer. The man looked tired, but he was thinking of a way to avenge their deaths. She couldn't explain how she knew it, but they shared a goal: to help the detectives find their killer.

71. Brenda Smith

It was one of the three bars near the abduction scene. The other two were more upscale and didn't feel like the right match. Brenda had to drive around for a few minutes to find a parking spot, but the place wasn't crowded.

Her plan was ridiculous, but what the hell? Her certainty had only grown. The killer lived nearby; she knew it. She'd spent all day thinking about it as she organized her notes on a felony assault case going nowhere and followed up on some of the missing persons she still hoped to find. Mary was busy tonight, and Brenda felt the urge to do something.

Wood counters, cozy booths—the place was nothing special but clean. An older man with a long white beard and a broad, bluish, vein-riddled face nodded on and off at the other end of the bar. The bartender should've cut him off sooner.

"Bourbon, please." Brenda wasn't quite sure why she had the taste for bourbon tonight. She sat on one of the empty stools, looking around.

With every minute, the pressure inside the killer's head must be building—building up to the next execution. The pressure in Brenda's head built up accordingly. The thing with the evidence in Dmitry's desk wasn't leaving her mind. This job was a weight on her soul. A bag full of stones. It would surely drown her, one way or another.

The killer might not be a drinker. There were many ways to numb oneself. Drugs of all kinds were readily available in a metropolitan city like Portland. Marijuana had been legal since 2015. Or the killer might be downing espresso shots at the Starbucks across the street. He could be anywhere.

Brenda peered at the Starbucks to check it off the list. The glass front made the whole place open to her scrutiny. An older woman at one of the tables and a teenager in the corner, neither a conceivable candidate for her serial killer.

No, no, she should trust her hunch. It was as if a voice in her head was telling her this—her voice. She should stick with bars. The killer was not a coffee drinker. Detective's work: being wrong most of the time but not always.

The bartender slid over with her drink.

"I have a question for you." Brenda took a sip. She pulled out her badge, and the bartender didn't seem surprised. He was a youthful man—tall, with a small mustache. His face was pleasant but not too friendly—perfect for the job. His long, curly blonde hair hung around his shoulders like Robert Plant's.

"How can I help you?"

"Have you heard the one about the bartender and the cop?"

"No." The bartender grinned. "Tell me."

"A cop comes into a bar. She asks the bartender: *have you seen a limping man?*"

"A limping man?" The grin on the bartender's face hung tight.

"Yes."

"What's the punchline?"

"There's no punchline. A male with a limp."

The bartender's brows went up in a funny but cute way, and he laughed. "I can't think of anyone recently. People don't come here to dance, you know. Most just take their seats and don't get up until it's time to go. And if they stumble on the way to the men's room, it's usually for other reasons."

"Right. Will you please keep an eye out?" Brenda handed him her business card. "He might be on the larger side."

"Hmm..." The bartender seemed to be trying to recall something. "What has he done?"

Brenda considered how much to reveal. It had to be substantial if she expected this guy to take her seriously. "He's wanted for three murders. We need to get him before more people get hurt."

"I'll keep an eye out for a limping dude." The bartender nodded. "Thank you."

Brenda felt better for no reason she could think of. She was excited, blood rushing through her, her heart up-tempo. She pulled out her cell phone and texted Mary a handful of hugs, hearts, and more hugs.

THURSDAY, NOVEMBER 21

72. The Corrector

The Corrector leaned over his mother's body to listen. A strong smell of disease streamed from her, but he was used to it.

"She's just sleeping." With his luck, today's visiting nurse had to be Black. Not as bad as some of these fucking Muslims, but still...At least she seemed to know what she was doing. She used a stethoscope and nodded with her lips pursed. Mom's heart was still beating.

"You have to prepare." The nurse looked sad, like she cared. They sure trained them well. "You have to talk to her."

The Corrector wanted to explain that his mom refused to talk but stopped himself. This one should mind her own business.

"You see this kind of thing a lot, don't you?" he asked instead.

"Yes." Her voice was flat but pleasant. She didn't make eye contact.

"How long does she have?"

"Hard to say. Could be a week, could be less."

"Shit." Something broke inside The Corrector, even though he expected this.

"I'm sorry." She gave him a sad look. "It's tough. Call us anytime."

They sat on either side of his mom's high-tech bed for a while, the nurse typing something into her tablet.

"Can she hear us?" The Corrector asked.

"She's going in and out of sleep." The nurse rose and began packing up her kit. "If you keep talking to her, she might hear. Other than that..." She kept talking, explaining something, but The Corrector couldn't help tuning her out.

A minute later, she was out the door.

"Oh, Mom." The Corrector took his mother's dried hand in his, like a wad of paper from a new shoe. Had he felt a squeeze? "Mom?" But the feeling of connection was gone. She either couldn't or wouldn't confirm it.

"I did it for all of us, Mom," he tried. "You gotta know that."

But she said nothing. It was weird to think she'd be gone a week from now.

He didn't hide his bottle of bourbon anymore, so he just took a big gulp. Her eyes were closed anyway. He took another gulp. He needed to get out badly, or he didn't know what he might do.

"See you, Mom."

She didn't react.

The Corrector couldn't find his keys. Must be upstairs in his room. He left the front door unlocked. Let them come and steal his mother if they wanted. Ungrateful old crow. No wonder she and Dad had never gotten along. He walked briskly down the street, not noticing the passerby. The pressure was on; he didn't have much time. The faces from the last few weeks crowded in his mind. He didn't know which one would speak up next. Dad, or that old Muslim dude, or even someone he didn't know. Sometimes, he couldn't tell if they were real or not.

If only he could go back to his plan. He'd had a plan, but Sania Jamison messed it up. It wasn't quite right, her being an American. He had to do better next time. But where the fuck should he look for his next prisoner?

Duh. The place Muslims go to do their worship. A mosque.

Perfect.

He'd have to be careful and stay a reasonable distance away. He needed a pair of binoculars. Luckily, he'd pocketed one back at Straight Nail. He laughed to himself as he admired his brilliant move. The thing would have cost him $29.99 if he'd paid for it. Juan and the rest of those creeps could choke in their sleep for all The Corrector cared.

73. Azar Bayat

Azar sat on a bench in Willamette Park, thinking about her classes. The bench overlooked a small wetland, Portland's buildings modestly perched in the distance on either side of the calm river. A beautiful view and a leisurely bike ride from the Portland State University campus. Her red Schwinn bike was chained to the nearby rack. Her first bicycle had been stolen. She'd used a flimsy lock, an error pointed out by fellow students. She went to Goodwill for her second: old and cranky, a model less likely to be stolen. The city of bikes, the city of bike thieves.

Azar's thoughts turned to her term paper. She was determined to explore the intersection of religious fundamentalism and women's rights studies by contrasting them to communism, a topic that may have been ambitious for her sophomore year. But she was not one to shy away from challenges. She wanted to do well at school, not just for herself but to repay her parents for their money and effort in sending her here. The thought of not excelling was more than embarrassing; it was unacceptable.

In her lap lay *The Argonauts* by Maggie Nelson, a book about identity and responsibility. Azar was immensely impressed by the freedom and grace with which Nelson revealed her intimate secrets. Where Azar came from, people were far more secretive. She looked forward to feeling open like Americans seemed to feel.

Her phone buzzed in her pocket, and Azar took it out, dreading what she was about to see. Another WhatsApp message from Soroush.

> *Azar, call me back. Why are you not responding?*

Fair enough. Azar felt terrible, but that only made her even madder at herself and this clueless dude back home. *Dude.* In her developing US English, she was beginning to embrace this unpretentious word. What time was it in Iran, anyway? Middle of the night.

She couldn't let this Soroush cloud hang over her forever. She pressed the green button to call.

"Azar?" Soroush sounded more surprised than happy. He must have been up.

"Yes. Sorry I didn't call sooner. School, you know."

"Couldn't you just take *a minute* to call back? Or at least text?"

"I need more than a minute to talk to you." Azar heard the edge of irritation in her own voice.

It had taken only ten seconds for Soroush to begin blaming her. But was she really going to break up with him over the phone? She couldn't even hear him very well, his speech missing a syllable here, a vowel there.

"I'll take a minute over nothing." Derision in his voice—or was she imagining this?

"How's everything back home?"

"Same. Everything is always the same, as you know."

"No." Momentarily, Azar was out of thoughts, unsure even what her *No* negated.

"Anyway, don't change the topic on me. Please explain why you didn't return my calls. It's simply rude."

What a spoiled brat. Azar pictured him pouting on the other end of the line, his face tight with self-importance. *I'm done with him*, she thought. *I am.*

"Look, Soroush. I'm sorry." Azar was sweating, her heart beating anxiously. Her hands shook a little. "It's not going to work between us. It's just not. You're too far. And I don't want to go back to Iran."

"What?"

"I don't want to go back."

"When did you decide that?" He sounded like a grownup talking down to a child. Still, she had to think for a moment to answer accurately.

"Since the day I made it here. It feels so different. Why don't you want to emigrate?"

"I...I can't imagine living someplace else where I don't know anyone. Or the culture. Why should I?"

"You're a man living in Iran. Why should you? What can I say?"

"I'm a man living in Iran? That's your reason? After everything we've been through together? Oh well..."

Click.

He hung up.

He might have meant it as a slap in the face, but to Azar, it was a relief. Her former affection for Soroush surprised her. She didn't want to think about him anymore.

She checked her email: nothing but spam. On the bright side, a WhatsApp message from Bahar.

> hey sis! going dancing tonight at my friend's apartment, wish you could come. 80s disco theme. love you sis. good studies today.

Azar smiled as she read. She missed her sister more than anyone else. Bahar wasn't too fond of Soroush; she would not be distraught about Azar's breakup. But Azar wasn't ready to share the news yet. She'd write back when she had a few moments to think.

It was a sunny fall day. Portland continued, busy and casual all around her. Azar's life was ahead of her, not behind her.

74. Dmitry Volkov

Dmitry felt depressed as he unlocked his front door. The tension between him and Rita had been palpable since last night's confession. The case tormented him, Brenda's disappointment tormented him—and, worst of all, Misha's threat hung over him like a guillotine blade. He hadn't dared to show his face at the police department. Instead, he drove around town, thinking of his deteriorating situation.

If he was honest with himself, life might never return to normal on the home front. Still, he'd try it. He would fix his money situation, and then things might improve. He hoped they would, desperately.

"I'm home," he announced from the foyer.

Silence rang in response.

It was Rita's turn to pick Natasha up from school. Dmitry went to the kitchen and pulled a beer out of the fridge without switching on the light. The glare from the refrigerator cast an uncommon set of shadows in the small space as if the kitchen had seeped through to the other side of the looking glass. Dmitry shut the refrigerator door, enjoying the darkness disturbed only by the city glow outside.

He felt hot, constrained, captured too tightly in the net that his life had become. He couldn't breathe. He pushed the window open; cool air rushed over his face, a slight relief. The evening was mild. No rain. Dmitry watched the pedestrians, more numerous than on most fall days. An old lady in a dark gray jacket captivated him with her slow progress. Supporting herself with a cane, she moved one step at a time as other people zoomed past her; she paid them no attention. She reminded Dmitry of his mother, who was never in a hurry for anything. He wished they had a healthier relationship, but that was impossible in this life.

When the old woman finally crossed the visible area, Dmitry sat at the table. Only now did he notice a notepad, a pen abandoned nearby.

> *We're done. You betrayed me. I don't know how to forgive that. You'll never get out of debt. And even if you do, how do I know you won't hide things from me again? How? I can't do this anymore. I'm so angry I could kill you. I don't deserve it; Natasha doesn't deserve it. N and I are at Mom's until we figure it out. Don't call. I'll call you when I'm ready to talk.*

His hands shook as he pulled out his phone and pressed his wife's number on the speed dial.

One ring, two, three, four. *You have reached Rita Volkov. Please leave a message, and I'll call you back.* He loved the way she'd Americanized her last name, *Volkov*, instead of *Volkova*, the female equivalent back in their Russian life so many years ago.

He felt nostalgic for those days.

"Hey, listen," he said into the phone after a delay that felt too long. "I found your note. Give me a call." He thought for a few more seconds, wondering what else to add. His mind was blank. He hung up, a state of confusion reigning in his soul. He was fucked; that was the word.

His legs didn't behave when he got up and returned to the window. The old woman was crossing his view again, on her way back from wherever she'd gone. From his angle, Dmitry could see her wrinkled face, her eyes on the ground before her.

75. Brenda Smith

It had been an empty day catching up on minor cases as Brenda considered her experience at the bar and puzzled over where Dmitry might be. She and Mary cuddled on the couch in Mary's small, elegant living room. The enthusiastic wide-screen TV flickered a river of color at them, getting in the way of their conversation. Mary pressed *Pause* on the remote. A red luxury car froze on the screen, two women in Barcelona mid-journey and mid-dialogue, like a crooked mirror reflection of the two of them.

"We should go there together," Mary said as if Barcelona were a place anyone could stop by whenever the whim struck them.

"To Barcelona?"

"I love that city." Mary's eyes were bright with excitement, so contagious. "Have you been?"

"Not yet. I've seen it in movies." Brenda felt a pang of insecurity on account of her lack of worldliness. What was she doing with this intelligent, educated woman?

"I fell in love with Barcelona before I ever went. Has it ever happened to you, falling in love with a place you've never been?"

"I don't think so." Brenda shrugged. "I'm always too busy, but it's not a good excuse."

"No, it's not." Mary smiled. "But you'll get around to it. *We'll* get around to it."

"That sounds lovely." Brenda squeezed Mary's hand. The fact that Mary was proposing shared plans filled Brenda with bliss she'd not expected from a romantic relationship at her age.

"How's your case going?"

"Can I tell you something big and nasty?"

"Ooh...I love big and nasty."

"It's not the kind you may be thinking." Brenda turned her head to face Mary. "I think my partner is a dirty cop. Scratch that: I know he is. I just found out."

"What? Or no." Concern in Mary's eyes. "The Russian dude? Dmitry? What did he do?"

"I found evidence in his desk from a financial crimes case we have nothing to do with."

"Shit. Did you confront him?"

"Yeah."

"How did it go?"

"It's hard to say."

"Shit, Bren." Mary repositioned herself, her back to the opposite edge of the couch in a way that made it easier to keep eye contact. She looked like a doctor or a therapist, prepared to listen to Brenda's concerns. "That's above my pay grade, but wouldn't you get in trouble if you didn't report him?"

"I might. But most importantly, I have to do what's right."

A quiet spell followed. Brenda felt peaceful, Mary's hand in hers, the two of them breathing together. Would this last? As Brenda's thoughts meandered, her eyes scanned the modern Danish furniture, the expensive-looking rugs, the art, and the carefully placed gadgets.

"How can you afford all this?" The second Brenda said it, she felt alarmed that the question might come through as a challenge.

"My dad was a bridge engineer." Mary sounded matter-of-fact; clearly, she'd taken no offense. "So full of energy and commitment, he could *not* refuse a project. He'd consult on one while completing another. Worked extra hours even if he didn't have to. He'd saved up a lot of money that way." Mary sighed.

"Worked? In past tense?"

"He burned out. He was supposed to build a bridge across Hood River, with a few other projects in discussion. But it all went south. He got fired for being drunk on a bridge construction site. His reputation was destroyed. So, he and Mom moved back East and took my little brother with them, but I decided to stay. Dad has kicked the booze since, but he never worked again."

"Oh. Why not?"

"In some professions, you can't just disappear for a while and then return to the same level you were on." Mary shrugged. "He was too old to start again."

"Poor guy. But I'm happy you stayed. Otherwise, we would've never met."

"You're sweet." Quick as a cat, Mary moved over to Brenda's side of the couch and took Brenda's face in her hands, looking at her with admiration like she was a museum exhibit. Mary kissed her, slowly and tenderly, until Brenda's body felt as if it had melted away.

"I'm not sweet." Brenda tried to catch her breath. "Just honest."

"What about your parents?" Mary pulled away and faced Brenda with interest, her eyes attentive and awake.

Should Brenda mention her father? It could be too soon for the two of them, but she wanted to be able to talk about serious things. Otherwise, what good was a relationship? She and Jessica had never really talked, never discussed their lives. They'd merely shared information—but mostly, they'd gone places together. Their lives had driven them. Brenda didn't want this to happen again. She wanted words between her and Mary, always.

"My dad is dying," Brenda said.

"What?" Instantly, all joy was wiped off Mary's face.

"We haven't been in touch. My Mom told me last night."

"Ouch. Baby!" Mary squeezed Brenda's hand. "They're no longer together, are they?"

"No, not since I was a kid."

"Who's taking care of him?"

"I didn't ask. I know I should call him, but our relationship went to shit so many years ago. He's an asshole. He couldn't deal with me being gay, with not going to church, all of it. No way to repair this in just a few months."

"A few months?" Mary visibly tensed at that. Those hazel eyes. Mary cared, even if Brenda herself felt distant from this drama.

"Pancreatic cancer." She shrugged. "Sorry to load all of this on you."

"I want to know things about you." Mary looked Brenda straight in the eye, her face intensely serious. "Why wouldn't I?"

76. Dmitry Volkov

"Hey, Borya," Dmitry said into the phone. "I'm in. Let's do it."

"Ha. Now we're talking." Boris sounded excited. "We can discuss the rest when I see you."

Not only did Dmitry need the money desperately, but he'd been desperately lonely since Rita had moved out. The house felt large and empty without her and Natasha and all the noise they made. Running feet, slamming doors, those horrible cartoon voices blaring from the TV. He even missed the stupid doll, Mercury.

He was the one who should move; they'd have to talk about it.

Dmitry wondered about his brother's plan, but he was afraid to find out the details. Odd, this mixed place, contemplating a crime while trying to solve another. The smell of eggs that had wafted from the kitchen still lingered. He was so hungry he scrambled half a dozen and wolfed them in one sitting.

He sat on the couch for a while, trying to focus on the murder investigation. His thoughts were unglued. He and Brenda knew too little about the killer. The killer had them by the balls. Dmitry wished he had an idea, a thread, a direction in his head. He felt like a good plan was there, hiding, revealing its fragments at night, but he didn't know what it was yet. He could hear the victims speaking, but their voices were indistinct in his dreams.

He wondered what Natasha was doing. The loss of his daughter's presence next to him every day gnawed at his heart, carving a massive hole in it. He missed watching her talk, breathe, laugh, eat breakfast. He missed her thoughts and questions. He missed the family routine.

The worry was worse. He'd gladly give up the chance to see his daughter again if he could be sure she was safe from Misha. Dmitry didn't have it in him to tell Rita about Misha's threat and hoped with all his heart and everything else in his body that Misha wouldn't hurt a child.

Rita's move wasn't going to make a difference. It would take Misha's guys just a day or two to find her. Dmitry was sweating as he thought this, his heart rate escalating. For the hundredth time, he asked himself: was it his fault, the disease's fault, or both?

His mind kept returning to the last time he and Rita went out, a couple of months earlier. They ate burgers, drank beers, and walked around downtown Portland holding hands, happy like children. Why did that moment keep coming up in his memory? It was as if no other day lived up to this one.

The doorbell interrupted his thoughts. He rose, but Boris was already opening the door, his black leather jacket wet from the rain. A jerk move, using his key when he knew Dmitry was here. Why ring the bell at all?

"How's it hanging, brother?" A huge grin on Boris's face.

"It's hanging." Dmitry shrugged. He didn't know where to start. He returned to his spot on the living room couch.

Boris tossed his jacket on the floor and sat across the coffee table from Dmitry, his eyes on his brother, as if trying to read what was inside Dmitry's soul. But Dmitry no longer had a soul. He didn't believe in it anymore.

"A shitty night out there," Boris added as if Portland rain called for a special mention.

"Yes." Dmitry nodded.

"What made you change your mind about the job?" That huge shit-eating grin on Boris's face again. Dmitry wished he could hit his younger brother on the head with a tennis shoe as he'd done in their childhood. He'd gotten in trouble with their parents for that, but it was worth it.

"Dude, I'm fucked. I owe money to this Misha guy." Dmitry felt terrible sharing this with his brother, the family's petty criminal. He was supposed to be the cop.

"Misha? Misha Petrov?" Boris's brows went up like he was impressed.

"You know him?" Dmitry wasn't sure if his brother's reaction made the whole thing more or less scary. He desperately wanted Boris to reassure him but knew he couldn't trust Boris's opinion. It was a shaky position to be in.

"Yeah." Boris looked at him with some concern. "He's a serious guy; he doesn't fuck around. What does he want you to do?"

"Nothing, right now. I just helped him out with something." Dmitry continued sweating as he shared these truths about himself. "But he'll want something sooner or later. Sooner, I think."

"Hmm…" Boris scratched his chin. "He's pretty well protected. I wouldn't go against him. How much do you owe?"

"15K." The conversation weighed Dmitry down like a ton of concrete on his chest.

"That's all?" Boris looked like he'd just heard a joke. "Bro, I'd thought you were in for millions. This is nothing. We'll do this one job, and you'll be golden."

Golden?

"What's the job?"

"You sure you're not wearing a wire?" Boris squinted at him, his brows tight with worry.

"What the fuck are you talking about?"

A second or two passed as Boris kept staring with intense suspicion, an angry priest glare, until all at once, his face collapsed into a laugh. "Just fucking with you."

"Fuck you," Dmitry said. "Tell me about the job."

FRIDAY, NOVEMBER 22

77. The Corrector

Sania Jamison was there in the room with The Corrector. The other woman, too. Both were the same, like a double ghost. The Corrector rubbed his eyes, but the ghost didn't go away. Spooky. He had begun to doze off. The ghosts must have been a dream. He needed another drink. He felt around for the bottle, but it wasn't in bed with him as he preferred. He stretched his arm to explore the carpet next to the bed. No luck.

The Corrector lifted his face off the pillow, a wet stain where his gaping mouth had been. He took in his bedroom, the trash and the dirty clothes, and the empty bottles strewn all over. At least his eyes had cleared up. No more women in hijabs, thank God.

He picked up a bottle, examining the contents against the light from the window. Empty. He picked up another. Shit. Only half a finger of liquid at the bottom; The Corrector drowned it in one gulp. Shit, shit, shit. He'd have to go downstairs. Good thing he'd picked up a case the other day.

Or had he already gone through it?

The Corrector thought about it for a minute. Fuck it, he'd confused it with the case from the week before. He remembered now: at least two or three bottles were still intact.

A wobble in his legs as he walked down, a buzz in his head. He held on to the rail, the old wood rough under his fingers. As he turned around the curve in the stairs, it came as a shock to see Mom lying there in the big high-tech bed with all the knobs and switches. He'd forgotten. Strange what sleep did to people. Half the memory, gone.

A small body in a large bed, the same spot he'd left her. Where the hell would she go? All tucked in under her covers, but her hands on top looked withered. It was fucked up that this shrunk thing, like a pickle, had given birth to him years ago. Had it been worth it? He sure hoped so. He'd make America a better place; that was for sure.

It was curious, the body shutting down like an old engine that was finished. He walked up to the bed and leaned over his mother. The smell was the same as before: disease and cleaning supplies. Mom's eyes were closed, her features relaxed. Must be having a good dream, the old bird.

A worry stirred inside him. She looked too still, each crease on her old face unchanging. What the fuck, what the fuck, what the fuck? His eyes shifted to her chest under the covers.

It wasn't moving.

Right then, The Corrector knew. He'd seen a few dead bodies. Finding his mother before him like this, a dead thing, hit against a whole lot of emptiness in his heart.

He didn't feel anything.

He walked over to the corner where the bourbon was stashed. Shit. Only one bottle left. The supplies in the garage were gone as well. The Corrector's legs ached as he made his way upstairs. His lungs struggled for breath. His foot hurt like a motherfucker.

The hospice nurse would be back Monday. He could wait until then to deal with the whole thing. At least he didn't have to worry about changing Mom's stinky diapers or feeding her one bite a minute as she stared into space. What a fucking relief.

The bottle of bourbon in his hand felt solid, real. Full. He would plan his next corrective action in the morning. Nothing stood in his way now.

78. Dmitry Volkov

Dmitry parked on a side street. His car smelled like coffee and Boris's sweat. Rain pounded on the hood of the car. The street looked washed anew under the streetlights. The most die-hard bars had closed, and the earliest risers were still in bed. Few crimes were reported during these hours.

He could say goodbye to his career if this didn't go well. He'd be in prison. He knew their odds of getting caught were incredibly high. As a cop, he was familiar with the many ways crimes like this usually went wrong. But he had to keep Natasha and Rita safe. And he was running out of options.

From their vantage point, they could see the shabby jewelry store on Hawthorne with its green sign that looked gray in the dark and its barred, shuttered window, revealing nothing of what might be inside. Boris had explained that much of the merchandise was left in the store overnight; it was all insured anyway. But could he trust Boris on that?

What would his friend Ivan have said back in his USSR *militsia* days? As far as Dmitry knew, Ivan might still be working for law enforcement in Putin's Russia. There, one was expected to be corrupt from the get-go. Here in the States, Dmitry had started with different expectations. He'd genuinely fucked it up.

"This is crazy." Dmitry felt jittery. "I'm sure they have security cameras in every corner."

"Dah! They would, wouldn't they? Except your brother knows just the right people. This dude from Novosibirsk I know from way back is a computer genius; he hacked into their system. Crashed it a few minutes ago. We're safe, don't worry."

"Are you sure it worked? Shouldn't you double-check with your guy?"

"Done." Boris pulled out his phone and showed Dmitry a text that said *Done*. Was it even from the same person? Dmitry couldn't be sure; he never was when it came to Boris. "Remember that time in Leningrad when I got drunk and fell asleep on the bank of the Neva and got arrested, and you had to come pick me up?" A wistful smile was on Boris's face as he spoke, as if this memory was dear to him.

"I remember."

It was a nuisance, having to drop whatever Dmitry was doing with his girlfriend, though after all these years, he no longer remembered what it was. He wasn't a brother's keeper. But when he'd seen the fear on Boris's face, the anger had left Dmitry all at once. Boris had been a shy kid, nothing like his current gregarious self.

"Why did you think of that now?" Dmitry asked.

"We used to live in the same crappy apartment, you know. Every day waking up, eating, talking, shitting, smoking, going to sleep in the same small place. Where do those things go?"

"Into our memory, I guess." Dmitry wasn't sure what had brought up this sentimentality in his brother. Boris still surprised him some days.

"Anyway..." Boris sighed. "Don't forget to show your badge if anyone gives us any shit. Ready?"

"Ready."

Dmitry wasn't ready, but what else could he say? By contrast, Boris seemed utterly relaxed, as if preparing for a day at the beach.

What was wrong with his brother?

Boris got out of the car; Dmitry followed. The rain hit him vigorously, plastering his hair to his scalp. Already, Boris's lock pick was in his hand. The old-fashioned wood door. The lock looked like nothing, odd for a joint with so many valuables inside. Cops saw so much disregard in the world. People being careless. And now, he was the one taking advantage.

As the door yielded, loud ringing cut the silence. A jolt of cold cut through Dmitry's body. Both he and Boris froze in place.

A second later, the panic dissipated: it was only the door chime.

"Don't turn on the overhead light," Boris whispered.

Dmitry could barely see him, a silhouette against the faint background of the shuttered window. A trickle of light seeped in through the cracks. The whole thing was idiotic. Now, in the middle of it, this felt clearer than ever. Dmitry pulled out his phone; it took his fingers a second or two to get it to work. The beam came on, startling in the darkness.

"Point it down." Boris's small light joined his on the floor.

The store smelled stale: cardboard boxes, dust, silence.

"Where's the storage area?" Dmitry should have remembered it from their planning, but he didn't.

"Right over there." Boris pointed his light deeper into the store, exposing a long expanse of space fading away toward the back wall.

They approached. A dark curtain: Boris felt around with his hand, found an opening, and pushed the heavy velvet aside. In the feeble light of their two phones, a massive steel vault faced them with its large metal wheel on the door.

"Fuck." Boris's voice was a note or two higher than usual.

"What? Don't you have the code?"

"Hmm. Don't worry, Dimka. We'll figure it out."

"Figure it out?" Dmitry was getting pissed, warmth rushing to his face. "You said there was a storage area here. Didn't you check it out?"

"I did. Of course, I did." Boris's voice hovered between distressed and his usual conciliatory tone. "They must have just installed this shit."

"You're kidding me." How could he have taken his loser brother's plan seriously? They should go before they got caught.

The sound was nothing more than a rustle. Then, a crack split the air in half.

Shit.

The small room exploded into slivers of sound: crashing, collapsing things. The smell of gunpowder and also a sharp pain in Dmitry's side. Oh, fuck. Oh, fuck. He leaped into a corner, rolled onto his back, desperately felt for the light button on his phone, found it. In the darkness, he held his breath. His brother's phone must have fallen; Dmitry couldn't see its light. His right hand reached for the gun in its holster; his left felt the wound. Already, the cloth around it was wet. Dmitry held on tight as if doing so would reduce abdominal bleeding. He knew he was badly hit. The pain was fucking hell.

A second shot rang out. Dmitry considered shouting, *Police, drop your weapon*, but it was too late to be police. He held his gun before him, even though he couldn't see anything.

He didn't want to shoot anyone. He put the gun down on the floor next to him, feeling the blood seep from under his left palm.

Another shot cracked the air somewhere on his left.

"Fuck." Boris's voice: surprised, perplexed. Then, a thud of a body falling.

79. Brenda Smith

Brenda was at work early. The small office felt oppressive today; every place did. She had to make a decision about Dmitry, the kind she'd never expected to face. And she had to call her dad. She didn't know which was worse. Rain pounded on the window, sliding down the glass like an octopus's arms. The smell of coffee was inspiring. Brenda looked up her father's number and dialed.

"Hi, Dad."

Brenda was irritated by the need to have this conversation. She'd tried to sound at least friendly, but that wasn't working. Her hand was on her forehead, clammy and hot. Just knowing that her father was on the other end of the line made Brenda sick, as if a callous hand were compressing her heart. He still had a stultifying effect on her.

"I guess you've heard about my condition?" A weak voice.

"I've been meaning to call. I'm sorry you're sick." She didn't feel sorry.

"Well, Bren. Shit happens. Maybe it's fair."

Was he referencing his situation? Their relationship? What was she supposed to say to this?

"I don't know, Dad. We will all die someday. It's neither fair nor unfair." How abstract it was, her father's impending death.

"I wish we had more time." His scratchy voice.

"Yes." Brenda didn't want more time with him. She could barely get through this conversation.

The phone call had barely lasted three minutes, but Brenda already craved an interruption and hoped another call would give her an excuse to cut this one off. She didn't want to think too deeply about her dad and his sad ending. From the way he'd treated her, it was fair. Her Nixon-Reagan-double-Bush-Trump voting dad, the homophobe.

"I know you think I've been a bad father to you," he said as if reading her thoughts. The elephant in the room. "I tried to do what's best for you."

"Best for me? Bullshit. That's why you wanted me to be something I'm not?"

"It's true, we disagree about some things." Now, he sounded resigned, unemotional even, as if reading from a script. Manipulative asshole.

"You don't get to disagree about what I want to do with my life. It's none of your business. It's just not. It never has been." Brenda had to work hard to resist the urge to hang up. "Do you expect me to give you official forgiveness or something? After all these years? You haven't even changed your mind."

"I should have done things differently." He was contradicting himself now. What in the world did he mean? Of course, he should've done things differently. Of course. "You see, my parents never gave me a model to follow. My dad was a drunk, and my mom—well, you've met her."

Grandma was a pleasant, blank-faced woman whose actual thoughts never penetrated her stoic facade. She didn't seem unhappy, just absent.

"I know, Dad. I know. What do you want from me?"

Impatience boiled in Brenda. Here he was, still looking for excuses. She'd heard all about her grandparents. She was wasting her time. She should be out there, looking for the murderer. On the other end of the line, her father continued talking, going on and on about his life and his circumstances. Brenda had no attention left for that.

"Dad, I've got to go."

"What, so soon? I thought...I thought we were going to talk."

"It's work, Dad. I'll call you back." Even as she said this, she doubted she would.

"Well…" Her dad broke off as if he were still hoping for something positive from her. Another friendly word from his estranged daughter.

"Bye, Dad." Brenda hung up.

She shouldn't have called. Better to put the whole thing out of her mind, to push her dad's toxic presence out to the edges of the known universe. She was good at this mental trick; her father had given her plenty of opportunities to practice. Already, all her thoughts were on the murder case.

Something about Wednesday night's bar visit was sticking with Brenda. A feeling, but one she couldn't quite decipher yet. She felt even more confident that the killer lived close to the Jamison residence; some clue in her, still maturing, pointed in that direction. As if the victims themselves insisted, pumping her full of conviction. This made no sense. Still, Brenda trusted her intuition. She had to go back. Try another bar in the neighborhood or even the same one. Yes, the same one. The bar felt right.

Dmitry was not returning her calls. And if he did, what would she say? A sense of clarity dawned upon her. She couldn't carry her father. She couldn't carry Dmitry. The only weight she could carry was her own and a little of Mary's. It was a broken world with dead bodies and red business cards. It was a bag full of stones; she could carry only a few.

Brenda looked up the number for Internal Affairs. She would not be stuck in hesitation. She dialed.

80. *Azar Bayat*

The Sunni mosque on 86th Ave was a modest brick building with an elegant dome and a minaret that didn't reach the middle of the nearby stand of pines. The rest of the architectural features were generic in a Western way, especially in contrast to the opulence of Tehrani mosques. All Azar needed for her paper was a personal experience.

As much as she had hoped to be open-minded about the whole mosque business and the apparent right of others to decide what to believe, the notion of separate men's and women's sections was a punch in the stomach. To be respectful, she did wear a headscarf.

She chose Maghrib, the evening prayer, which started right after sunset at 4:51 p.m. tonight. As Azar walked up to the mosque, something inside her resisted; she felt the anxiety one feels when something vague is amiss, even if no objective danger is present. She had to use a separate unmarked door, like a service entrance. The women were relegated to a balcony, much smaller and shabbier than the picture of the men's section Azar had found online. This felt like stepping into a self she didn't want to be.

She took her shoes off but skipped her ablutions. No one was watching. The seven or eight women in attendance sat apart as if each had come here following her separate path, which was probably true in this cosmopolitan city in a Christian, or formerly Christian, country.

Awkwardly, Azar approached the middle of the room and kneeled on one of the pink octagons lining the floor. The other women faced the Mihrab, each in her private world. No one met Azar's eyes.

The Imam appeared in the men's section below, already intoning

Allahu Akbar. Azar was irritated by the questionable intentions hidden behind the pretty words and prepared to hate every minute of this. She would get through it, she would, she promised herself. She started counting. The numbers added slowly in her head, like a pile of zeros.

81. The Corrector

The Corrector parked across the street from the mosque and turned off the windshield wipers. The view became blurry in no time. He was ready for his corrective action. It would take a wizard to see him in his car.

He got out and moved to the backseat, then slid all the way to the right. He would be even less noticeable in the back, and he could quickly grab any Muslim that might walk by on the way out of the stupid mosque. The whole thing would be easier if he parked by the entrance, but a video camera hung over the door.

The mosque was a two-story brick thing. Pretty small for a place of worship. A Muslim tower in the center, whatever those were called. A construction site next to it, a new apartment building from the looks of it. The artsy sort with too many lines and mixed colors. They kept rising all over Portland like poisonous mushrooms. The fucking real estate boom, it brought all kinds to the city. The Corrector missed the good old days when Portland had been the city of Portlanders and America was a country of Americans.

The rain had been pouring non-stop for over twenty-four hours and wouldn't let up anytime soon. A perfect night. On his side of the street was a florist's shop with a huge sign made of neon roses, *Pink Petal*. The Corrector gave Pink Petal the finger. Up yours. Who cared about flowers when the nation's future was at stake?

In any case, a *Closed* sign was on the door. Next to the flower shop, a regular house, then another store. Gifts or some nonsense, from the looks of it. The Corrector couldn't read the sign from where he was.

Not a busy street at all. Good. In his rearview mirror, a coffee shop that looked as empty as hell's asshole. A red outline of a cup glowed, topped by a little green cloud. Was that supposed to be steam? Fuck! The Corrector didn't trust people who spent their money on stupid four-dollar coffee drinks.

His car smelled of stale cigarettes. He grabbed the pack of Marlboros from the console and shook one out. The fresh smoke would kill the stink. He lit a cig and took a deep drag, exhaling slowly. It was lovely to sit without worrying.

He was on his own path, his own person. The Corrector. He wasn't going to be Junior anymore.

82. *Brenda Smith*

Brenda was wrapping up at the office, feeling guilty about turning Dmitry in. She hadn't heard from him in over twenty-four hours. Internal Affairs could not have approached him yet, so where the fuck was he? The office smelled of coffee. Brenda was on her fourth cup, her body jittery. She held a fresh cup in both hands, a sacred object. She should've talked to Dmitry more and forced him to open up.

Her phone rang. Nervously, Brenda grabbed it from her desk.

Her boss, Lieutenant Manes.

"Smith, something came up. You need to know." He sounded thoughtful, puzzled. "Are you still in the building?"

"Yeah."

"Can I please see you in my office?"

Brenda walked down the long corridor, dread in her heart, her hands shaking, rain pounding the tall windows. This was about Dmitry. So soon. She knocked.

"Come on in."

Lt. Manes raised his eyes from a pile of papers on his desk, his broad middle-aged face pale and tired. It was a corner office; light burst in from both sides. The ample space was organized unwisely: too much furniture. Bookcases shy with their gaping holes, like missing teeth. The office looked and smelled dusty and unoccupied. Wasn't it vacuumed every day, like the rest of them?

"I got a call from Internal Affairs about Volkov." Manes' attentive eyes were on her. "Thanks for doing the right thing."

The fist of worry tightened inside her as Brenda examined her boss's face. You never knew how police higher-ups would react to a cop ratting out another cop. Loyalty was a significant value in the force, sometimes overrated.

"Volkov is at the hospital with a gunshot wound." The lieutenant's bushy brows converged in a worried look.

"What?" Worry cut right through Brenda, too. She still cared about Dmitry deeply. How could she not? She wasn't sure what this said about her.

"Shot during an armed robbery at a jewelry store."

"Armed robbery?" What in the world? So many questions bounced about in Brenda's mind. "Is he going to be okay?"

"They don't know yet. He has an abdominal wound. The victim is even worse off. He may or may not survive."

"The victim?"

"Yes, the store owner."

Brenda's thoughts raced ahead of one another, not connecting. "Did they get the perps?"

Manes shook his head sadly. "Your partner is one of the perps."

83. The Corrector

Most Muslims had arrived before 5 p.m. The Corrector noticed that the women used a separate door. Weird. He'd been here half an hour; darkness was coming on fast. In just a few minutes, it would provide the protection he needed. He shook the ashes of his cigarette off onto the floor of the car.

For a while, everything was quiet. The Corrector thought of his mother's body back at home. He'd taken care of her while she needed care, and now he was done. One day, his own body would lie somewhere on a slab of metal, and that didn't bother The Corrector one bit. He looked forward to it—not in a suicidal way, just as a finishing touch. He had to make room for death if he was serious about serving his country.

The Muslims began trickling out. Men in their suits and women with their covered heads. The colors turned shades of gray as they stepped into the darkness. A woman his age met her husband by the entrance, and the two crossed the street, passing within yards of his car.

As the Muslims dispersed, The Corrector dreaded a wasted night. He might be leaving empty-handed. Two guys were still hanging near the mosque, blabbering, their voices in a foreign tongue so loud The Corrector could hear them from inside his car.

They shouldn't have come here.

84. Azar Bayat

The Imam finished, and the women turned to the left and the right and gave blessings. A mishmash of male voices rose from the main floor. Azar felt ill at ease, even though no one was watching her. The women's faces were directed inward; several had tears in their eyes.

Azar rose from the rug. Already, the women were filing out, some speaking to one another as they headed down the stairway. Azar felt intensely out of place. Who did she think she was, pretending to pray so that she could write something clever for her class?

She was the last to the exit. The heavy door had closed, leaving Azar alone in the room. She felt trapped, as if any second, she would run out of air to breathe. Her heart beat fast as she walked down the narrow stairs to the women-only lobby. Desperate, she pushed the large women's door open, expecting it to be locked. It flung open from the excessive effort. Fresh air hit Azar's face.

It was like resurfacing after being underwater for too long. She tore off her headscarf.

85. The Corrector

As the Muslims dispersed in small groups, The Corrector just about gave up hope for tonight. He'd have to think of something a little different. He lit another cigarette. As soon as the cig was done, he'd hit the road.

He glanced at the stupid steaming coffee cup sign in his rearview mirror. Way too far for anyone to get a good look at his car. Barely any traffic, too. No one has noticed him. Such a good fucking spot.

And what do you know: just then, his lucky card again. A woman, all on her own, stepped out of the mosque through the smaller door. The moment she got outside, she took off her headscarf. Her long hair fell onto her shoulders. She just stood under the mosque's awning. Didn't seem to be going anywhere, like she was waiting for the rain to end. Good luck with that here in Portland.

The Corrector sat in his car, watching, waiting to see what she would do.

86. *Azar Bayat*

Azar stood under the awning, getting ready to step into the rain. The darkness had settled; only the very edge of the sky above the buildings still bore a trace of light. She felt wrung out as if she'd crossed a desert or heaved a massive rock up some hill like a naïve al-Masih or a misguided Sisyphus. What an encounter with the past, this Maghrib service. And not even her past, but rather the past and the present of an entirely different category of Iranians. She felt uneasy and disoriented.

It was a quiet street, with more bird calls than traffic. A few quaint stores, closed at the moment, mixed with residential buildings on the other side of the street. Half a block to her right, a coffee shop was still open. The elaborate neon sign featured an ornate, steaming espresso cup. Azar could use an espresso.

Out of respect, Azar had powered off her phone inside the mosque. As soon as she turned it back on, she saw a WhatsApp notification, a message from her sister in Finglish.

> maloos peed on Baba's book again. bad
> kitty. miss you. xxxooo
>
> ps: how's my smarty-pants sister? send
> me a new reading list

Two years her junior, Bahar was much brighter than Azar ever hoped to be. Azar was so impressed by her sister's intense learning curve. Soon, Bahar would be ahead of her in reading and keeping track of films and art. Azar would be the one asking her little sister for a reading list.

Dad must have been mad at Maloos for about a minute before ordering another copy. Dear old Dad, with his books and his tea.

Couldn't go through a day without eight or ten cups. No wonder Azar had turned into a caffeine junkie.

What were her parents doing now, without their favorite daughter by their side? Sleeping, of course. It was around 5 a.m. in Tehran, with the ridiculous time difference of eleven and a half hours. The irritation at her homeland for the extra half hour and everything else flooded Azar's head with a wave of heat.

She imagined her parents in their bed with its imposing cherry bedframe and the rugs on the walls. She missed them, but in a soft way that didn't cut her heart as sharply as other pains. She missed Bahar more.

She opened the app and typed,

> poor maloos he may have a urinary infection. you wouldn't believe where i am...a mosque... a mosque! it's for my paper. i'll tell you all about it in the morning. miss you baby sister xxxooo

Poor cat. What was he, twelve? Thirteen? Azar had been a kid when this independent calico creature entered their lives. On many nights, Maloos would sleep on her chest. She hoped he was okay. She wasn't ready to lose him.

The rain slapped her face as Azar stepped out from under the awning. She didn't try to hide. Instead, she turned around to face the mosque and snapped a picture with her phone. She attached the image to her message and pressed Send.

87. Dmitry Volkov

A suspicious kind of brightness oppressed Dmitry's eyes like snow on a sunny day. He was a child back in Leningrad. He wasn't allowed to go out and play with his friends in the courtyard between their building and the five-story hotel that hung over the yard like a dull goose, its gray windows concealing the mysterious foreigners who came there on business—or, more often, communist party officials visiting the city of Pushkin and Dostoevsky.

But then, Dmitry was in the yard, anyway. A sandy path snaked between two strips of lawn. Snow covered the grass, except for the very edges, bare due to some whim of nature. What was the cause? He scanned his head for an answer; he should remember it from physics class back at school.

His hand was squeezed tight around something warm. Something beating. He brought his fist closer to see, but at once, panic struck him. This didn't feel right. He didn't have it in him to open his palm. Seconds ticked in his aching head. There it was, the hidden thing, in his fist, and he couldn't even see it. What kind of detective did that make him?

"Daddy?" Natasha's voice. "Daddy, are you okay?"

Dmitry looked, but Natasha wasn't there. His eyes were still closed. He made an effort to open them just a slit. White all around him. Snow. But soft, like a bed. He wanted to explore the softness around him, the white room, but the other scene was already drawing him in. His brother walked out of their building. He wore his gray coat and the shoes Dmitry had outgrown. A crooked hat crowned Boris's head. He was so small and ridiculous in that attire; they lived in a land where everyone was ridiculous. The USSR.

"Borya!"

Boris stopped and turned around, confusion on his face. "What do you want? Who are you?" A perplexed grimace.

As Dmitry looked on, puzzled, his brother turned and resumed walking away. Dmitry didn't want to insist on a conversation. He felt empty in his body, as if every bit of intention had been removed. His muscles no longer worked. Wait, this must still be a dream. But why couldn't he wake? A cold hand on his forehead. *Mom,* he thought with tenderness, but his mouth made no sound.

There'd been something between him and his parents, some disagreement. How could that be? If he hadn't obeyed them, they'd give him a spanking and lecture him about Jesus, who'd died for our sins, and so we shouldn't sin anymore, period. Jesus was excellent and childish, like Santa. The smell of wild mushrooms enlivened the apartment. His grandmother was drying them again.

88. The Corrector

Holy fuck! The Muslim woman was about to cross. She looked left and right like a good pedestrian, then stepped into the street. The Corrector slouched and squeezed himself into the backseat. He could barely see her figure through the downpour.

The woman crossed the street and walked along the sidewalk toward The Corrector's car, probably headed for the coffee shop. Luck was on his side again. No time to waste. The Corrector tore off a piece of duct tape from a roll he'd left on the backseat. He'd practiced this move. Still, somehow, the tape adhered to his fucking thumb. He tore it off with his other hand, and it stuck to that one. Shit! It took him forever to get it right. She had almost walked by, still not noticing him in the backseat, when The Corrector pushed the door open and jumped out. His hand snapped the duct tape to the woman's mouth, and the next moment, he forced her in. She must have been half his weight; she had no chance.

The whole thing went extra smooth this time. The woman fit just right, her head at the far end of the backseat. Her purse slid to the floor, a colorful thing. She was trying to scream, but the duct tape turned the screams into mumbled nonsense.

The Corrector looked around. No one was out, and the nearby windows were all dark, like no one lived there. Just huge puddles of emptiness. Only the stupid coffee place remained open, but it was too far for anyone to see him in all this rain. He lifted the Muslim woman's feet as he slid onto the backseat under them and shut the door behind him, like turning the volume down on the rain.

Already, his prisoner had pulled her feet free, and her red and blue sneakers smashed into his left side with a force he hadn't expected from this tiny person. Feisty. The Corrector smiled, barely registering the pain. He grabbed her ankles and held them both with his left hand. She tried to free them, but his hand was strong. He had to show he was in control, didn't he? His right hand drew the gun from his jacket's inside pocket and pointed it squarely at her face.

89. *Azar Bayat*

The black gun looked enormous. Azar froze, her heart beating so fast it might explode, her mind a whirl. She wasn't ready to die. She was out of her mind with fear in the backseat of the stranger's car.

"Stop fucking kicking. You're as good as dead if you try anything stupid." The voice was higher than she'd expected from such a big man.

Azar froze. He put the gun away, but she felt like the barrel was still pointed at her. The kidnapper quickly wrapped layers and layers of duct tape around her ankles, then let her feet fall on his lap as he grabbed her purse and rifled through it. He pulled out her phone and turned it off, then dropped it back in, zipped up the purse, and tossed it over to the front.

What do you want? She tried to say, but with the tape over her mouth, all that came out was a mix of mumble and moan. Azar shivered, breathing fast through her nose. Her awkwardly bent legs were a gruesome parody of reading in bed. The man's face was broad and blurry: a messy beard, a baseball hat, bushy eyebrows. A round, imposing face. She tried to punch him, gun and all, but her fists wouldn't reach him. She squirmed, trying to push herself up with one arm, but couldn't find a way to defend herself from her position.

She screamed into the tape that covered her mouth.

90. The Corrector

The Corrector sure didn't want her to free herself and scratch his eyes out from behind as he drove. He leaned in and wrapped her hands together with duct tape. It was awkward with her legs on his lap like this, but at least she couldn't kick him anymore.

She struggled to pull her arms away, but her strength was no match for his; he held her arms together with his left hand as he ran the tape around them with his right. Then, he used a piece of rope he'd had in his pocket to tie her hands to the safety belt buckle. She'd have some room to wiggle around, but not much. He was getting good at this if he said so himself. Done in under five minutes.

No trick to it, with the rain pouring like piss from Hell. The Corrector exited the backseat, shut the door against the woman's Adidas sneakers, and looked around. No one. A pained cry above him; The Corrector looked up. Two geese slid across the background of a black sky like ghosts.

The Corrector walked around to the front, got in, and started the car. He turned his wipers on and carefully pulled out into the empty street.

As he drove, he moved his rearview mirror to check on his prisoner. Her big eyes were directly on him. Spooky. The Corrector wasn't in the mood for that. He moved the mirror back. Better to focus on the street ahead. Rain and nothing but rain.

It wasn't a long drive. Down the numbered blocks on Sandy, crossing 82nd and a right on Fremont without hitting a single red light. He couldn't even hear his father's voice. His house was on a narrow side street. Not much happening on the block; a suitable location for his mission.

The Corrector's house looked bright as candy in all that rain. Nice and pink. Knowing that his mom lay dead inside sucked, but his successful corrective action helped make sense of his life. The Corrector pressed the button on the visor and watched the white garage door go up before him. He pulled in, relieved he'd made it home, safe as a peach.

He didn't feel like dealing with his prisoner now. He didn't have the passion for whatever reason. He'd done the risky part; that was enough. He had to set his mind on killing her. She'd wait until he was ready for her.

It was the result he was after: one less Muslim on American streets. Not the act itself. Especially after that American girl, Sania. But he owed this to his country. He pressed the button and watched the garage door slide down in the rearview mirror. The woman's eyes were still on him, but he didn't want to look. He got out of his seat and slammed the car door behind him.

As The Corrector entered the house, the stink hit his nose like a fist. It had gotten worse while he was away. Mom, what the fuck! Only a day and a half. He opened the window a crack to help with the smell.

His foot hadn't bothered him all day, but now it throbbed like a motherfucker. He needed a drink. As he crossed the living room, he tried not to look at his mother's body. She was a little green and sagging, not rigid like the first day. The house was cold like a fucking tomb, so The Corrector pushed the thermostat up a notch. Then he picked up the cleanest glass from the sink full of dishes and headed upstairs. He'd moved the two new cases of bourbon up there this morning after a drive to the liquor store. Might as well keep them in one place.

In his bedroom, he turned on the light and poured himself a drink. He dropped into his chair, thinking of Dad, who should just shut up and never speak again. What did the old man care anyway? Especially now that The Corrector had made it far ahead of anything his father had ever achieved. With each successful action, The Corrector was safer from Dad. Good riddance.

91. Azar Bayat

Everything inside Azar ached as she shivered, her body and mind tied up, her thoughts rushing around in circles, seeking a way out. The man would be back any moment. Was he going to kill her? Through her inflamed, burning nose, she inhaled the cigarette-smelling air.

Azar remembered the news report from the other day. A killer targeting minorities. Wasn't there a Yemeni immigrant involved and someone else? She should have read it more carefully. She should have acted more carefully. Desperate, she rubbed her face on the car seat, working her jaws in a frenzy, hoping the duct tape might come off. For a second, it felt like an edge of the tape was coming loose, but no... whatever she tried, her mouth remained sealed. Every few minutes, Azar had to lie still for a while to catch her breath through her nose. Tears streamed from her eyes. She'd nearly torn her hands off trying to pull them free, and at the moment, her wrists tortured her more than the other pains.

Minutes passed. Was the kidnapper awaiting instructions from someone else? Azar's legs were tied, but she could move them in constricted space. She put her feet up against the side window. There was plenty of bend in her knees to kick the glass out.

Think. Think. There'd be a loud noise. Would anyone hear? She'd have to be able to get out fast.

With her arms tied to the seatbelt buckle, that was unlikely.

Azar lay there, feeling the remaining moments of her life speed away.

92. The Corrector

The Corrector sat in his chair, gloating and smoking a cigarette. Fuck! He was dying to share his progress with someone who felt as serious about the future of the United States as he did. He hadn't been on Discord for over a week, not since he almost fell into that trap, but he didn't care anymore. If the cops hadn't caught him by now, they never would.

His friend WhysKrak had just posted.

WhysKrak
Liberals are traitors man. They should all go to fucking jail.

Nice to hear from good old Krak again. The Corrector had missed the man, even though they'd never met. What a fucked up world they lived in.

The Corrector started a new thread. Just a little teaser. Seeing his name in bold letters was half the fun.

The Corrector
Get ready to here about another corrective action in Portland. Down with Muslims & terrorists. Make America Great Again.

93. Dmitry Volkov

Dmitry's eyes opened, and the white ceiling stared at him. Where was he? His head was hazy. A vague pain in his torso, somewhere to the right of the middle. He couldn't keep his focus.

What happened? Flashes in his head—a street at night, sitting in the car with Boris.

Was Boris here, too?

"Borya?"

With much difficulty, Dmitry raised his heavy head from the pillow and scanned the room. No one. His body was filled with fatigue; his abdomen burned in pain.

He'd been wounded.

He was dead, wasn't he?

Slowly, he ran his left palm over the right side of his body. His body was there; he felt it; it felt his hand. He was still alive.

He let his head fall back on the pillow. A picture, repeating. A dark room. Was it before or after that moment in the car with Boris? He couldn't connect these episodes. A metal door with a large wheel. Something the two of them had planned. But wasn't Boris still at school? Wait, wait, no. It was 2019. He just needed a little more rest; that was all.

Dmitry's eyes closed.

94. The Corrector

The Corrector sighed. His mouth was dry as a motherfucker. How long had he been sitting in his chair like this? Hell if he knew. He might've fallen asleep. Good thing he didn't have to be at work. His job at The Straight Nail already seemed like the distant past.

The future was now. The Corrector had to grab it by the throat. The immigrant problem had gotten bad enough. The President said, *They're bringing drugs. They're bringing crime. They're rapists.* And the President knew what he was talking about. The Corrector couldn't wait for Trump's second term. He would let loose on all the fucking liberals and hopefully outlaw all immigration.

"Why don't you get this thing over with?" Dad asked, and The Corrector had to turn around to face him. The old man was lying in The Corrector's bed, his gray, disheveled head on his son's pillow.

"Dad? What do you mean?"

"You know what the fuck I mean." Dad didn't have to raise his voice to sound scary. "I mean the fucking girl."

Then Dad was gone. The Corrector rubbed his eyes. They were playing tricks on him. And the smell, as if from inside him, not from downstairs.

Who cared if his prisoner was still in the car? He got out of his chair and stomped about, pumping his fists in the air to relax. It didn't help. He had to get out. A drink or two away from the stink; that was all. He had to do something about his mom's body soon, but tonight wasn't the night.

The Corrector pinched his nose and closed his bedroom door before walking downstairs. Just in case, he approached the garage door and listened. Nothing.

His foot was fine, the pain gone, just like that. He'd walk to the bar, only a few blocks. It was still raining, but The Corrector didn't give a fuck. He put his jacket on. One of the buttons was missing, but who the hell cared? The rain might feel nice, for a change.

95. *Azar Bayat*

Azar heard a door slam, and heat rose in her body. Now, her chest hurt more than her wrists. Her face was hot. She waited, shivering, each second creeping into the next, her heart punching a double beat.

Seconds kept dripping; nothing happened. Azar listened. Like before, no sound inside the house. She had to do something—even if it was pointless. The side window. Azar lifted her legs, brought her knees to her chest, and smashed her feet into the glass. The angle wasn't quite right, resulting in a thump, not a hit. Azar aimed again and struck. This time, the impact felt more substantial, the seatbelt tugging at her bound arms.

Still, the glass resisted.

Azar took the time to inhale and exhale through her nose, then struck again. With a pop, the glass dissolved into a cloud of fragments.

A rhythm in her ears: the sound of rain hitting the garage roof. It was so typical, this rain. Frustration flashed through her like fire, and Azar began banging the top of the car with her feet, adding to the noise. She desperately hoped for someone to hear: a neighbor, a passerby. Surely, someone would help. She had to pause after a few blows to get a good breath, then start again. Pause and start again. The physical strain was a relief. The car lining was getting some damage. The brown plastic had caved in several spots, dirt from her sneakers smeared on it. Absurdly, that made Azar proud.

The rain outside intensified. She was working against the rain. Then, all at once, she was exhausted. No one would react to banging inside a garage. Screaming was the only sound that would help. She wanted to scream. She needed her mouth free to scream.

Something stunk in the garage. A dead mouse? Why wouldn't the man remove it? Or was it worse than a mouse?

96. Brenda Smith

Mary pushed the bar's heavy wooden door, and the smell of grill grease invaded Brenda's nostrils. She nodded to the bartender, and he mirrored her nod. Something about his face was different. Then it hit her: his mustache was gone. He looked better without it.

She and Mary took a booth, the brown wood well-polished and sturdy. Despite the hour, the bar was nearly empty. Two couples, a man in his sixties, and three students at the dartboard. Immediately, a server approached to take their order. White, in her twenties, athletic.

"A screwdriver, please." Mary smiled at her.

"Same for me, please," Brenda said.

"Two screwdrivers. Coming right up."

The smell of the place reminded Brenda of the burger routine with Dmitry. She missed the good moments with Dmitry. Her day had passed in a fog as she waited for news about her partner's condition and sifted through the scarce evidence.

"Mary, listen. If something happens, I must be sure you won't get involved. Promise me."

Mary's grin suggested that she wasn't taking this very seriously. "I promise."

"I mean it. I shouldn't have even brought you here. I could be in deep shit if anyone found out."

"Ouch." Mary laughed. "I'm just a private citizen, doing whatever the fuck I feel like doing in a public place. Anything wrong with that?"

"Okay then." Brenda dropped her jacket on the seat next to her. "I'll be right back."

She walked over to the bar. A tall male in his forties in a dark blue sweatshirt had taken the seat two down from where Brenda stood. His shoulders were broad, and his neck as wide as his skull.

"Detective." The bartender gave her a friendly look.

"Hi."

"Mind if I get this gentleman's drink first?"

"Go ahead."

The bartender moved over to take the man's order.

"Bourbon," the man said.

The bartender poured, and the man began sipping his shot as he stared at the row of bottles over the bar wall or at something inside his head. The bartender walked back over to Brenda.

"Anyone matching my description?" she asked.

"I would've called you." He pulled Brenda's card from behind a counter and held it for her to see. "Still got your number."

"Okay. Thank you."

"You bet."

Brenda returned to their booth.

"Remind me, how do you know he has a limp?" Mary asked as Brenda sat down.

"The forensics. His footprints. Don't share any of this with anyone, please."

Mary rolled her eyes.

"Thank you for coming along," Brenda said.

"Sweetie! I'd come along with you anywhere."

Brenda knew Mary was sincere. Her beautiful hazel eyes saw Brenda. She grabbed Mary's hand from the table between them, brought it to her lips, and held it there.

"Two screwdrivers." The server's voice arrived from a separate place that included the whole world apart from Brenda and Mary.

Brenda let go of Mary's hand and took a long sip. The bitter taste felt like a reward on her tongue. "Do you think I should visit Dmitry?

Even though I'm the one who turned him in?"

Mary contemplated, her lips pursed, her eyes on Brenda's. "Do you *want* to visit?"

"I don't know." Brenda imagined being in Dmitry's hospital room, next to his wounded body. "It'll be awkward."

"Maybe you should give him a chance to tell his side?" Mary frowned, thinking. "There may be more to it. How's he doing, anyway?"

"Out of intensive care, probably looking at a prison sentence."

97. Azar Bayat

Azar had spent a while trying to scream through her taped mouth, and now she was exhausted, still gripped by panic but lacking the energy to thrash about anymore. She felt like a sack of vegetables in the back of the car. The stink of stale cigarette smoke and sweat and decay spoiled every forced breath she pulled through her nostrils. Her bound hands were limp on her chest. Her eyes stung, her head was splitting, her legs sore.

A wave of regret poured over her. Why had she come to this country, this crazy city? The faces of the Proud Boys from the other day assembled in her mind. This man could be one of them. Had they followed her? She couldn't tell which possibilities made sense and which didn't. Azar closed her eyes tight, trying to stop the mad carousel of thoughts in her head.

Her childhood in Tehran flashed through her, a swoosh of feeling, a longing. Her naïve happiness was later replaced by disdain for her country. Her teenage years were confused and full of self-searching. She'd hoped to become a respected thinker, an intellectual—all for nothing.

No, it couldn't be.

She was mad at herself for going to the mosque. Mad and terrified, her body sweaty and shivering. Think of something, think of something. For the hundredth time, she scanned the gray fabric under her, the pockets on the backs of the front seats. A shabby paperback of *Dangerous* by Milo Yiannopoulos, an author Azar wasn't familiar with. A window scraper, a receipt, a pair of black leather gloves—nothing useful to a captive, especially one whose hands were tied. The roll of duct tape still lay there on the car floor.

Azar imagined herself as a superhero. She'd pull apart her bound arms, tearing the tape. She imagined something sharp in her hands. She imagined piercing the attacker's throat with a thin blade and watching all the blood escape. She knew she would do it if an opportunity arose. She imagined being relieved but shocked by the gore of it.

No matter what, she wasn't ready to give up. She shouldn't just assume the worst. If the guy wanted to kill her, why wait? The longer she remained alive, the more likely she was to survive. At least she hoped, desperately, that this was the case.

The small of Azar's back began to hurt. At least she'd worn pants and a shirt under her overcoat instead of a dress. It was odd to be glad about a thing like that under the circumstances. Her brain was going off in all directions at once. She appreciated the reprieve. She hated the reprieve. The balance of fear and relief and muscular pain was a unique blend of torture. She was deathly tired and anxious, and scared to the core of her body as she waited for the kidnapper's next move.

98. Brenda Smith

"Let's order some food," Brenda said. "I need a burger."

"Me too."

Brenda was delighted to discover that Mary liked burgers. They'd been at the bar for about an hour. As they talked, the cop in Brenda scanned the room. A few more people had come in, but no one walked with a limp. Two youths took the next booth and held hands, obviously as much in love as Brenda was. The tipsy students laughed their asses off over darts. A young woman in the booth behind Brenda kept complaining in a squeaky voice, upset about everything from her boyfriend to the human condition.

But the tall man at the bar activated something in Brenda. He seemed to be monitoring them now. Another homophobic asshole in this LGBTQ-friendly city. He pulled out his wallet, and Brenda saw a driver's license, a red credit card, and some folded bills. He left a few on the worn wood of the bar and walked out.

"Bren, where are you?" Mary waved her hand in front of Brenda's face.

"What?"

"She was asking what you wanted with your burger."

"Sorry." Brenda blushed as she looked up at the server. "Fries, please. Light on salt."

"Coming right up." The young woman departed with a nod, and they held hands.

"What a place," Mary said.

Brenda didn't quite know what Mary meant. Looking around, she noticed that the large man had dropped something. Brenda released Mary's hand, jumped from her chair, and walked to the bar. With each step, she was increasingly sure.

Holy shit.

It was the killer's red business card.

"I'll be right back," Brenda mouthed to Mary, who watched her with an ironic smile. Uncertain if Mary had understood, Brenda took off toward the door, narrowly avoiding a collision with a bar stool. Her head buzzed. Two twenty-something guys got out of their booth, accidentally blocking her way.

Exasperated by the delay, Brenda finally reached the door and pushed it open. No one outside. He'd had plenty of time to get into his car and drive off. Brenda ran north to the nearest street corner, nearly wiping out as she stumbled on a root growing through the sidewalk.

An empty street.

The man was nowhere. She'd found the killer; she was sure of it. And then she'd lost him.

99. *Azar Bayat*

Azar drifted in and out of sleep. Her mouth felt like sandpaper and tasted like a bad memory. She was so exhausted she barely had the energy to be scared. Thirst was becoming her primary concern. Still, how lucky that she hadn't had too much coffee or water this afternoon. Azar knew this didn't affect her chances of survival, but she couldn't have handled the additional humiliation of peeing her pants.

She thought of Bahar. Soon enough, her sister would text her and be surprised by the lack of response. At some point, Bahar would share her worries with their parents. Azar had mentioned the mosque and even sent the picture. But that wouldn't be much help. Their car ride had felt long; they were nowhere near the mosque.

Then she noticed something.

The corner of the duct tape covering her mouth was loose. Azar could feel the air coming through as she inhaled. Could she get the rest of the tape off? She rubbed her face on the back of the seat without success.

She wasn't about to give up so easily. She kept trying.

And trying.

And then, it happened. A slight tug on her cheek. Carefully, Azar moved her head an inch or two in the opposite direction, then back. The duct tape was coming off. All the drool she was producing must have helped dislodge it. Unbelievable: one moment, she was struggling with her face against the seat, and the next, her mouth was free, the tape hanging limply on the back of the seat next to her face.

She could breathe.

She could also scream.

Azar screamed.

A croak came out, and she coughed and coughed. Her throat was sore. Soon, an actual scream arose from her chest, hesitant at first, then enormous in the small space. Azar coughed again and screamed again, competing with the sound of rain. If she didn't save herself, who would save her? Azar visualized someone hearing her. A neighbor walking a dog. A delivery driver. A mom with a stroller.

Her throat became dry sooner than she'd expected. She couldn't scream forever. She just lay there, breathing, listening to the sound of rain on the garage roof. She counted her breaths until she reached three hundred. All the movement had warmed her up, but she was getting cold again.

There must be a way out of this. She'd give anything to be Proust's Albertine, a prisoner by agreement who briefly tries to appease the hesitant Marcel before returning to her own story. How absurd it was, thinking of Proust at a moment like this. Her life, with all its intellectual pursuits and ambitions, seemed light years away. Azar's mind was blurry. She forced out another scream through her parched mouth.

100. The Corrector

The Corrector felt great as he unlocked the door and entered the house. He was getting used to Mom's smell and might even miss it when she was finally done and buried.

He heard the bartender call that woman *Detective*, and something told him that it was him, The Corrector, that she was after. He watched her and her girlfriend for a while, picking up snippets of their conversation. Fucking lesbos.

As he sipped his drink and watched them holding hands and all, he kept hearing: *the murder case, the killer.* Each time, he had to stop himself from grinning. He'd fooled them all; he had. They would never catch him. They had nothing on him. They were only there because Sania Jamison lived nearby. Big deal. Nothing connected her to The Corrector. He winced, remembering how it had gone down. But that was another story. Better keep it where it belonged: in the past.

Hesitantly, The Corrector approached the garage door. Not a sound. His prisoner must have fallen asleep. Just as well. He was too elated by his brush-up with the lady cop to worry about the next steps in his corrective action.

He danced to the kitchen and stomped around, his big fists in the air. A couple of his red business cards lay on the counter. Just a reminder for himself to stick to his mission. He liked to look at them. They made him proud.

The Corrector was out of breath from all the stomping, and his head spun. As he stood there, leaning on the counter and catching his breath, he wondered if his latest action had made the news yet. He walked upstairs, feeling the effort in his ankles from the long day. In his bedroom, he sat on the edge of the bed, poured himself a drink, and flipped his laptop open.

He googled *Portland, kidnapping,* and *Muslim,* and nothing recent came up.

Too soon. Tomorrow, the world would know.

SATURDAY, NOVEMBER 23

101. The Corrector

The Corrector awoke and stretched without opening his eyes. He was in his bed, still fully dressed, his half-open laptop next to him. It was dark outside, the rain's patter constant on the roof. He had no recollection of going to sleep. He pressed the button on the laptop, but the stupid battery was dead. He pulled out his phone.

2:02 a.m.

Shit, the Muslim girl. He'd better get her out of the car. He sure didn't want to have to clean her poop or have the backseat soaked in piss. Fuck.

With some effort, he shifted in bed until he was close enough to the edge to swing his feet over. He pushed himself up with his arms and sat there. He'd hit a home run picking up his latest target. It couldn't have gone any smoother. He felt around in bed for a bourbon bottle and found one, still half-full. What a relief. For now, The Corrector took only the tiniest sip. Too much work to do. He took another, sealed the bottle, and tossed it aside.

He'd bring her into the house. He wanted to interrogate her. To ask her what the fuck had made her come to his country. He wanted to understand her motives, that's all. He was curious why these people believed those fucked up things, whatever they were. He'd tell her about the real America, the country he was fighting for. Would she listen? Hell, of course, she would. What choice did she have?

The living room was a mess. Now that he didn't have to take care of Mom, he really should pick up all this crap. It surprised him, but he was embarrassed about how his prisoner would feel. A hell of a way to spend her final hours. But it wasn't like he could toss his mother in the garbage bin and leave her on the curb for pickup.

He'd take her to Mom's old bedroom upstairs.

The Corrector rose, plugged his laptop in to charge, and walked down the hall to check the room. It sure was an excellent fit for the task. Mom had been paranoid about intruders and had him board up the windows. A crazy idea, but she'd preferred sitting there in the darkness, watching her little TV. The bathroom was tiny as fuck, but who cared.

The medicine cabinet made him worry. Too many metal parts, plus the mirror itself; she might break it and use a piece of glass as a weapon. He found a screwdriver in a pile of tools in the corner of his room and took his time with the cabinet, trying not to get frustrated. The rusty old screws resisted, but The Corrector was strong. He collected the screws in his pocket and took the whole cabinet out. He didn't know what the hell to do with it, so he just dragged it into his bedroom for now and moved some of his dirty laundry from under the bed to clear the space for it.

As he walked downstairs, The Corrector felt a little shaky. His foot buzzed with a steady ache, and he held on to the railing. The house was freezing, so he upped the heat on the stupid thermostat.

The prisoner of war needed a drink of water. He grabbed one of his empty bourbon bottles from the counter. As he rose, he almost lost his balance; his head was spinning. The Corrector leaned on the wall until he felt better. He went over to the sink and filled the bottle without bothering to rinse it first.

She'd want food, too. But what difference was food going to make? The Corrector was about to dispatch the woman, so where did the idea of feeding her come in?

"Stupid," Dad said.

"Stupid?"

Was this Dad? He looked a little weird. Shorter, smaller than

271

Dad. Hell!

"What the fuck are you doing here?" The Corrector asked.

The man grinned. "You know what."

The Corrector wasn't interested anymore. The bottle in his hand felt like a joke: good old bourbon replaced by water. The fucking opposite of a miracle. He paused by the garage door, his hand on the knob.

102. Azar Bayat

A squeak jolted Azar awake. The light slapped her eyes with a shocking brightness. For a moment, she was blinded. She wished she could rub her eyes, but her arms were still bound.

It took a few seconds for her eyes to adjust. Shivering from the cold, Azar scanned the upper parts of the garage she could see from her position in the backseat. All sorts of boxes, and on the wall opposite her, a target, as if the kidnapper practiced shooting right here. She couldn't see the man himself, then his figure rose next to the broken side window.

Something was about to happen; unbearable tension hung in the air. The man would be mad about the damage. To anger him like that, without anything to show for it, might have been a colossal mistake.

He stood there for a long time as if zoned out. Then he leaned over the car door, his hand on the door handle. How large that hand was. And his face, terrifying yet distant, as if he was thinking of something else. His baseball hat was gone, exposing a short haircut on a balding head. And his face, round, imposing, inexpressive. Everything collapsed into tightness inside her.

103. The Corrector

The side window, broken. Fuck. He should've expected it. The damn Muslim must have kicked it out with her feet. Now, The Corrector would have to take the car in. All he needed in the middle of the rainy season.

He stood there for a minute or two, looking at the girl. Her eyes were on him, too. They were serious, not distracted like most people's.

He found himself smiling once he calmed down about the whole glass thing. At least she'd tried something. She wasn't like most Muslims; he could tell there was spunk in her. He opened the car door and leaned over to untie her hands from the buckle. She was shivering; the garage was cold like a motherfucker. He'd forgotten about that. The duct tape was already gone from her mouth. An oversight, he had to admit. He'd left her in the car too long.

"No screaming, or else." His voice came out scratchy; he cleared his throat.

The Muslim girl was quiet anyway, her face red. She looked so different, like another species. For a moment, The Corrector wanted to ask her name, but he changed his mind. Better off not knowing. He'd check her purse later.

"I'll free up your legs," he said. "No funny business, you hear me?"

"Funny business?" Her accent was strong. She was awful young. In her twenties, narrow-faced, her long dark hair a loose bundle all around her. The Corrector remembered how she'd taken off her hijab as soon as she stepped out of the mosque. Where was the fucking thing? Her purse? For a minute, he was worried she might have dropped the hijab when he grabbed her, but in the end, it made no difference.

She stared at him like she was lost or something. The Corrector cut the duct tape around her ankles with a box cutter he'd picked up from his dad's toolbox. Then he scrambled out of the backseat.

"Get out."

"What will you do to me?"

"Get out."

It felt awkward to watch her squirm to make it out of the car with her hands still bound by the duct tape, so he didn't look. Out of the corner of his eye, he saw her shuffling along the backseat until her feet fell to the ground. Her body kept sliding until it collapsed in a sitting position right there by the car door. Oops.

"Free my hands." She looked up at him from the garage floor, challenge in her dark eyes.

"If you say so." The Corrector was amused by her forwardness. He planned to do that anyway. There were rules about treating prisoners of war. He bent over her to cut the tape.

As he rose, blood rushed to his head. For a second, he was afraid he might faint. If he did, surely, she'd escape. She could open the garage door just by pulling the string. The fucking thing just hung there; she didn't have to be a brain scientist to figure it out. The Corrector held on to the side of the car, waiting for his moment of weakness to pass. Luckily, she'd missed it.

"Water," she said. A statement, not a question.

He walked over to the side of the car where he'd left the bourbon bottle he'd filled for her. "Here."

She looked surprised for a second, then took the bottle into her hands and began gulping like the world was ending. She drank and drank until the bottle was empty.

"I'm freezing." Desperation in her eyes as she looked at him. "I need the bathroom."

"It's upstairs." The Corrector pointed up. Who knew how much English she understood.

It didn't seem like she had already gone in the car. Nice. He felt bad about leaving her there for so long. His duty to his country was one thing, but this was a little sloppy. Oh, hell. Who cared at this point?

104. Azar Bayat

Azar was trying to read the man. If she could read him, she might find a way to save herself. He seemed preoccupied with something else. Was he waiting for instructions? For inspiration? Was he on drugs?

"This way." He pointed toward the door leading inside the house.

Azar obeyed at first, but she slowed as she approached the door. This seemed like a puzzle. If she went in, she'd never get out again, but if she refused to go in, she'd never leave the garage. Both options were unacceptable. Azar was drawn to the warmth she expected to feel inside. Her nose was still stuffed, but the smell of rot in the air had not gone away. Did he keep a garbage bin inside the garage?

"Go ahead." The man's voice behind her back was strangely high and tense, as if he wasn't sure what he was doing. His hand was on her shoulder, large and heavy.

Azar didn't want to look back. She turned the handle and pushed the door open.

When she raised her left foot to step inside, air rushed in from the house, and Azar's hand went up to her mouth. Warmth and the smell of decay amplified. She turned her head at her kidnapper in a silent question, but the man's blank face offered no answer. Azar worked her hardest to push down the nausea.

"What's that smell?" She already knew. The bodies of other victims.

"It's my mom. Sorry about that."

"What?" Azar was lost. *Mom?* She must have misheard. She shouldn't ask random questions. She shouldn't.

"Come on, come on." The man's big hand on her shoulder again, pushing.

Should she collapse right there on the floor or be propelled forward? Azar let her feet carry her in.

105. Naseem Nazari

Naseem lay in the morgue and thought about his life. The more time passed, the less concentrated his thoughts were. Now he was thinking, living, remembering—and now he was as if in suspense for minutes, even hours. Little happened until the next thought arrived, interrupting his growing stupor.

None of this bothered Naseem. The progression from life to death was natural, even if he hadn't expected this period in between. What bothered him was the unfairness of taking the life of another.

The young woman in the row below him kept sending strong intuitive signals to the detective. He felt those signals going through him, too. The young woman was much more upset by her death, and, at her age, this made perfect sense. Naseem would've felt the same had he not already believed, ever since he'd come to the United States, that his life was nearing its end. Not because he hadn't liked living here— quite the opposite. His life had become too comfortable for the past he came from. This was too complicated to explain, but Naseem no longer owed anyone any explanations.

His present state reminded him of the time when Aisha's cancer had taken a final turn for the worse and all the medical options were exhausted.

"I'm relieved," she'd said.

The sweat on her forehead, her pale skin. The chemo had taken her hair long before.

"Relieved? Don't you want to live?" He immediately regretted saying this.

"I do, but not like this." Aisha moved her palm horizontally over her prone torso.

Naseem didn't know what to say to that.

And now, there was something appealing in this: existing without having to worry about his body. He wanted to use this time well. As well as he could. He wanted his murderer to be arrested. He focused on helping the young woman below lead the detective to the killer. He still didn't know how this worked, but he could feel the detective receiving their message.

106. Brenda Smith

Brenda lay in bed, unable to sleep. Her head was splitting. Next to her, Mary made a soft rhythmical murmur, a cute version of snoring. Through the window, the sky was dark. No stars tonight, only the omnipresent city glare.

Brenda hoped she could get a hold of the sketch artist in the morning while the perp's face was still fresh in her memory. Unfortunate, to sit within five yards of the killer all night without knowing. But Brenda couldn't blame herself for that.

She was happy her intuition was correct. She was getting close. The killer wouldn't drive to a bar across town. He lived in the neighborhood.

A car honked outside; the arc of lights crossed the ceiling. Brenda was sweating; she pulled the covers off and lay naked, her skin taking in the apartment's cool. She should get a thinner blanket. She'd forgotten how much heat was generated by another person in bed. How different her life was becoming. Brenda was afraid to feel happy, but she did.

With a bite of guilt, she thought of her dad. Should she call him again? She hated the thought and was in no mood to keep considering it. She turned to her side, facing Mary's sleeping figure.

107. The Corrector

Holy fuck. His prisoner was throwing up. Hell. Was the stink that bad? As she vomited, The Corrector just stood there, not knowing what to do. It was taking forever. He didn't want to watch but couldn't walk away either. She retched and retched, producing little. By the time she was through, she was out of breath.

"Done?"

She looked at him in a funny way, like his question had made no sense.

"Up there." He pointed at the stairs that led to the second floor.

That's when she saw his mom, just lying there.

"You..." That was all that she managed to say. Didn't finish it.

"I'm awful sorry about that."

"Did you say...did you say it was your mom?" She looked at him like she was trying to see the answer inside his head.

"She died the other day." The Corrector wasn't quite sure how many days had passed. It seemed like a long time. Who the fuck cared, anyway? The old bird was dead and gone, that was all. And before too long, this Muslim would be gone, too. Now here, now gone. How quickly things changed.

"What happened?" she asked.

"What's with all the fucking questions?"

She said nothing.

"Heart failure. She was on hospice care." The Corrector pointed at the huge high-tech bed and the whole mess around it.

"I'm sorry."

Ha. She was sorry like he was a rubber duck. But it was a nice thing to say. The hospice care nurse would be back on Monday. He'd have to process his prisoner by then. That was plenty of time.

"Upstairs." He pointed.

And just like that, she went. Reasonable-like.

On the landing, she stopped and turned to him, her brows raised. Asking for directions. Still, The Corrector couldn't help noticing her eyes darting about, taking things in. Thinking on her feet. Anyone in their right mind would do that.

"Second door over there." He gestured toward Mom's bedroom. "There's a bathroom in there. I'll get you food." It occurred to him that there was no need to bring her water in a bourbon bottle. Oh well. "If you try anything stupid, it's over, you understand?" The Corrector dragged his index finger across his throat. He'd seen an actor do it in some movie.

"Why are you doing this?" she piped up.

Curious as hell. What was it they said about cats and curiosity?

"Shut up and go in." His voice was louder than he'd expected.

"There you go," Dad's voice.

So, Dad was around, too? The Muslim girl obeyed. She opened the door and walked in. Her hand grabbed the handle on the other side as if she was about to close the door behind her instead of waiting for him to do it. The light in the room was still on.

"Wait," The Corrector said.

She stood there, her hand still on the handle.

"What's your name, anyway?" The Corrector regretted asking the moment he did. Slippery slope. But her purse was still in the car; he didn't feel like fishing for it under the seat just now.

"My name is Azar." She looked straight at him, her eyes like lakes of darkness. "Azar Bayat."

108. Azar Bayat

A small room, three by four meters. Shabby gray paint on the walls, a nondescript brown couch along one of them. A chair. A window boarded up. Azar shivered, considering the people who might have passed through here. Had any of them survived? Unlikely. If they had, the kidnapper would have been caught by now.

She went to the window and tried to pull on one of the boards. It was nailed in solid. She couldn't get a good grip in any case: not enough space between the boards to fit her fingers—just enough of a gap to see the darkness behind the window, the fence around a dusty backyard.

Azar examined the nail heads sunk into the wood in a way that made it impossible to get them out without a tool. She pushed and pulled on the boards this way and that. They wouldn't budge. Her insides were still cold from the hours in the garage, but her extremities began to warm up. She took her coat off and dropped it on the couch. The nauseating smell from downstairs was strong. The bathroom was minimal, just like the room: a narrow shower stall, a toilet, a sink, a bar of soap, and a stained old towel. No mirror. Too bad; she might have been able to break it and use one of the shards as a weapon.

Azar sat on the toilet.

When she was done, she drank and drank from the tap until she felt like her belly was about to explode from all the water.

With the satiation of thirst, Azar felt exhausted. Her body didn't hurt as much anymore. The fatigue dulled the panic. She tried to push fatalism away. Her fate was *not* out of her hands. It wasn't. The rain kept pounding on the roof of the house, different in tone up here than down in the garage but no less persistent. Heat poured in from the vent in the floor.

Azar was tempted to scream but constrained herself. No one would hear except for her kidnapper. She'd already tried that. No, she had to be shrewd and do something unexpected. She had to be patient.

How could she?

Azar tried to remember abduction scenes from books and TV, but her mind was disjointed. She had to find her own way out. She couldn't seem to catch her breath. She paced the room, her inhales shallow, her chest tight. Her eyes couldn't stop scanning the space for something she could use to her advantage.

109. The Corrector

The Corrector was relieved as fuck to have the prisoner in Mom's bedroom. A weight off his back. Now, he had time to plan. He sat there, next to his mother's body, thinking. Mom's colors had gone darker and bluer; he tried not to look.

The Corrector opened his eyes. He must have dozed off. It came back to him that he'd promised the Muslim girl some food. Oh, hell! What was her name? Azar Bayat. It had stuck in his brain for some reason.

He was torn about feeding her. She didn't have much longer to live, so it didn't matter. Still, he wanted to come through on this one promise. What on earth would he feed her? For a moment, his head was blank. He'd been buying takeout for the most part when he bothered to eat at all. Then he remembered. He had tons of juices, sauces, and other nonsense left over from Mom. The old bird sure didn't need them now.

The Corrector walked to the kitchen. Half a loaf of bread in the fridge. Nice. He dug around in the cabinet next to the sink and pulled out two jars of applesauce, a can of tuna, and a bottle of apple juice. Not too fucking shabby. He was happy with this solution as he carried the food upstairs, the bread bag under his arm, the small jars held tightly in his large hands. He didn't have a free hand for the handrail, so he walked up carefully. It would be dumb to fall and break his neck when his corrective action was going so well.

The Corrector was a little winded by the time he reached the top. He stood there for a few seconds, catching his breath. His hands began to sweat. The apple juice jar, a glass thing, might slip out and fall. Hell. In any case, he had to unlock the door. He put the whole bundle on the carpet by the door and pulled the key out of his jeans pocket.

She would've heard him coming, so The Corrector carefully pushed the door open and stood there a second to ensure she didn't surprise him with some clever trick. But there she was, on the couch, a small figure.

"Why are you keeping your dead mother here?"

110. Azar Bayat

Azar wasn't sure why she'd asked that. She was shaking, and still, an ironic voice in her head said, *A non sequitur if ever there was one.* She was mad at herself for that question. She'd spent too much time with her nose in books, and now she might never... Azar stopped her thoughts from entering that spiral. She had to stay in the moment.

The man stood in the doorway next to a small pile of cans, jars, and half a bread bag. His broad face didn't have much of an expression. Azar's mouth began to water at the sight of all the food, but the edge of nausea she felt from the smell also sharpened. Her body did its own thing, however determined she was to survive this ordeal. How long had it been since she had anything to eat? She had no idea what time it was.

"I...I'll take care of my mom later." The man seemed stumped by her question, his lips pursed.

"What are you going to do with me?"

He stared at her for a few seconds. "Don't ask too many questions."

The smell of alcohol from the kidnapper cut through the smell of death. Azar's thoughts ran in random directions. If he was a drinker, her chances were better. She'd seen drunken men, their slow moves. He was bigger than most but seemed lost. Confused. He looked like some self-assured men in Iran when they crossed a line and stepped away from decency. Azar knew that look.

He kicked into gear again, enough to pick up all the items with his large hands. He entered and piled them on the other end of the couch. Then, without another glance at her, he stomped out, shutting the door behind him. The key clicked in the lock. Had she missed her chance to catch him by surprise? But how was she supposed to tackle a man twice her size, without a weapon, without anything?

Azar scooched over and examined the small pile. Applesauce, a can of tuna fish, apple juice, bread. As if there was a child in the house. This odd collage of food items sent her salivating; her hands shook as she removed the plastic knob that kept the bread bag sealed. Her hand made its way into the bag; two slices came out. Azar bit into both at once and began chewing quickly and without thinking.

Swallowing proved harder; she was too stressed. She had to force herself to relax and listen to the hunger. Her hands were already opening the applesauce, which joined the bread in her mouth. After being so hungry, eating in this room was life-affirming and humiliating. She remembered the sumptuous family gatherings in Iran, the tables overflowing with food, the happy faces. She wished she could subtract the last few months from her life and magically transport herself back there.

Azar reviewed the can. *Chicken of the Sea, Solid White Albacore Tuna in Water, 5 oz.* An underage mermaid with a mindless grin sat on the company logo, a butter stick torch in her hand. Azar pulled on the tab. The burst of smell momentarily cut through the stink in the house, sharp but alluring.

She had more bread but no tool for the tuna. Azar used her fingers. Once the tiny can was empty, she ran her fingertip along the edge, collecting the remaining small bits.

Five slices remained in the bread bag. Azar put them aside for later and laughed at herself. Her life might be ending, and she was saving bread.

On the deepest level, she didn't believe her life was ending. She'd find a way out.

She wanted to stay alert and analyze her situation, but the food made her groggy. Her eyes were closing.

111. The Corrector

Now that the prisoner was taken care of, The Corrector could relax. He threw a towel over the vomit near the garage door and headed upstairs.

In his room, he poured himself some bourbon and opened his laptop. Forty-nine likes on his last Discord post. Not too shabby. He reread his message, feeling proud of himself. A smile grew on his face.

> **The Corrector**
> Get ready to here about another corrective action in
> Portland. Down with Muslims & terrorists. Make America
> Great Again.

Two responses: *You said it man* from Krak, and *Don't mind if you do* from a new user, GoGetThem83. Nice. Knowing that his prisoner was in the next room at this very moment made The Corrector feel extra strong.

He needed a clever way to dispose of her. She might fit alongside Mom in her high-tech bed. But seriously, he wanted to do something cool with her body, something fucking spectacular. He'd already used a warehouse and a nature setting twice. He needed a good follow-up.

The Tilikum Bridge, with its fucked-up name? Ha! Good luck getting a body there. He'd have to settle for something simpler. The Corrector's mind felt dull, like a fucking safety razor with hair stuck to it. A nuisance.

He could take her to Mt. Hood and set her up amid the snow. That might work, but what if he got stopped for some reason with a body in his car? Fuck, a drive that long with a body sounded too complicated. And when he got there, it was not like the stupid mountain would be deserted, ready for The Corrector to do his thing. Fucking tourists all over the place, like this was California.

He had to think, really think. He should have planned, but he'd had no problem finding a good place the last three times. The fucking inspiration was not with him this time. He was tired. He poured himself another drink.

Everything was quiet in Mom's old bedroom across the wall. Good. He sipped his bourbon, thinking of his mother. Once Mom's body was removed, he'd never, ever see her again.

This thought caught in The Corrector's throat, and he began crying. Sobbing like a fucking baby. He couldn't stop.

112. Brenda Smith

Brenda tried to breathe to push the anger out of her. Fine, she'd call. She grabbed her phone and found her dad's number in her call history. As she pressed Call, she was already sweating, her chest tight.

A click. One ring, another, a third. She should have hung up but sat frozen, listening to the rings. Abruptly, a crackle broke the line.

"Hello." A female voice.

"I...My name is Brenda Smith. I'm trying to reach my father."

"Oh, dear. Brenda." A pause. "I've heard so much about you."

"About *me*?" Brenda repeated, feeling stupid. She didn't care if the woman had heard her dad's twisted, homophobic version of her life.

"Yes, about you. I'm so sorry, darling. Your dad died." The factual tone of this delivery didn't match the news, as if the woman didn't care. And as Brenda listened, she felt no emotion either.

No, that was wrong. She did feel something.

Relief.

The next moment, Brenda felt terrible about it.

She was relieved she didn't have to visit her jerk of a father and struggle to forgive him on his deathbed.

"When did he die?"

"Last night. He died in his sleep."

"Oh. I guess that's good?"

"As good as he could have wished for, under the circumstances."

"And you...are you his partner?" Brenda knew she sounded like a cop when she asked this, but it was a reasonable question.

"Your father and I have been together these last two years." The woman's voice remained flat as if none of it mattered. Maybe it didn't. Spending the last two years of Dad's life with him must have been something. It sounded like a miserable role.

"What's your name?" Brenda did her best to soften her voice. She didn't have an axe to grind with this woman.

"Lucy."

"Lucy. Hi Lucy. Well…" Brenda was at a loss for words to say to this person, the other side of the final cold, meaningless relationship in her father's life. "I'm sorry."

"I'm sorry too, darling." The woman said. "He loved you very much."

Bullshit, Brenda wanted to scream. *Bullshit. He never cared about me. He never saw the person I am, and he never will.* But she didn't have to explain any of that to the woman on the other end of the line.

"Thank you," she said instead.

113. Azar Bayat

Azar awoke with a start. The room was hot. With a soft hiss, the vent pumped warm air into the small space. Azar's shirt was soaked in sweat. She had no idea what time it was; then she noticed lines of light through the slats in the boards covering the window. She shivered, her stomach cramping. She rolled off the couch and pulled down her pants as she ran to the bathroom.

She made it just in time and sat on the toilet, panic beating hard against her chest, a whirring motor somewhere below the skin. Blood pulsed through her aching head. Everything was over; she was not getting out of this. And another thought rushed to fight it: she'd make it through. She'd find a way. She would not give up.

Azar washed her hands. Soap. The bar wasn't new; it must have been here before. There were no other personal items.

She approached the window and aligned her right eye with a gap between two boards. Why did she always use her right eye to stare into microscopes and her right ear to listen to the phone? And what did this have to do with her situation? Her brain kept spinning out these useless trajectories of thought.

The window looked out onto a trashy backyard. All Azar could see through her narrow viewpoint was an old lawn mower, a car tire, and an assortment of weeds growing over everything. A fence to her left. To her right, a blank white wall of another building. Crows perched on the trees, watching her. The rain kept pounding on the roof of the house.

Azar was hungry again. Slowly, she ate two slices of bread, trying to make them last. Only three more. She checked the tuna can, which sat awkwardly on the carpet beside the coach. She remembered finishing it off—and indeed, it was empty. She tossed the can over her head, surprising herself with this careless gesture.

Azar returned to the bathroom and drank some water from the tap. She would have loved to change out of her sweaty shirt. Something else was on her mind, but she couldn't quite pin it down.

114. The Corrector

Time went by, and The Corrector was beginning to feel sleepy.

"You're fucking up again, boy, ain't you?" Dad frowned from across his mother's dead body. The Corrector was startled; he'd thought he was upstairs in his room. He didn't remember coming down.

"Shut up, Dad. I've got it under control."

"Like heck you do. You have no spine; that's what's wrong with you, boy. I could break you with one hand." His father clenched his fist. "How long are you going to keep her alive?"

Something about this struck The Corrector in a weird way. Something was off. He looked closer, and his father's fist was tiny. Hell. The Corrector clenched his fist. How much larger it was.

"Bullshit, Dad." He was almost screaming now. "I've already achieved more than you ever even tried."

"See what you've done to your poor mother." His dad was small in the chair across Mom's body.

"Fuck you, Dad." He said it calmly; he wouldn't bother with his father anymore.

The Corrector considered the prisoner upstairs. The soundproofing in the house was not worth shit. She must have heard him talking to Dad. Hell, what did it matter? The truth was, The Corrector hated her. Azar Bayat. He hated her, but he wanted to understand why. It just didn't make sense for her to leave her own country and come live here. This nonsense irritated the fuck out of him.

Azar Bayat. Azar Bayat. He kept repeating it in a threatening voice until her first and last names merged into one big blob of anger.

Azar Bayat.

He hated her for getting him into this. Why couldn't she practice her fucking religion back where she came from?

He'd show her. He found the old Black Sabbath CD and popped it in on repeat. Ozzy's voice crackled in the air. It was evident from the voice that Ozzy and The Corrector were on the same page. He turned the volume to 6, 7, 8. Let her feel what hell sounds like. And if he happened to talk to Dad again, she'd hear nothing.

115. Azar Bayat

The silence exploded with drums and bass, shaking Azar out of her reverie. Something deeply familiar about this sound... after a few more measures, she recognized the album. *Sabotage.* She'd listened to Black Sabbath since childhood and loved Ozzy much more than the band's later vocalists. How shocking to hear this music here. She found herself on her feet, walking around the room. It was helping her think—and to feel less desperate. Her steps aligned themselves with the beat.

It occurred to her that she should take advantage of the loud music to check the door. She yanked the door handle and examined the keyhole and the lock frame. Solid. Azar crossed the small room and tried the boards on the window again. If only she had something to pry them off the wall. She growled in desperation.

Had she made a mistake when she obediently walked into the room? Azar forced herself not to focus on second-guessing and self-recrimination. She was shivering in her sweaty clothes even as anxiety burned through her. Her mosque visit seemed like months ago. She was thirsty again, so she entered the bathroom and drank using her palm. Then she resumed walking to the music, listening to Ozzy's edgy voice.

116. The Corrector

Fuck it. The Corrector knew he had to get out. Otherwise, he'd spend his day drinking, dozing, blasting Black Sabbath, and arguing with his father. He had no inspiration for what to do with his prisoner. Not yet.

At least his car was no longer occupied. He grabbed his wallet and jacket. He was a little wobbly on his feet as he entered the garage. Seeing the car, just sitting there, gave him a strange feeling, like nothing had happened. Had it? He hesitated, waiting for his head to clear.

Fuck. The broken side window. He forgot about it. The Corrector opened the back door and saw the roll of duct tape next to the seat. He reached into the car and threw the duct tape at the garage door. It made a thud as it bounced off the wall onto the gray concrete floor.

He examined the damage to the car's interior. Shit! He'd have to take the car in when he was done with Azar Bayat. Right now, he didn't care. He wasn't even mad. Hell, he would've done the same thing.

He got into the driver's seat and pressed the button on the visor. The garage door slid up behind him, opening into a gray, wet day. A hint of perfume or something else feminine was mixed with the usual smell of stale cigarettes. The Corrector had to grin at himself for how well things were going. He needed a little break; that was all. He pulled out of the garage, driving extra carefully in case his coordination was not up to snuff.

The funny thing was, he wasn't sure where he was going. Finding another bar out of the neighborhood was tempting as fuck, but with all the drink already in him, he'd just fall asleep if he had any more.

No, he'd just drive. He took a left on Martin Luther King Boulevard, heading south. A mass of gray hung over the city.

Not too many cars were out on this rainy Saturday afternoon. His backseat must be soaking by now, but fuck it. It would dry out. As The Corrector drove, he checked off the bridges in his mind. Steel Bridge, Broadway Bridge, Burnside Bridge. He'd been around these bridges all his life. He could walk to the Willamette from his house if he wanted to.

He was passing Morrison Bridge when he knew where he was headed. The place by the river where he'd laid Sania Jamison to rest. Something drew him there. He lit a cigarette and smoked, trying not to think about anything.

Hawthorne Bridge. The clusters of tents on the roadside by the overpass exit. The Corrector felt terrible about the homeless. They were good Americans. All these immigrants were flooding Portland and taking other people's jobs and houses.

As he passed Holgate, the river on his right veered away. Just another neighborhood, West Moreland or whatever the fuck it was. He knew he wouldn't see the Willamette for another couple of miles. MLK had turned into McLoughlin by now. It stretched out ahead of him, two rows of tall trees guarding the boulevard. Pretty, but something dark about it, too, like he was driving on the road to hell or something.

The Corrector didn't know why it struck him that way. A slow Audi ahead of him annoyed him. What was wrong with American cars? Fancy motherfucker. The Corrector switched lanes and gave the driver the finger as he pressed the gas pedal.

117. Dmitry Volkov

Dmitry's vision was blurry; the shapes around him contradicted one another, failing to form a single image. Rectangles, circles, shadows. White, so much white, like being inside a pillow. He rubbed his eyes, feeling the lead of fatigue in his brain. Why was he so tired? As he blinked against the whiteness, shapes began to materialize: the ceiling, the walls, the sheets. The smell of industrial cleaning supplies and plastic. At last, he could see a figure, a woman in a chair next to his bed.

Rita.

With an effort, he moved his heavy head and looked around. He was in a small white room with a compact sink by the door. Why were his feet facing the door? Cabinets lined the walls, a small label on each that Dmitry couldn't make out.

Through the glass window, he could see a uniformed cop stationed outside in the hallway.

Rita was reading a magazine and hadn't noticed that he was awake. Dmitry loved her face, so familiar after all these years. He loved the position of her head, a little tilted now, the way she always held it while reading. He'd missed her.

Brief snippets of memories came back. He and Boris in the darkness of the jewelry store. A shot. No, multiple shots. He didn't want to remember the outcome. The pain in his side pulsed to life. He moaned, and Rita dropped her magazine and jumped up from her chair.

"Dmitry! Are you okay? Should I call the nurse?"

"How's Boris?" His voice came out hoarse, and he tried to clear his throat. Another powerful blast of pain zipped against his ribs, and he moaned again.

"Oh, Dmitry! I'm so sorry."

Rita's face went expressionless; he could tell she was considering the best way to say it. And in his gut, he already knew.

"Boris didn't make it." Rita's hands covered her mouth.

"Oh, no. Oh, no. God, no."

This couldn't be real.

"What the hell were you two thinking?" Rita sounded more puzzled than mad.

There was no good answer.

In just a day, all meaning was gone from his life. His family was destroyed forever. He'd get years of prison time. His mom and dad would be dead before he was out. They'd never forgive him. Natasha would grow up ashamed of her father. He would never forgive himself.

He wanted to take it back, as in a friendly chess game.

"I'm sorry." He couldn't think of anything else to say.

"You're sorry?" Rita's flashing eyes—not the kind of fire Dmitry longed to see in them. But she contained herself.

He knew this wasn't a reunion. This was a final separation.

118. The Corrector

As The Corrector entered Milwaukie, the Willamette River appeared on his right again, a broad blue line. It made him happy, but only for a moment. Too much on his mind. That's what happens when you are committed to serving your country.

Twilight began to settle. Just by the bend in the river ahead, where he'd left Sania, he saw police cars, an ambulance, and blinking lights. Why now? Hadn't they already picked up the body? Wait, how long had it been? It was a Saturday. Last week or the week before?

His first impulse was to turn off the road, but no exits were ahead. Oh, well. He told himself to calm down. He was just another driver passing by.

As he approached, it became clear that the whole fucking thing was unrelated. A torn-apart blue Honda smoked by the side of the road ahead; an orange semi towered over it. Two bodies lay covered on stretchers.

This was fucked up. No trace of his corrective action in this place, and yet, someone else was already lying dead less than one hundred yards away. New death every day. The traffic had ground to a halt. Fuckety fuck! Why in the world had he driven here? Like flirting with danger.

His speedometer hovered around five mph. The smell of tires and something else burning reached inside his car through the broken window. The collision was fifty yards ahead, then twenty, ten.

The scene was laid before him. The Honda had no chance against the semi. The whole right side of the car was squashed to smithereens. The Corrector noticed a tall woman in a long blue dress meandering about in the drizzle, blood on her head and in her hair. The Honda's driver, maybe. Her face was expressionless, like she was absent from her body. He was surprised they let her stay so close to the accident site. She looked familiar, but The Corrector couldn't quite place her.

Everything was in slow motion, the woman's face just floating there. She knelt beside the two prone bodies, rose, and began pacing again. Nobody paid her much attention. The Corrector was so absorbed in watching her that he almost rear-ended the car ahead. He slammed the brakes.

He rolled ahead at one mile per hour for a while. This would take forever. He checked on the woman and was startled to see her standing barely two yards from him, her eyes intensely focused on his car. As he rolled by painfully slow, she put her hand on the edge of the broken window.

This was spooky as hell. He wanted to move on, to be gone from this scene, but the car ahead had barely crept, and now it had stopped completely. The woman just stood there, frozen, her hand on his car, her eyes on him in the rearview mirror.

119. *Azar Bayat*

Black Sabbath played on repeat for hours; Azar heard each song at least three times. Then, mid-song, the music stopped, replaced by footsteps heading downstairs.

That had happened a while ago. Since then, Azar had been pacing and sitting and pacing again. It was difficult to keep track of time. The heat was beginning to drive her mad. The more tap water she drank, the more she sweated, her clothes sticking to her skin. Yet, she couldn't take them off.

An idea was about to bubble up in her unconscious; it seemed important, but Azar couldn't quite capture it. Her brain was short-circuiting; she was having trouble thinking things through, her thoughts drifting to other topics instead: Bahar, her parents, Soroush. This cloud of dumbness must have been one of the effects of captivity. But Azar wasn't ready to give up on herself. She would force herself to think; she would. She couldn't overpower the kidnapper, but she could outsmart him, one way or another.

At least twenty-four hours had passed. Someone must have alerted the police by now. Azar had arranged to go for a walk with Becki. She wouldn't have left Becki hanging, of course not. Azar wasn't a flake. Becki knew this about her.

Were they supposed to be meeting *this morning*? For a second, Azar was uncertain. She could see darkness between the boards covering the window. In her head, she sent signals to Becki, to whoever else might be concerned: save me, save me. Then it came. The answer to the puzzle lingering just under the surface of her consciousness. The tuna can lid that had come off so easily with a pull on the small handle. With that lid, she might be able to cut the man's throat.

Azar picked up the can from the carpet where it had fallen, the lid still hanging at one end. She tore it off. The thing had a thin edge. Azar touched it with her finger; it felt sharp but not enough for a deep cut. She had no tools to sharpen it. Aluminum. Or was it steel? Azar began rubbing the lid at an angle against the edge of the can as knife sharpeners do. One, two, three, four, five, six. She rubbed and rubbed as she continued thinking. Was it getting any sharper? Azar tested it with her index finger and was unsure.

She would have to find the perfect moment to use the lid against the kidnapper. She'd have to act fast. Her heart accelerated as she imagined jumping him when he brought more food. *If* he brought more food.

All the while, her fingers continued to work.

120. The Corrector

Finally, all the bumper-to-bumper nonsense was over. The Corrector pressed the gas and watched the strange woman drift into the distance behind him. For a moment, he wondered if he'd imagined her. There was something spooky about her, like she was a ghost or something. He left the accident scene behind, feeling like she was in his backseat.

What a fucking relief to push ahead at regular speed. But he knew the road would veer away from the river again, and he didn't want that. He liked the look of the water through the trees, something real that was always there. The Corrector took a right onto one of the smaller streets between McLoughlin and the Willamette, driving slowly. A mixed area: half-park, half-residential.

To his right was a playground; ahead, a small parking lot. A nice fucking spot, with a river view and all. The Corrector pulled into one of the spots. It was sad to die like those two people in the accident. What fucking luck. Was it better than stretching things out into their sixties, like Mom had? Not much to show for it. Was that Dad's fault? Hers? Who the fuck knew? The Corrector had stopped trying to figure out his parents' marriage long ago.

He pictured Azar Bayat in his mom's bedroom and his mom's body in the living room. It felt good not to be there. All of a sudden, he missed Mom. He even missed Azar Bayat in a way he couldn't explain. Weird as fuck, but there was something about her. Confidence, maybe. Once he'd disposed of her, it would be just him and his mom's body again. Then, he could settle the whole thing with the hospice service and be done with it all. Focus on his mission. What a relief that would be.

He turned and looked over his shoulder to check if the strange woman was in the backseat. She was nowhere around. The whole area around the parking lot seemed abandoned. It made The Corrector sad. His life was abandoned just like this. Then it happened again, the fucking tears. He sobbed and sobbed. Embarrassing as fuck. Luckily, no one was around to watch it. What was wrong with him?

"Good question, son." In the rearview mirror, his father's grinning face from the backseat. His father's being a dick was business as usual, but The Corrector was relieved. At least it was someone he knew.

121. Brenda Smith

Brenda parked in a "No Parking" spot, one of the small privileges of being a cop. She walked around the Portland State University dorm, a nervous energy in her legs. A potential witness, Becki Anderson, was supposed to meet her at the small fountain by the Center for Student Health. Becki's friend was missing; Manes asked Brenda to investigate.

> A guy from the Interests Section of the Islamic Republic of Iran called Re Azar Bayat. Just a heads up. Let's follow up tomorrow.

The evening was unusually warm, with no rain for now. A cluster of students congregated on the edge of the narrow water rectangle, chatting and smoking. A young woman sitting by herself examined Brenda's face.

"Becki Anderson?"

"Yes."

"I'm Brenda Smith. We spoke on the phone. Thanks for seeing me at this late hour."

"Nice meeting you." Becki rose to shake Brenda's hand.

Two kids watched them with curiosity.

"Is there someplace more private we can talk?" Brenda asked.

"Yes, right inside."

Brenda followed the younger woman into the building, vast and empty at this hour. They sat next to each other by a flower bed in the lobby.

"I understand your friend, Azar Bayat, has been missing since yesterday afternoon."

"Yes. I'm worried about her." Becki looked it, her face sunken and sad.

"Please tell me everything. From the start." Brenda took out her notepad.

"We were supposed to go for a walk yesterday morning. She didn't show up, and I haven't been able to get a hold of her for over 24 hours. She's not answering her phone."

"When did you see her last?"

"Around 5 p.m. Thursday. I've waited." Becki Anderson sounded apologetic. "I know you guys want people to wait before reporting someone missing."

"Thanks for contacting us." Brenda liked this Becki Anderson. "Did she mention any unusual plans or anything else that may have surprised you?"

"She was planning to go to a mosque for her research."

"Mosque?" Brenda didn't like the sound of that. "What if she changed her mind about the walk? Made other plans?"

"She's very reliable."

"How long has she been in the United States?" Brenda asked.

"Since the start of the fall term."

"Can you think of any other place she might be?"

"Not really." Becki shrugged. "She studies a lot. Normally, she'd be in her dorm room by now. She told me she had relatives in Lake Oswego, but I don't know their names. I don't think she's even gone to see them yet." Becki stared at Brenda for a few seconds as if expecting reassurance.

"You mentioned on the phone that you had a picture of Azar? Can I see it?"

"Of course. I almost forgot." Becki seemed overwhelmed as she looked for the picture on her phone. "Here it is." She turned the screen toward Brenda.

Azar Bayat looked intelligent and determined, her eyes asking something of the viewer. Demanding that Brenda find her.

"Would you mind texting it to me?" Brenda asked. "And her phone number, please."

"No problem. I still have you in here." Becki fiddled with her phone again, and Brenda's own buzzed with the incoming text.

Brenda saved the contact, which made Azar Bayat feel even more real. Brenda pressed the Call button. Voice mail. Of course. A young, throaty voice with a slight accent. *You have reached Azar Bayat. So sorry. I'm running about, but I'm happy you called. Please tell me more, and I'll call you back.*

Could Brenda leave a message? Of course not. Technicians were monitoring Azar's account; Brenda didn't want to mess that up. She hung up. Why had she even considered that? And if she did leave a message, what would it say? *I'm getting close? I'll be there to save you? Don't give up?*

122. Sania Jamison

Sania was still mad at her killer, but being mad non-stop for so long was an arduous task. Atif's face stood firmly before her, Omar and Lidia's small faces floating around him. How she missed them all. And how they must miss her. Especially Lidia, such a mama's girl. Still, Sania knew they'd be okay, somehow.

Increasingly, she remembered a moment from her childhood. An expanse of moments. She was on the swing in their front yard, a kid, eight or ten. Her parents had just bought the house. What year was it? Sania couldn't remember years. Just the feeling of flying. The sky above, the carousel of clouds.

Oh, the flying. Her life ended up just like that: an ascent on a swing. The other half, the fall, had been removed.

SUNDAY, NOVEMBER 24

123. *Brenda Smith*

It was still dark when Brenda woke up. Rain pattered on the window, a boring monologue that would not stop. Mary breathed steadily next to her. Waking up with Mary by her side felt different. Even the room felt altered, more alive. It smelled more personal.

Brenda sat up. The wood floor was cold under her feet. She felt for her slippers and found the right one, but not the left. She used her phone's light to track down the missing slipper under the bed.

The events of the last few days came into focus in Brenda's mind. She didn't care about her dad's passing any more than yesterday, but now, a morsel of guilt was added to the mix, like she was *supposed* to feel something.

What she felt was a worry for the young woman who had likely been abducted, Azar Bayat. Brenda imagined herself in Azar's shoes, at the mercy of the large man from the other night. Brenda had no proof that Azar's disappearance was connected to the case, but intuition screamed that it was, insisting that Azar was still alive.

124. The Corrector

As usual, The Corrector's parents were arguing; he could tell by their angry expressions. For some reason, their voices were muted; he felt relaxed as he sipped his coke. Breakfast was good. Bacon and eggs, who could say no to that?

A knock-knock. He ignored it, but a louder knock with a click-click to it followed. The Corrector's eyes opened.

A flashlight in his face.

What the fuck? He rubbed his eyes.

A figure at the car door. He must have fallen asleep.

"Sir, please roll down your window!" A loud, deep voice.

Shit. A cop.

Fear and doom washed over The Corrector in a wave of heat.

He did what he was told. He could already see himself being led away in handcuffs.

"Officer." He nodded, trying to act polite. "What did I do?"

The Corrector's recovering eyes could barely see the cop's face, but he was a big guy, white. Not someone to fuck with. The Corrector froze as he waited. The seconds of silence were killing him. His heart beat like a motherfucker.

"Did you know that overnight parking is not allowed here?"

"Overnight…Hmm…What time is it? I fell asleep."

The cop's eyebrows went up. "Have you been drinking?"

"Not since yesterday morning." Fuck. The instant The Corrector said it, he knew it was a wrong answer. Drinking in the morning; he shouldn't be talking about that with a cop.

"Sir, do you have a weapon on you?"

"No." The Corrector had left his gun in the garage.

"What happened to your side window over here?" The cop pointed with a motion of his head.

Motherfucker. Things went blank in The Corrector's mind. Hadn't prepared an explanation for this. For a moment, he couldn't remember what the hell had happened, either. "Went shopping for some two-by-fours. Should have tied them down better, you know."

"Remodeling?" An unfriendly glare in the cop's eyes. It was still dark out. The flashlight made everything look dramatic as hell.

"Yeah. Some rot in my house, you know."

"Driver's license, please."

The Corrector knew to move slowly as he got the wallet out of his pocket. He'd make sure the cop didn't see his red business card.

What the...The red card wasn't there.

The Corrector felt heat rise in him again. The bar was the last place he'd opened his wallet. He was fucked, but this was no time to think about it. He pulled out his license and handed it to the asshole cop.

"Sir, please remain in your car. I'll be right back."

The Corrector said nothing.

125. *Azar Bayat*

Azar kept sleeping and waking, sleeping and waking. Then, a gap in time swallowed her. She opened her eyes. Her body tightened. Fear clutched at her gut. Something was about to happen today. She didn't know why she felt that way, but she did.

What would her parents do? She imagined each of them in this situation. Baba would refuse to cooperate and, in that way, would take on no responsibility for the violence that might result. Maman would talk and talk and try to appease the kidnapper. And Bahar? The thought of her sister being in this situation was too upsetting; Azar threw it out of her mind.

In the morning light seeping between the boards on the window, Azar took another look around. The tiny, nondescript room, the spartan bathroom. If she didn't survive this, if she didn't find a way to stop the man, someone else would be here next week. Someone just as desperate as she was now.

126. The Corrector

The Corrector's head was splitting as he drove. The river was on his left, gray like a rat's tail. He needed more sleep. He'd gotten away. A $140 ticket, but who the fuck cared on a day like this.

As he passed the accident scene, the strange woman's face came back to him. He thought she might still be hanging around, but not much remained of the scene apart from a few metal parts on the other side of the road.

The Corrector was mad at himself for losing his red business card. Must have dropped it at the bar. If so, the cop lady would connect the dots. So, she knew what he looked like. Fuck. But if he was caught—oh, well. Thanks to the fucking Democrat Governor for the moratorium on capital punishment in Oregon. Three or four murders made no difference.

127. Dmitry Volkov

Dmitry lay on his side in his hospital bed facing the wall. The door whooshed like air suction. A visitor. Dmitry didn't want any visitors. He felt sorry for himself. Rita wasn't coming back. Not today, not ever again. Someone must be here to interrogate him. He shut his eyes and pretended to sleep.

He was headed to prison, but this wasn't even half the problem. Boris. There was no way around it. Boris was dead. Dmitry had had a chance to stop his brother; instead, he'd endorsed Boris's doomed plan.

Whoever was in the room was taking their time. Dmitry hoped they'd just leave.

"Dmitry?" Brenda's voice.

Dmitry felt a flash of joy. He hadn't expected her to visit, had assumed she was mad at him, like everyone else.

"Dmitry, are you asleep?"

"Bren?" He turned onto his back and groaned in pain. "Bren. Oh, Bren. I'm so sorry. I fucked up."

"Yeah…" She hesitated. "Listen…I'm sorry about your brother."

"Thank you." Dmitry was grateful to hear condolences instead of accusations. He'd let Brenda down; he had. Still, she was being nice.

"Dmitry, why?" Brenda stared with big eyes full of puzzlement. "Why did you do it?"

"I was too much in debt." Dmitry was embarrassed to share this, but it was too late to worry about such things. He owed Brenda a straight answer. "This guy was blackmailing me."

"You could have borrowed some cash from me." She looked sad.

"Why didn't you say something?"

"It was too much money to ask for."

"Shit. I'm sorry I had to report you. You'd do the same if you were in my shoes."

Would he? Dmitry didn't know if this was true, but the whole thing felt like a remote past. His troubles were so much greater than stolen evidence.

"What are they charging you with?" Brenda must have read his thoughts. Too obvious.

"Armed robbery and attempted murder."

"No way."

Dmitry couldn't face Brenda's disappointed eyes. He looked through the door, where the shoulder of the uniformed cop remained in the same spot. The whiteness of the room was oppressive.

"They might drop attempted murder *if* they believe me. But I deserve it, to be honest."

"You don't deserve it, Dmitry. Don't be ridiculous."

"I don't know, Bren. I'm still trying to think it through. It's all spinning in my head."

"How long will they keep you here?"

"I don't know." He sighed. "A few more days. I'm not in a rush to get out of here, considering."

"And Rita?"

"Me and Rita are done."

Brenda stared at him for a few seconds. She was a good friend; Dmitry could tell she was upset for him.

"I'm sorry."

"Remember that thing you said? If you dive with a bag full of stones tied to your neck, you won't come out. That's exactly how I feel."

"Yeah, I hear you." Brenda looked uncertain about how to

respond. There wasn't much to say.

"Sorry I let you down with the case." Dmitry was tired of talking about himself. "Any progress?"

"We have another potential victim. An Iranian student who hasn't returned to the dorm since Friday night. Looks like a fit for our guy."

"No way." Dmitry would have given his head to be able to return to his detective life.

"And check this out. I had the killer within five yards from me that same night, but I let him get away." Brenda told him about the stakeout at the bar and the man with the red card.

Incredible. Dmitry felt a surge of excitement as he listened. He couldn't be a part of this anymore, but he was glad his partner was making progress.

"I'm sorry, Bren," he said when she was done. "But you didn't do anything wrong. Didn't miss any clues. You'll get him; I know you will. You're close."

"I hope so." Brenda looked around the hospital room, then back at Dmitry. Her face seemed disconnected, as if she hadn't taken it all in yet. Fair enough. Dmitry himself hadn't. From his first two decades in the Soviet Union, how had he laid a path into this guarded hospital room? How had this happened? It was his responsibility, wasn't it? But not much of it seemed like his choice. He was just a Russian dude in another country, stuck in a life he couldn't control, a life that had destroyed him.

128. Azar Bayat

Azar was in a torpor as she sat there, shaking despite the excessive heat in the room. She was trying to think and not to think about the approaching confrontation with her kidnapper. Her confidence had deteriorated. The tuna can lid was still in her hand. Could she really use it as a weapon? No, it was ridiculous. Azar dropped it on the floor next to her feet. She needed something better.

She had already made mental apologies to her family for coming to this crazy place, the United States, only to perish here. But then, she imagined their encouraging voices. *Don't give up. You're smarter than him; you'll get out of this.* If she did, she would call her parents every day. She'd never ignore their messages just because she was busy. She'd go home for her school break.

Azar heard someone walking up the stairs, slow and steady, her heart rate rising with each footfall. The steps got closer, then stopped. The man must be standing in the hall, just behind the door. Azar got up from the couch as if to fight. She didn't know what she might do.

129. Brenda Smith

Brenda was distraught as she left the hospital. She hated finding Dmitry in this situation, even if it was his fault. The next time she'd see him might be at the trial. She'd have to testify. His sentence would be long.

A gust of wind threw a handful of rain in her face. Brenda rushed to her car and got in. So what if she'd spent the whole morning driving around with no result? She was convinced that Azar Bayat was still alive.

Brenda turned the key in the ignition and pulled out of the parking lot, careful not to hit anyone or anything in this onslaught of rain. It took only nine minutes to get to Fremont. From outside, the bar looked the same, but it was not. The killer was not coming back. Brenda turned one corner, then another. Intuition had brought her back here. Any house on these blocks could be where Azar Bayat was being held.

130. *The Corrector*

The Corrector was mad at his fucking hesitation. He didn't have all day. Finally, he came upstairs, planning to kill the girl and be done with this part. That was his duty. He still had to decide what to do with her body. But now a new question stopped him: should he do it right there or take her to the garage? He spent too long on the landing, debating what to do next.

"Don't be a pussy, Junior." Dad was back so soon. "Just do what you came to do."

"I will, Dad, I will. And fuck you, by the way."

He walked to the bedroom door, getting the key from the pocket of his jeans. As he unlocked the door and pushed it open, he stayed alert in case his prisoner did something crazy. She stood in the middle of the room, her face tense, her black hair all over the place, her thin arms hanging at her sides like sticks.

"What are you going to do with me?" Her English wasn't too bad, but her accent was strong. The Corrector was still shaken by the fuck-up with Sania Jamison. At least this one wasn't an American. "Did you kill those other people?" A challenge in her eyes as she said this.

He didn't feel like replying.

"Who were you talking to out there?" the prisoner asked.

"No one. Mind your own fucking business and come with me."

The Corrector would bring her back down to the garage and shoot her. At least she'd be out of the house. He'd had a good reason to put her upstairs for the night, but now he couldn't quite remember.

"Where?" Azar Bayat's question interrupted his thoughts. He

needed a drink.

"Shut up." He gestured toward the door. "You first."

131. *Azar Bayat*

The man ushered her toward the stairs and remained right behind her, the gun in his hand. If she tried to turn and punch him, surely the kidnapper would overpower her. The large hospice bed sprawled below, to the left of the stairs. Azar tried not to look as she descended.

One step.

Two.

Three.

The doorbell broke the silence. Azar started, then froze.

The man's hand gripped her shoulder. "If you make any noise, you're dead." His whisper in her ear was barely audible, and when Azar instinctively turned her head, the gun was inches from her face. "And so is whoever's out there."

Azar glanced at the front door. Ten meters from the bottom of the stairs, at least. Her heart was exploding, her gut in a fist. Even if the door were wide open, the man would have plenty of time to catch up with her or to shoot her in the back.

No. This wasn't her way out.

They stood motionless on the stairs, the stench of death ruling the air.

The doorbell rang again.

The man kept his gun on her as he carefully made his way around her. Azar was tempted to grab the weapon and push him down the stairs. Anything, anything. But he watched her carefully; the moment to act had passed. The kidnapper tiptoed down the stairs and half-crouched by the window, looking through a crack in the Venetian blinds.

132. Naseem Nazari

Naseem noticed how detached his thoughts were becoming from his life. He could still see and feel everything, but he found it difficult to connect what he saw into a continuous picture, a world, a polyphony of lives. He was drifting off. He imagined a gigantic chessboard. On such a board, he might be able to beat Igor Pechorin—how about that?

He still thought about Aisha, but even her dear face was losing its contours in his memory. There were only two people he was able to track clearly. One was the middle-aged detective in charge of his case, her face focused and beautiful as she crisscrossed the area next to the killer's house, her car a lonely boat in this ambush of rain. The second was the young woman held at the killer's house, very alive and terrified, sweat glistening on her forehead, the killer's gun on her. Naseem could feel her rapid heartbeat. And in her eyes, he saw the determination that made him optimistic. He kept his focus from sliding away.

133. Brenda Smith

Brenda was on her fourth pass around the neighborhood and beginning to lose patience. She should go home, spend time with Mary, think—or not think—about her dead father. Instead, here she was, looping through the rain like a crazy person. Still, she couldn't let go. A voice in her head said, *Keep looking, keep looking.* Some streets felt cold for reasons she couldn't explain. Others, warmer. She began focusing on these.

The search drew her into a smaller area in Northeast, between Failing and Shaver. Failing, what a street name. Brenda kept driving, turning into smaller streets, examining the houses, their open and closed structures, their light and dark windows. She wished she had Dmitry's help.

134. The Corrector

The knocking didn't sound right for the cops. They would've been pounding on that door. The Corrector looked through a crack in the blinds. Fuck! It was the Black nurse from the other day. He'd almost shit his pants for nothing. She was already walking back to her car. Now he heard her voice from her last visit about coming on Sunday, Tuesday, and Friday instead of Monday, Thursday, and Saturday because of Thanksgiving. The Corrector hoped she hadn't smelled Mom through the door.

"Don't tell me you're not cut out for your task." Dad's giant hairy arms were folded on his chest.

"Shut up," The Corrector turned away from the window and walked to the kitchen. "I'm better than you. I'm better than you."

"Better than me?" Azar Bayat frowned.

"Shut up."

135. Azar Bayat

"Who was that?" Azar would not submit silently to whatever violence the man might do to her.

"Mom's nurse." He seemed more likely to respond when their tense conversation touched upon his mother. He must have loved her.

Talk, keep talking, Azar instructed herself again. *Be Scheherazade.* She did her best to ignore the nauseating stench.

"Why did you leave her body lying around like this?"

"I...I'll take care of her after...after this." The man shrugged and pursed his lips almost apologetically as he selected a bottle from a row that dominated the kitchen counter and took a long swig.

"After this?" Azar repeated, still standing in the middle of the stairway. "What do you mean, after this?"

Should I run for the door?

No, not yet. Too far. The kitchen's open layout allowed the man to reach the outside door in three or four steps. Azar would have to run three times the distance from the bottom of the stairs. The counters were covered with dirty dishes, plastic containers, and trash. Could she hit him on the head with something? The indecision was infuriating.

136. The Corrector

The Corrector knew he should finish Azar Bayat off, but instead, he was chatting to her like they were fucking pals. He relaxed a bit. If she had screamed, she would be dead, that's for sure, but she would've also made a hell of a mess for him. He would be in police custody by now.

He didn't feel as angry anymore. Those drinks had helped. He didn't even know *what* the fuck he felt. He was dealing with too many things at once. He remembered the cop from this morning, the fucking ticket. Something about the scene of the accident had stayed with him. The spooky woman with her empty eyes and her hand on the edge of his broken car window.

He grabbed the bottle. About a third left. Azar Bayat stood at the bottom of the stairs, near Mom's bed. When had she come down? She covered her nose with her hand.

"Why are you doing this?" Her eyebrows rose as she spoke. "Don't you think you at least owe me an explanation?"

What the fuck. Ballsy of her to keep asking all these questions. "Why did you come here?" he said. "Why couldn't you just stay in your own country?"

Azar Bayat just stared. She had nothing to say.

137. Azar Bayat

Why had she come here? For three months, she'd pondered this.

"Because where I come from is hell. Because if you're not religious, you're fucked." It was strange to share this with her captor, of all people. But she wanted to give him time to get drunk, and for that, she had to keep talking.

The man looked at her funny. "What? You're not a Muslim?"

So that's what he had assumed.

Of course. How ironic.

He seemed to be disappointed. Good. Maybe she still had hope if things weren't going according to plan. Could she use his mistake against him?

"Me? Muslim? Oh, no." Azar inhaled, barely able to get enough air. "I hate religion." Her heart raced as panic washed through her blood. Anything might happen any second.

"Then what the hell were you doing at the mosque?" The man took a drink from the bottle.

Azar wasn't sure how to answer. Trespassing? Wasting her time? Acting on a death wish? No, no, she wouldn't dip into negativity.

"Working on a paper," she mumbled.

"Paper?" The kidnapper stared uncomprehendingly.

"College paper. About Muslim women."

How stupid her high-brow effort seemed to her now. Overblown.

"Fuck." The man frowned. "Where're you from?"

"Iran."

"Isn't that where all that shit's happening with the shah and all?"

"Right. Ayatollah." Azar did her best to answer affirmatively. She had to build a rapport with her captor instead of challenging him on the details. "We had a shah back in the 20th century."

"Yeah, ayatollah. The guy with the beard." The man played with his own beard as he said this, grinning, a happy child impressed by his erudition.

"Why did you kidnap me?" Azar was repeating herself, rephrasing, trying to confuse him. Her heart kept pounding like a mad train, and her throat hurt.

The kidnapper took another long swig from his bottle.

138. The Corrector

The Corrector felt like someone had hit him in the gut with a fucking log. The girl wasn't even a Muslim? Holy shit. The one before, Sania Jamison, came to mind again with her American accent. Both prisoners were wrong, one way or the other. How had it come to that?

"You're fucking up, Junior," Dad said.

"No, I'm not."

But he was fucking up, wasn't he? Should he pack it up and call it quits?

Muslim or no Muslim, she was an immigrant. Wasn't that enough?

"Get her to the garage and blow her brains out," Dad insisted. "You'll figure out what to do with the body later."

"You shouldn't have come here," The Corrector told her.

"What do you mean?" Azar Bayat stared with those big dark eyes of hers.

"You shouldn't have come to this country."

"I love this country. That's why I came here. I wanted to contribute. You're going to kill me for that?"

He didn't say anything.

"Plenty of people from other countries have come here." Azar Bayat kept chattering. "People from everywhere. Maybe even your great-grandparents."

"Don't talk about my great grandparents, you hear me? Muslims are the suicide bombers, ain't that right? Have you heard of some white dude blowing himself up?"

"But I'm not a Muslim."

Wasn't she? She might be lying about that, like everything else.

Who the fuck knew? The Corrector was tired of trying to sort it all out.

"What about your family?" Azar Bayat asked. "Didn't they come from somewhere?"

Fuck fuck fuck! Too many questions. His head was splitting.

"My family has always been here." As he said it, he remembered all the crap about the Indians and the cowboys and the English people with wigs coming on ships with big sails. How long ago had all that been? Much too long ago to worry about if you asked him. The bitch had no fucking point, no point at all. He took another sip, the bourbon an old friend on his tongue. But even the drink failed to clear the dread The Corrector felt.

"Were you born here in Portland?" Azar Bayat asked.

"Yeah. Oregonian, born and bred. My folks are from the South."

"South? Where?"

The Corrector tried to remember. In one gulp, he finished off the bottle. Luckily, there was another in the kitchen, among the empties. His hands shook a bit as he opened it. Azar Bayat kept staring. Something about her face, like she cared—but she was fucking pretending; he knew it. And Mom knew it, too. He waited for Mom to say something, but she kept silent, lying in her big bed.

"What happened to you?" Azar's face softened as she kept talking. Something in it was like Mom's face on her good days. "Why did you decide to do *this*?"

"Someone has to." He scoffed.

"But *you* don't have to. You can just let me go."

139. Sania Jamison

Atif, Omar, Lydia. These names were sharp in Sania's mind, but now and then, she had trouble remembering who they belonged to. They were her family; she knew that. But the meaning of *family* was growing vague in her mind. Sania had been trying to hold the world in her grasp, but it insisted on wrangling itself free.

She couldn't remember how many days she had been dead. Days no longer made a difference. Fewer things concerned her now. With its many unsolved problems and continuing tragedies, the world would flow unimpeded, separate from what she, Sania, had become.

Sania. She tasted the name on the frozen edge of her motionless tongue. *Sania.* She'd been Sania for so long. Now, she was leaving her name behind. She was becoming something bigger, something outside herself. For whatever reason, all she wanted before she left the world was to help find her killer. The detective was getting close.

140. *Azar Bayat*

Azar saw how deranged the man was. Deranged, deluded, and deeply traumatized. Half the time, he seemed to be talking to someone else who was not in the room. She had the privilege of sanity, intelligence, and common sense. The conversation was going in circles, and she liked it that way. *Why had she come here?* She'd explain another hundred times as the man took gulps from the new bottle. Soon, she'd be able to make a run for it.

Something in the kidnapper's face reminded her of the ayatollah's stubborn refusal to allow for the validity of conflicting opinions. Something beyond the scraggly beard and the wrinkled, pale face. His narrow-minded squint as he stood there, leaning on the kitchen counter, the bottle in his hand. The contempt. She had to keep talking.

"You must miss your mom. What was she like?"

"She didn't have a happy life," the man said after a second. "Dad was a dick to her. Punched her around a lot."

"Why?"

"I don't know." He sounded defensive, almost insecure. "How am I supposed to know?"

"What was her name?"

"Nancy." His face sagged as if thinking of his mother's name made him mourn her differently.

"That's a lovely name." Azar checked and re-checked her position relative to the door. Too far to breeze past him and escape. The dead body in the large hospice bed next to her felt like the center of dark gravity. The blinds let in gray slits of light.

"I just don't know anything anymore." A pained grimace on the man's face. He seemed to be disintegrating before her, his expression collapsing. Tears rolled from his eyes. A second later, he was sobbing, rubbing his face with his shirt sleeve. How perplexing. Azar remained indecisive, watching. What was the right move? He would collect himself if she tried to run or attack. His gun was right there, black and glistening next to him on the counter. Her hesitation was torture, like tooth pain, the dread of time melting away without an attempt to escape.

"What's wrong?" She'd keep the conversation going while she tried to choose her next move.

For ten or twenty desperate seconds, the man didn't respond as he fought tears. Then he huffed through a tight mouth, "Why should I tell *you?*"

"Because I care." Azar had to work hard to keep her voice level. "I want to understand."

The man sighed. "This woman I killed, Sania Jamison." He fell silent again, his mouth open like a tunnel into darkness.

Sania Jamison. Azar remembered the name from the news. Her body was found next to the Willamette. Is this where Azar, too, was headed? The thought made her shiver.

"What about her?"

"I thought she was an immigrant. One of those suicide bombers. But she was an American. An American. I got the whole thing wrong."

Could she run now? *Don't rush it,* Azar told herself.

"I thought I owed it to my country." The man sighed deeply and cleared his throat.

He was almost a person before her, but Azar wouldn't be fooled. More than anything, he was a threat. Her eyes fell upon an empty bottle next to the wall just a few steps away. She could use it as a weapon, but to cross the remaining distance between the bottle and the man, she'd have to run another eight or ten meters and get around the kitchen island. Plenty of time for him to react. *Don't rush it.*

"You can't change the past. What you've done makes sense. I get it." Azar felt a pang of guilt for betraying Sania Jamison like this, but she had to gain the man's trust. "I'm not the right person for you. I'm not a Muslim. You have to let me go. You have to do what's right in this situation."

"What's right?" The man took another huge gulp. "Fuck if I know what that is anymore." Tears still rolled from his eyes, and he sniffled like a snotty child.

"No one ever loved you, did they?" Azar hadn't planned this; it just came out, and she bit her lip. "No one ever loved me either." Untrue, in her case, but she had to say it.

Azar held her breath and sensed every edge of the moment on her goose-pimpled skin. Her words might have angered him when he was beginning to calm down. But the kidnapper just stood there, leaning on the counter, rubbing his face, and staring at her with deep, empty eyes.

"What am I supposed to do now?"

"Do the right thing," Azar said.

141. The Corrector

The Corrector felt disoriented like a fucking baby. *Do the right thing?* In one of his ears was his dad with his angry shit; in the other, this weird Muslim who wasn't a Muslim, Azar Bayat. What the fuck was wrong with her? And what the fuck was wrong with him?

Embarrassing as hell to cry like this in front of the girl. But it was too late to worry about small shit. If he was going to kill her, who cared if he cried? And if he didn't kill her, then what? Could he let this one go? His gun was right there, but could he shoot her? He hadn't shot any of the other three. Besides, there was something about this Azar. Something different. Like she understood him in some way.

Fuck! His thoughts were running away from him. He couldn't think beyond the next step; his head was exploding. He needed a fucking break, or another drink, or both. Maybe he needed to stop drinking. Hell. He didn't have it in him to deal with her the way Dad wanted him to. Not this moment. Or did he? *Do the right thing?* What did that mean, anyway? *The right thing.*

His mom knew what to do, didn't she? She just lay in her bed without moving. Why wasn't she moving?

142. Azar Bayat

Azar felt the moment with all her body. Her chest tightened, and her skin embraced her like a snake's. Electricity ran through her hair. *Don't rush it.* She counted to five in her head. The man just stared at her, his eyes welling with emptiness.

"Call me Junior."

Azar struggled to understand. Then she just went with it. "Do the right thing...Junior." With confident steps, she walked past the living room, her eyes on the door. She forced herself to keep that measured gait. *One...two...three.* "Do the right thing."

Any moment, the man would leap to grab her.

Five steps, six, seven. A few more, and the door would be within her reach. She didn't want to look at the gun on the counter.

Eight. Nine. Ten. Azar flipped the lock, intensely listening for something fatal the man might do. The lock clicked, releasing. Still, the heavy door wouldn't give. Sweat ran down Azar's back, each bead distinct, urgent. How sad it would be to die here, right by the door. *No, no, no.* She pulled again. With a slight woosh, the door came open. The cool, fresh air from outside was like a new lifetime. The street was covered in puddles.

Now. The man would shoot her in the back, now. She visualized the gun's angry mouth, a black hole. She didn't want to look; it would give him another chance at power. She wouldn't look.

She raised her right foot and stepped outside.

143. Brenda Smith

Brenda had taken this right turn a few minutes earlier, but something in her insisted. One of the unpaved Portland streets, terrible for driving. Brenda slowed down to navigate the enormous gravel potholes filled with rainwater. More rain was coming down, pounding on her windshield. *Barcelona. Barcelona.* The city of her and Mary's planned vacation kept coming up in Brenda's mind.

Just then, the door of a pink house ahead on her right opened. A young woman emerged, walking stiffly, her black hair disheveled. Brenda squinted as she pressed the brakes. Already, she knew.

Azar Bayat.

Azar wore black pants, a blue shirt, and an old-fashioned pair of red and blue Adidas. She walked briskly down the porch stairs, looking around, uncertain which way to go. Brenda's wet brakes squealed as the car stopped amid a vast puddle. As silence leaked into her ears, she felt as if all air had been sucked out of her lungs. How should she handle this crime scene without her partner? She was already calling for backup. She had to get to Azar and keep her safe.

Brenda turned the engine off, pushed the door open, and jumped out.

144. Azar Bayat

Azar's mind was in overdrive. Part of her remained in the pink house. Had she gotten away? Could this be true? Everything was happening too slowly and too rapidly at once. She wiped something wet off her forehead. Rain. It came in a steady flow.

Car brakes squealed like a dying creature, sending a shiver down Azar's spine. A black car was approaching through the puddles. A woman driver. She must have a phone. Azar started running toward the car, her legs filled with lead, like she'd just run ten miles. Rain washed her face.

The woman got out and showed a badge. "Azar?"

A police officer.

She wasn't wearing a uniform, just a puffy blue jacket. She looked genuinely concerned. Her face was gentle, and her short, curly hair reminded Azar of Maman. She was the same age.

"I'm Detective Brenda Smith. Are you okay?"

A whoosh of feeling through Azar. She would not die today. She'd see Maman again. Could this be real? Her arms were around Brenda Smith. She was safe.

"Are you okay?" the detective said again, patting her back.

"Yes," Azar heard herself replying. She wasn't as sure as she'd made it sound.

She made an effort to let go of Brenda Smith.

"Is he inside?" Brenda asked.

"Yes." Azar focused. She didn't want to think about the man anymore; she longed to push him out of her head. But this was important. "He's a little out of it, but he has a gun."

"Backup will be here any minute." The detective drew her gun and held it pointed down. "Just in case." She made eye contact, and Azar felt reassured. "I need you to wait in the car." Brenda Smith gestured toward her vehicle, a ship in the middle of an enormous puddle. "For your safety."

"Okay."

The door of the pink house stood open as Azar crossed the puddle and got into the passenger seat. Her sneakers were soaked.

145. The Corrector

The Corrector knew. As Azar walked out, he could have stopped her with a single shot. No way to miss, at this distance, even with a few drinks in him. But his arms hung unmoving before him; all he could do was watch her. Dad was right. He didn't have it in him to shoot her like that. She was kind of like Mom. He couldn't shoot Mom, could he?

Once Azar was gone, the rest of his energy left him. The drink must have gotten to him, but this wasn't the happy drunk feeling he had hoped for.

"Run after her," Dad yelled, but there was no force in The Corrector's legs.

He'd fucked up. His mission was a failure. The world was a cold place. No one understood him. He was alone against everyone. He'd tried to change things, but there was only so much one man could do. He was crying again as he thought of this. The sound of sirens in the distance grew louder.

"Mom, tell me you understand." His hand reached for the gun on the counter next to him as he waited for her response. "Tell me you understand."

146. Azar Bayat

"I need to let my family know," Azar said. "How will I get my phone? I don't know if he still has it."

"Let's just wait a few minutes," the detective replied.

So, she would live? Keep going to school? Reading books? Thinking about art, literature, religion, politics? Drinking coffee with bear claws?

How was this possible?

Azar's body was abuzz with adrenaline, her muscles and throat sore, her clothes stuck to her skin. She remembered the promise she made to herself. She'd go home for her school break. She'd see Maman Feri again. Bahar wouldn't leave her sight.

Azar cried as she imagined this. Her own life became a gift. Wasn't that something? The sound of sirens reached her from the distance.

147. Maharani Kapoor

Maharani had been dead for so long she was used to it. Little of her former life bothered her now. Her shape was gone from the world, and now it was mostly gone from her memory.

She'd helped disorient her murderer by appearing as a ghost at the accident scene. How lost he was. A baby in an oversized frame. It was an effort to manifest a complete body when hers was so fragmented. She didn't know why she was able to do that or how. It felt like her final responsibility in the world.

And now, the young woman, the last victim, was safe.

Maharani watched as her killer collapsed on the floor, sobbing, any semblance of power or force gone from him. He wore jeans and an old black T-shirt with stains on it. He rested his back against an old-fashioned stove, his face age-warped, his teeth yellowed. He held a gun in his pale hand. As Maharani watched, she already knew what would happen next. The man stuck the muzzle into his mouth and painted the white stove in ragged, organic splashes of gray and red.

This scene reached Maharani from a rapidly increasing distance. By the time the man's body collapsed on the kitchen floor, she could barely see or hear. Her job was done. She was not upset about being gone from the world. It was unfair, but unfair things happened to everyone. The world was a bag full of stones. So few of them were touched by the hands of gods.

Acknowledgments

I am grateful to Booseh Jafari for her invaluable help in fleshing out the details about Iran.

It's been a pleasure to work with the Apprentice House team. Thanks to Matthew McCarney for kindly acquiring the novel, to Sarah Gilmour for her many superb editorial suggestions, to Maxx Lao for the cover and the layout, to Emily Metheny for the marketing plan, Gianluca Secondi for promotions, and to Kevin Atticks for everything else.

My most humble thanks to my weekly critique group, The Guttery: Jennifer Brennock, Brittney Corrigan, Jessie Glenn, Michael Keefe, Jackleen de La Harpe, Shari MacDonald Strong, Cheyenne Montgomery, Tammy Lynne Stoner. Respect and gratitude to my agent, Laura Strachan, for all her efforts on my behalf and for appreciating literary fiction.

Respect and gratitude to Laurie for putting up with my literary struggles and the antisocial hours I spend typing in my room.

About the Author

A. Molotkov is an immigrant writer. His poetry collections include *The Catalog of Broken Things*, *Application of Shadows*, *Synonyms for Silence* and *Future Symptoms*. His novel *A Slight Curve* is forthcoming in 2025. His album "Can You Stay Forever?" was released in 2001 and is available on most streaming platforms. He co-edits *The Inflectionist Review*, loves to take photographs with dogs and mirrors, and plays the Armenian duduk in his free time. In the late 1990s, he was part of the San Francisco multidisciplinary group, Discord Aggregate.

Apprentice
House Press
Loyola University Maryland

Apprentice House is the country's only campus-based, student-staffed book publishing company. Directed by professors and industry professionals, it is a nonprofit activity of the Communication Department at Loyola University Maryland.

Using state-of-the-art technology and an experiential learning model of education, Apprentice House publishes books in untraditional ways. This dual responsibility as publishers and educators creates an unprecedented collaborative environment among faculty and students, while teaching tomorrow's editors, designers, and marketers.

Eclectic and provocative, Apprentice House titles intend to entertain as well as spark dialogue on a variety of topics. Financial contributions to sustain the press's work are welcomed. Contributions are tax deductible to the fullest extent allowed by the IRS.

To learn more about Apprentice House books or to obtain submission guidelines, please visit www.apprenticehouse.com.

Apprentice House Press
Communication Department
Loyola University Maryland
4501 N. Charles Street
Baltimore, MD 21210
410-617-5265
info@apprenticehouse.com • www.apprenticehouse.com

www.ingramcontent.com/pod-product-compliance
Lightning Source LLC
Chambersburg PA
CBHW050123030726
47505CB00007B/2007